Praise for the writing of Terri Pray

Focused On Love is an absolute page-turner. The poignant heart-tugging characters touch the heart in such a way that it is hard releasing them once the book is finished. Dani and Steven make such a delightful couple and the way they seek to conquer the odds stacked up against them is well-written. Ms. Pray pens a sharp and intense read that keeps the reader mesmerized.
-- Linda L., *The Romance Studio,* on *Focused On Love*

Ettore's Women is a beautifully written and perhaps deliberately fragmented story of women who work in a brothel. Terri Pray's voice fascinates me. I want to read more.
-- Catherine H., *Novelspot,* on *Ettore's Woman*

The novel flows extremely well. There is never a dull moment and the sex is blistering hot. *Sweet Deceptions* is a great way to spend a lazy afternoon. Full of intrigue it keeps you wondering what is happening and who did it.
-- Leyna, *Fallen Angel Reviews,* on *Sweet Deceptions*

...[A]n enjoyable fast read with the premise of being able to unleash the magic within yourself, if you have enough faith.
-- Aggie Tsirikas, *Just Erotic Romance Reviews,* on *Green Dreams* (Mojocastle Press)

2

Focused on Love

Terri Pray

Terri Pray

Warning

This book contains sexually explicit scenes and adult language and may be considered offensive to some readers.

Published by Under the Moon, LLC
Pelican Rapids, MN

This book is a work of fiction. Any resemblance to actual events, locales or persons, living or dead, is completely coincidental.

Focused on Love
ISBN: 978-1-938339-34-9
Copyright © 2016 Terri Pray
Cover Art Copyright @ 2016 Sam and Terri Pray
Editor in Chief: Terri Pray
All rights reserved.

Dedication

To my Sam, thank you now and always for your help, love and support.

Prologue

Sunlight played through the thick covering of leaves, leaving a dappled pattern across the forest floor. It didn't matter how often she stood beneath the trees—the simple beauty of the park never ceased to bring a smile to her lips. Spears of light pierced the canopy, reflecting from the leaf and bracken-covered ground, touching the granite rocks that marked the small campsite. Others could have their cities, their cars, restaurants and shopping malls. For Danielle, this was how life should be: a walk through the park at the end of the day with nothing but the sounds of the birds for company—well, almost nothing. She glanced back at the man who had entered the glade after her, before looking back at the calm beauty that surrounded her.

His hands reached about her waist as he leaned against her back, his breath caressing her cheek. "I'm going to miss this place, Dani," he said. But his words lacked the regret she had still half-hoped she would hear.

"You don't have to go, Bear." How often had they had this discussion in the last year? Arguing with him made no sense, but she felt she had to make the attempt, if for no other reason than to leave him believing a part of her did still love him. "You could stay here with me. You don't do well in cities—don't you remember the last time you spent more than a week in one? By the end of that visit, you were nearly ready for a straitjacket." She could remember how nervous he had been for close to a year afterwards, the near shakes that had threatened every time they had talked about returning for even a day.

"That was a long time ago. I've grown up since then; we both have. Maybe I still don't do too well in cities, but I want to finish my training, and that means leaving here. The local college doesn't exactly have the courses I want, and the clinic wouldn't qualify as a hospital even if they did run an intern program." He whispered against her neck, brushing against her skin with his lips. "You could come with me."

"No, you know I can't. I promised Gramps that I'd always listen to my heart," she explained, though they both knew it went far deeper than that. Things had changed; his dreams of staying near the park, near his family, had faded over the years, whereas she had remained content within the park, the small town and her life here. He no longer even mentioned returning home to start his own practice when he completed his time as an intern.

He'd changed, far beyond his drive to now return to the city. His dreams had adapted from the simple ones of their shared childhood, transforming into something she barely recognized. She didn't doubt that he would make a good doctor when his training was completed, but he was no longer the man she thought she had known.

"I could make you happy, Dani. If you come with me, I know I could..." His voice trailed off.

"Could what, turn back time? It wouldn't change anything. This is where I belong and we both know it." Could he hear the lack of conviction in his words, the way she could? What had been between them had turned into a friendship with fringe benefits over the last year, and though a part of her wanted to regret that, in all honesty she didn't.

"We could try?" His arms tightened about her waist, a moment of that old and passionate possession in his words. "If we both really wanted to, we could give it just one more try. Don't you remember what we have shared, all those times together, some of them right here?"

"I don't want to discuss that anymore—not right now, Bear." No—what love they had shared had faded, and neither of them had the courage to admit it. His grip on her body changed, turning her around to face him, his gaze meeting hers.

"For what it's worth, I'm sorry. I just can't let this chance slip by for me."

"I'm not asking you to," she protested in the heartbeat before his lips moved to cover hers. For a brief moment she forgot all the arguments, the endless battles over who was in the right, which one of them had made the mistake, the hurt they had caused each other. All of that faded in the heat of his kiss.

His arms tightened about her waist, hands cupping her tight buttocks until he half-lifted her into his grasp, her breasts pressing tight against his chest as her nipples hardened beneath her shirt. Her body remembered his touch, even if their hearts had taken separate paths. Her hands tightened about his shoulders, his tongue dancing within her mouth, teasing along the inside of her lips before he broke the kiss, leaving her wanting more. His smile beckoned her closer for another kiss, one she wanted to take, sink into and never come out of, just as she had so often sunk into his deep brown eyes, or inhaled that familiar smell of soap and clean air. Somehow she stopped herself from reaching for that second kiss and ran her fingers across his jaw instead, her touch unhindered by even a trace of bristle.

"We could. I mean, just one more time wouldn't be so bad." His hands smoothed back over her ass, settling in the dip of her waist. He leaned so close, offering that kiss she remembered, the comfort of his touch. He'd never leave her—that had been his promise, and now that was exactly what he was doing. It didn't matter than he had invited her to come with him, he had chosen his work over her, despite everything they had talked about in previous years.

"No." She didn't even hesitate. As much as she wanted to feel his touch again, to be held by him one last time, she knew it would not be wise. If she gave in, she would start hoping he would change his mind and stay. She still had the belief that maybe, just maybe, if she let him make love to her again, it would alter his decision to leave. The sane part of her mind knew better. And what's more, even if he did decide to stay, he would always hold a grudge against her for keeping him from the career he wanted to follow. Even with his given word, it wouldn't have been right to keep him there. She didn't say it—not verbally—but in that moment, her heart released him from his promise. "It wouldn't be a good idea, Bear."

"I guess not." But that didn't stop him from lowering his lips briefly to hers in a soft kiss, catching her lower lip between his teeth before he broke the kiss and spoke again. "There's no harm in asking, though."

"There seldom is." She nodded, stepping from his grasp, a knot forming in the pit of her stomach. It didn't matter that they had both known this was coming for some time. It still hurt, still felt as though she were losing a little of herself.

"I'll give you a call when I get to the city, Dani." He started to walk away from the small campsite. "Maybe you could come up for a visit sometime?"

"Sure." She didn't turn to look at him. The call wouldn't come; he'd find excuses for himself for a few weeks, and then he'd forget to even do that. Maybe in a few years, if he came home for that visit, there would be that momentary stumble when they met back up, a muttered unmeant apology. But she doubted even that would happen.

"Just remember to stay safe, will you?" Bear's soft voice carried through the trees.

She could hear him walking back towards the main path. He couldn't even stay long enough to wish her good luck or whatever to her face. This hadn't been a goodbye, for all he had claimed it would be when they had set the meeting up—nothing more than one last attempt to get laid.

"I always have in the past," she replied, though he was no longer in hearing range. She leaned down and picked up her jacket from the rock, slipping it back on, her fingers lingering over the park ranger badge. He might have changed who he was and what he wanted in life, but she hadn't. The distant sound of a car engine starting reached her ears—his car. For a moment, it gunned almost too loudly into life, the noise sending up a flock of wood pigeons into the air; then it faded, the car moving away down the access road

"Goodbye, Bear." It didn't matter that he couldn't hear her farewell. If the truth be told, it hadn't been said for his ears. No matter where he went, her place was here. Her gaze moved over the small campsite, the fire-touched leaves of fall lining the forest floor earlier this year than many before. What would her Gramps say? That an early fall was the sign of a long, hard winter to come—well, perhaps she needed just that. "Look after yourself, wherever your path takes you."

Chapter One

The wind tugged through her hair, pulling it behind her in a living banner. Ahead the path narrowed, leading her further into the park, growing steep and difficult to walk along, following the route upwards towards the cliff. She knew the area well—all its raw beauty, the hope and danger the view over the river offered— but the reason she took this path right now eluded her grasp. Further she climbed along the increasingly narrowing trail, the trees thinning out, permitting her a better view of the vivid blue sky overhead. A playful wind tossed the small, scattered clouds across an azure expanse.

A familiar cry broke through the soft background noises of the park, one that turned her gaze towards the sky above the river. There, dancing on the air currents with outspread wings above the snaking river, flew a bald eagle. How many years had it been since a bald eagle had flown over the park; twenty, thirty? Long enough that she had only heard tales of their building nests here.

Why had they returned now?

The bird circled, wings majestically spread, his call filled with a deep-seated loneliness as it echoed over the park. Where was his mate? His long, slow circles widened over the span of the river, widening his search; his cry resounded in her heart, tearing at the emptiness within her and calling back to the eagle. With a piercing screech, the eagle dived towards the water, far faster than she had imagined the bird would be able to move with any degree of safety. *Pull up*, she wanted to cry, but her throat locked, breath trapped in her lungs, a knot tying in the pit of her stomach. *Pull up, please!* Perspiration beaded across her brow, her fingers tangling in cloth as her gaze followed the steep path of the bird. Fear, excitement and disbelief mingled at the spectacle, her heart missing a beat when the eagle soared back upwards only a breath away from the surface of the river. And she saw a figure by the edge of the river, a human looking up to the sky, then towards her own form on the ridge. The distance between them vanished, the impossible happening as she met his gaze, locking with a pair of eyes as blue as the very sky the eagle soared through so effortlessly...

Her grip tightened into the cloth she had thought to be her uniform at first as the images shifted, fading into a haze of colors. The dream eagle becoming a blur, then a moments' darkness before her eyes opened. A dream; it had been nothing more than a dream, but it had been years since one had affected her so deeply. Even as the images slipped from her memory, her body still remained tense. The haunting call of the eagle, alone in the clear sky above the park, had torn at her.

Had it been a dream or a vision? It could have been either or both. Eagles, like so many other creatures, had mixed meanings according to what her Gramps had taught her. She tried to sort through the images, searching for the clues before the memory retreated to the back of her mind. The eagle searching, the unknown man—it could have all been nothing more than her desire to see the park once again become home to that majestic bird. Some still hunted the eggs and, within the parks, the birds and their nests could be protected. However, that still did not explain why the man had been a part of the dream.

Blue eyes; whom did she know with eyes of such an intense color? Dani's breath caught in her throat. Her entire body tingled at the memory of that powerful gaze, and despite the sense of sorrow that had marked the dream, she still felt alive in a way she could not explain. Never before had someone's gaze affected her like this. Her heart pounded within her chest, and a near static electricity traveled across her skin, leaving her nipples hard under the thin nightshirt and her thighs pressed tightly together. Not in the year since Bear had left for the city had she felt this aroused; no, it had been longer than that. Even in the last six months they had been together, nothing had stirred her that deeply.

The "why" slipped from her mind with the first touch of her fingers across her body, seeking what pleasure her sensitive skin now offered. A low moan escaped from parted lips, heat building from the lips of her already slick vulva long before her first touch against her clit. Beneath the light covers, her thighs parted to welcome her self-caress, arching up against her fingers, her light rub becoming harder, the need building with a speed that left her breathless. Her nipples throbbed under the light nightshirt, catching the soft material with each new rock of her hips, her body arching beneath the covers. Her fingers cupped at her covered breast, squeezing lightly into the small mound, feeling the press of the tight bud against the palm of her hand, each throb matching the now rapid beat of her heart.

Her bottom lip caught between her teeth, hips rocking upwards against the deepening touch of her fingers over her heated pussy lips. Blue eyes, even now she could see the blue eyes from her vision, watching her on her bed, never leaving her form though her finger circled her clit. He wasn't there—she knew that. Whomever he was, he couldn't see what she was doing. Yet heat rose in her cheeks at the very idea that he could somehow view her moment of wanton play.

She groaned, the torment growing, a swift kick sending the covers from her bed as her thighs parted wider on the soft cotton. Two fingers eased within the tightening confines of her eager cunt, her thumb playing circles over her clit, hips rocking upwards to meet her deep thrusts. She wanted this, needed the release it would bring, that moment of bliss she could remember. It had been too long since she had permitted herself even this self-love, this delicious time of exploration of her own body. She couldn't even remember why she had stopped playing—only that sometime after Bear had left she had stopped, the habit dying. Now it returned, her need given fresh life, hips rocking with an increasingly demanding pace.

Focused on Love

Her fingers grasped at one tight, ripe nipple, tugging on it, keeping pace with the thrusts within her heated walls. Her breath quickened, ass tightening, rising from the bed, her feet planted on the covers lifting up with each thrust within the tight confines of her willing cunt. She could feel it building, that desire, the need to let her passion release, a pulsing that throbbed from her nipples down into her clit and into her pussy. Nothing else mattered in this moment—not the work that waited for her or even the dream that had awoken her, only the slippery play of her fingers across her own body.

A low cry escaped her lips, her hips arching from the sheets, heels pushing down into the bed as her thighs clamped shut, trapping her hand between them. Perspiration beaded across her breasts, her breath ragged as she felt her heartbeat repeating in her clit. Lights sparked across her vision as she slowly lowered back to the bed, the tension easing from her thighs, releasing their grip on her trembling hand. Whatever beast had been awoken within her body had been sated—for the time being, at least.

Late. Thanks to the dream, she was going to be late for her breakfast date. With a groan, she dashed for the shower, barely casting a glance towards the open letter on the dresser. The last of the images washed away in a welcoming embrace of warm water and soap. It didn't prevent her thoughts from drifting towards the talk she knew would take place over breakfast in some form or another. Her Gramps would want to talk about what she had done with her life since Bear had left. He would never understand why it hadn't worked between them, why he hadn't stayed; nor did she have any desire to explain it to him in detail.

With a sigh she closed her eyes, wishing the water would wash the memories of his betrayal away with the soap.

"I was beginning to wonder if you had forgotten our breakfast date," Silver Fox commented as she slid into the chair opposite him, his smile crinkling the deep lines across his face.

"I took a longer shower than I had planned and lost track of the time. Sorry, Gramps." She reached for the menu. With any luck, he wouldn't catch the small rush of heat she could feel spreading across her cheeks. "I didn't mean to keep you waiting."

"It's not like you, but even the best of us lose track on occasions." He watched her over his cup of coffee, the local paper folded at the side of his silverware. "You need to eat more, Dani—you're all skin and bones. One stiff breeze and you'll blow off the ridge next time you're up there."

"You still worry too much about me." She smiled, setting the plastic-covered menu down. The town diner had to be one of the most popular places within a ten-mile radius, but they were past the normal breakfast rush, and it was far too early for lunch time. So at least she wouldn't have to wait too long to be served.

"I'm family. I'm supposed to worry about you—it's part of the job. That's something you'll find out for yourself one day, when it's your turn to raise a family.

"And you're still young enough that I get to play the concerned elder every day, if for no other reason than I remember what type of trouble your mom got into at your age."

There it was: the old argument. Her mom had made mistakes—everyone did at some point in his or her life—but the cost of her last one had been fatal. Her mom had walked away when it had become too much, leaving Dani in the hands of her Gramps, which she had long since accepted had been the better path. It didn't stop her from feeling angry when her Gramps spoke this way, though. "I'm not my mom."

"Blood runs true—your mom and I had our fallings out, but even she admitted that the call in her heart got her into more trouble than anything else. Sooner or later it will pull you, just as it did her, and her mom before her." He folded his hands on the table, looking calmly at her. "No point denying how things work. If she had accepted it, then maybe we could have resolved matters between us before she passed away."

Focused on Love

"If it is as inevitable as you claim it is, Gramps, there is also no point in discussing it every time we have breakfast together." She tried smiling, but the conversation had grown old long before today. There were times she missed the closeness that others had enjoyed with their mothers, yet at the same time, she welcomed the calm reassurance of her grandfather's guidance. "How are things out at the cabin?"

He shrugged and looked for the waitress. "So so. The pipes need wrapping again before winter, but I got that leak in the roof fixed a couple of days ago."

"Don't tell me you climbed up on that roof on your own again, Gramps." One of these days he was going to kill himself.

"Fine, so I won't tell you," He replied, mirth shining from his eyes.

"Gramps..." she began to protest.

"Wind Dancer." He rarely used her tribal name, and whenever he did, she knew a lecture or some form of reminder wasn't far behind. "If I hadn't gotten up there to do it, just who do you think was going to? Would the Spirits or one of the bears have lumbered his way over with a bucket of pitch? No wait, of course—how foolish of me not to have realized that the roof would have fixed itself." The piercing gaze he focused on her only added to her growing desire to sink into the floor. How did he always manage to find exactly the right words to turn her back into a squirming child? It never failed—they could be almost equals one moment, the next she might as well have still been eight years old, explaining how she managed to spill paint all over the front porch.

"I could have come out to help," she protested.

"And then you would have had me watching you, worrying about you falling from the roof. No point in giving this old man a heart attack now, is there? I didn't fall, the repair is done and the matter is over with." He finished with a stern nod that made it clear he would not be argued with.

"Coffee?" the fair-haired waitress inquired, the full pot held in her left hand.

"Yes, please." She looked up at the woman, smiling. "I'll have the waffles, bacon, two eggs sunny side up." With the length of day she put in, a good breakfast had become a must, and the look of approval from Gramps helped. If he wanted to believe she was ordering it to please him, then so much the better.

"What about you, Silver Fox? Did you want anything else this morning, or just a refill on the coffee?" The waitress set the silver pot down before she scribbled the information across the small notepad, her pink uniform already stained from a spilt drink.

"I'll just take my normal eggs and hash browns," he replied, lifting up his coffee mug. Like many of the regulars, he had his own larger mug and didn't use the standard white cups reserved for Rangers. "The extra coffee would be welcome—and you still make the best in town, Darcy."

"You only say that so I'll put extra hash browns on your plate." Darcy laughed as she refilled the mug from the coffee pot.

"Maybe so, but it works, doesn't it?" The banter between the two brought a smile to her lips. "It's either that, or you have a secret need to creep out to meet me at my cabin for a night of endless passion."

Darcy chuckled, looking about the small diner. "Well now, you old rogue, maybe I would do just that if I didn't think my Tom would notice."

"I'll just smuggle you in when he's not looking." Silver Fox winked at her.

"Your Gramps is a riot, Dani. Be right back with these orders." Darcy laughed as she sauntered off through the tables with an extra sway in her hips. Whatever else she thought of the older man, he had the ability to bring a smile into the lives of those around him.

"So, what are your plans for the day?" She took a sip of the coffee before speaking. "Have you got anything interesting in mind?"

His hand reached for hers, grasping it gently. "I'm worried about you, Dani."

She bit back the words she wanted to say, seeing little point in snapping at her grandfather. "I'll be fine. I'm eating, taking care of myself and getting on with my work. There's nothing for you to be worried about with me."

"Then answer me this: if everything is fine, then why haven't I heard about you going on a date since Bear left?" His gaze held hers in a long, unwavering stare. "It's been over a year since you and he parted ways. Don't you think that is more than long enough for you to start dating again? It's not normal for a woman of your age to be without a man."

"Isn't that my business, Gramps?" Her jaw tensed as she spoke.

"I'm concerned, that's all." His grip on her hand remained. "You're a good-looking young woman, and I don't believe that keeping yourself like this is healthy for you."

She wanted to ask "like what," but that would have opened the conversation up into realms she didn't want to face with anyone, let alone her Gramps. "Gramps…"

"I know, it's not my concern, but you are my only kin. I have a right to be interested in what you are doing with your life." How could she argue with that without making it seem as though she really did not want him to be an active part of her life? However, any further discussion thankfully came to an end with the sound of a familiar voice.

"Dani, Fox, good to see you both. Is there any room for one more at your table?" Henry Stones smiled, approaching the table quickly, a large brown envelope tucked under his arm.

"Sure, pull up a chair," she replied quickly before her Gramps could say anything else that would only add to the embarrassment she already felt. "I'm just waiting on breakfast. Anything new come into the station overnight?"

Henry sat down, passing the envelope to her. "A lot of work coming in our way. It seems some fashion company want to use the park as a background for a big shoot. All the permits have been filed, just appears that they forgot to forward them on to us. They're due into town tonight, a whole posse full—they're bringing in trailers, lights, teams, and knowing people like this, more than a dozen models. Most of them will be staying up at the motel, as the one permit that they were denied was their mobile home unit, or whatever they call those things. They're far too heavy for our park roads."

She flipped through the paperwork, her frown deepening the further she read. "Are they serious? There have to be at least fifty people coming in according to this, maybe more. Have you seen the list of places they want access to? Just how do they expect to get to them? Do they even know if locations like this exist in the park?" She looked over the list again, frowning. "Two of these locations are inaccessible except through half-a-day's hike. They can't expect a bunch of models to reach these locations, let alone the gear they will need."

"That, Dani, is where you come in." Henry grinned.

"Oh no, not me. I'm not trailing after a bunch of citified airheads looking for the right location for some dumb picture." She protested, looking up from the papers.

"Yes, you. I can't—I've already got that scout camping group on the other side of the park to look after, and Ben won't be here for at least five days of the shoot." Henry replied calmly, though the grin gave away just how much he seemed to be enjoying dropping this onto her shoulders. "Blue Skies Photography and the agency they are working with will be here tonight, and by tomorrow, you better be ready to show their lead photographer around or we will never hear the end of it. You know this park better than anyone else, myself included. Well, with the exception of your Gramps. Believe me, if I thought I could enroll him into helping out here, I would"

"Don't even think it." Silver Fox didn't even look up as he spoke. "I have no interest in babysitting. Those days are done, thank you."

"You can't blame me for trying." Henry smiled. "So that means it's up to you, Dani. With your help, maybe we can get these people in and out of the park quickly, with as little disturbance to our lives as possible."

By the time Darcy sat the plate of food in front of her, her appetite had long since vanished. The list of locations covered half the park, stretching out miles, and she had a hard time believing these people would be equipped for the type of traveling involved. Especially the models. The first time a bug came near one of those women, she'd be able to hear the scream across town—and that would be her fault, no doubt, for not showing them to a better location without the bugs, snakes, and dozens of other small residents of the park that city folk called pests.

"They're insane," she declared, shoving the papers back into the envelope.

"Perhaps, but they have their paperwork in place, and we have been told to provide all the help they need, so that is exactly what we will be doing," Henry insisted.

"What about any potential damage to the park?" Gramps inquired, one hand reaching for the papers which Henry quickly picked up.

"Now you know better than to go looking through these." He folded them in half and stuffed them in his coat pocket, smiling as Darcy set a coffee mug in front of him. "Look, it might not be that bad—they will be operating under some very strict rules. Dani will get a copy of the agreement before the end of the day, and any infraction of those rules will have them removed, and fined to cover the damage to the park. They agreed to that right off the bat."

"That's something, at least. It might make them behave so we only have a small mess to clean up, along with a dozen or more sets of wounded prides." Dani shoved the food around her plate, trying to regain her desire to eat; but the more she thought about the arrival of the crew, the less she liked the idea. "Tomorrow... well, at least I get today to go out to the ridge. Fire points will need looking over as well."

Fire points—those would be the least of her concerns by tomorrow. If Ben hadn't had those days off planned, then maybe she could have avoided the assignment. No, even then she would have ended up doing most of the work with them, Ben wasn't a people person at the best of times, and that was one of the reasons he had chosen to work in the park. Henry worked better with children than she did, which was why he had taken on the task of working with the scout troops—which now left her with the oh-so-pleasant task of babysitting the models.

"Somehow, I don't think my granddaughter is overly fond of the work ahead, Henry," Fox commented, a merry sparkle shining from his eyes. "Though she might come around after a few days of working with those visitors?"

Danielle speared a waffle from her plate as she looked directly at her grandfather. "Right. I have everything to look forward to in babysitting a bunch of high-heel wearing, perfumed and makeup coated models. Can't you just tell that I am going to enjoy every complaint they make about the park, the snakes, bugs, toads and the wind blowing in the wrong direction? I can't imagine anything I would rather be spending my time doing over the next few days... can you?"

Her Gramps had been right. For all that Dani had tried to embrace her independence since Bear had left, it didn't feel right. Self-preservation had been the driving force behind her desire to remain single. After all, if she couldn't trust someone she had grown up with, whom could she trust? She pulled the letter from her pocket as she walked towards her waiting truck, the temptation to read it one last time all too great. Tears stung her eyes as she opened the letter, her gaze moving over the familiar handwriting.

My Dearest Dani,

I wish I had the courage to tell you this to your face, and I will always regret lying to you over my reasons for leaving. Except I didn't lie to you, not entirely. I had to leave in order to finish my training—but there was more to it than that.
When I sat down to write this letter, I had hoped to just tell you how everything was going out here for me, but that wouldn't have been the right thing to do. Leaving you the way I did was bad enough, waiting a year to be honest with you even worse. I only hope you can find it in your heart to forgive me one day.
I'm getting married to a woman I have known for three years. I don't know any other way of saying this except bluntly: we were seeing each other before I moved out. I'm sorry, I should have been honest, ended things between us sooner, but I was afraid you wouldn't be there for me. Selfish, maybe—but you were always there for me, Dani, and I didn't want to lose that.
I don't expect to hear from you again, not after this. I just couldn't hold onto the lie any longer.
Bear

The paper crumbled in her hand. It wouldn't matter how many times she read it; the letter wouldn't change. The lies remained revealed, neatly scribed across watermarked paper. He hadn't chosen the notepaper—it wasn't his style. A note hurriedly scrawled on a piece torn from a yellow legal pad would have been more in keeping with the Bear she thought she had known. The paper was one of the trappings of his new life with the woman he was marrying—or already had married, for all she knew.

He hadn't even mentioned the woman's name; he hadn't needed to. Kelly Markham had left to go to the city only a week before he had. That smug parting look from the woman in a brief encounter the day before she had left should have been a warning. There hadn't been a man in town she couldn't have if she had put her mind to it, not a man who wouldn't have dropped everything he was doing to be with her, and she had known it. So why Bear? Why, out of all of the choices she had laid out before her, had Kelly taken her Bear?

Because she could—because he was the one man everyone thought would never date outside of the tribe, and because he had been the only man in town with a future, a career that could offer her a higher status in life. Kelly could be a doctor's wife, someone who could be looked up to, if Bear went into the type of medicine she believed he would. If he made it and became a surgeon, she would have all that her greedy little heart had ever dreamed of And he had fallen for it. The Bear she had known had ceased to exist, turned from a good and honest man into a liar. He had been right—he had lost her, but she doubted he even cared now.

It wouldn't have hit her so much if he had not been there through some of the darkest days in her life. He'd been the only one other than her Gramps who hadn't turned away from her or whispered mumbled words of sympathy when her mother had died in the fire, nearly fifteen years ago now. She'd clung to him because of that, and he had stayed with her because he needed her support. It had been the wrong form of dependence—she knew that now.

She shivered, the memory of the fire still burning at the back of her mind. For years it had haunted her dreams, until her Gramps had sat for three nights in the medicine lodge, making a dream catcher with three butterflies woven into the design. Night after night he had held her, stroking her hair, singing in a language she had never taken the time to learn beyond a few words here or there. Chasing the dreams away—until Bear had been old enough to chase them away with another form of touch.

Focused on Love

They'd never found out for certain who had started that fire—perhaps the same teenager who had been responsible for later ones, but no name, no blame had ever been placed.

"Goodbye, Bear," she murmured, closing the door one last time on the man she had called both lover and friend. "Goodbye and good luck."

Chapter Two

Clouds scattered in brief wisps of white across an otherwise clear sky, the breeze a welcome caress in what might have become a stifling day within the small valleys. For now the peace remained, but by tomorrow she could well imagine it would be gone, and her time in the park would turn into a nightmare of questions from people who would be better off remaining in that mess they called a city.

It wasn't that she hated cities—they just weren't for her. The amount of people within them made it difficult for her to breathe; the smell of the cars, the noise, it all combined into a clogging, moldy blanket that wrapped about her far too tightly for her to cope with. If the models and photographers' reaction to the park was similar to that she had to the city, it would make for an interesting assignment.

Still, she could understand why the area would make the perfect, dramatic backdrop for a shoot of this kind. The all-too-perfect models in the wilderness, draped over logs, against rocks, under the canopy of the maples, was far too good a photo-op to pass up—but that didn't mean she had to enjoy it or the work it now involved for her. There were better things she could be spending her time on, instead of babysitting the models.

The air was so clean up here—no smog or chemicals tainted the air, and the dirt had a rich black color. If the area hadn't been set aside and protected, it would have become a sought-after area by farmers. Others might have fought to build out here, ruining the area for most so a few could enjoy the view.

And what a view it was. She stood at the edge of the ridge, looking out over the forest-covered valley. Photographers, developers, hikers, picnic-goers, partiers; they all made their way out here eventually. Each one looking for something a little different, never aware that they hunted for the same thing. A place of peace.

It took a moment before Dani realized her path had taken her to the very spot she had seen in her dream that morning. That shouldn't have been a surprise, as she spent more time out at the ridge than she did any other area. Like others who ventured into the park the place called to her—a dreaming spot, her Gramps had told her more than once. The old ones had trekked their way out here in generations past, so they could sit on the ridge and wait for a dream or sign.

But the time for dreams would be later—she had work to do and couldn't sit out here all day, even though she wanted to.

Sunlight reflected across the valley, blinking at her from a spot by the river. Someone was down there—a camper, perhaps? Well, whomever it was might not know the area and the dangers that went with it. The water could run swift in the narrowing sections; all it would take was a piece of the bank crumbling beneath an unwary hiker's feet, and she'd have a rescue on her hands. Dani looked out over the ridge once more, making sure she knew roughly where the unknown walker would be before she set out, half-walking, half-scrambling down the steep rise.

Her steps were swifter than those of someone who was unused to the area. She, like her Gramps, had spent half her youth here and knew most of the pathways better than she did the sidewalks of the small town. But even so, it took her close to an hour to make her way to the edge of the river. In places the brush had overgrown on the narrow paths; one of the routes had been laid aside for the less-experienced walkers, and showed signs of needing repair thanks to a recent storm.

Noting such things was also part of Dani's work—a badly worn path or damaged rail could lead to injury or death. All it would take was the wrong type of publicity and the park's funding could be cut, visitors would drop in number, and eventually, the money needed to maintain the area would dwindle into nonexistence.

"Hello?" she called out, the small signs of passage through some of the brush clear to her. A few broken twigs, a bush that had shed some leaves a little sooner than it should have, a rock turned out of place, exposing bugs and worms to the sunlight. The hiker might as well have left a road map to guide Dani to him. By the edge of the river, half-crouched down, a camera held to his face, she spotted him. "Hello. Park Ranger here."

He rose, turning to look her as he spoke. "Afternoon—it is afternoon, isn't it?" Blond hair, longer than she was used to seeing except on other men of the tribe, was caught in a ponytail at the nape of his neck. His eyes were a deep blue, matching the color of the sky on a summer's day, claimed by a natural smile that already tugged at the corners of his lips.

"Yes, it is. Welcome to the park; did you find what you were looking for out here?"

She took a step closer, looking him over as she did so. He was certainly dressed for the area. Good walking shoes, and a canteen of what she hoped was water hung from his belt. A backpack, lightweight and no doubt if the newcomer had any experience in the parks, waterproof, sat on a flat, stable rock some distance from the river bank. He carried a good utility knife, the securing strap closed, on the other side of his belt. It all suggested this was not the first time he had explored an area like this.

"Thanks. It's a beautiful area," he replied, replacing the lens cap over the camera. "You must feel very lucky to be able to work out here every day."

"That would be a good assumption." His underlying accent suggested he had been born out of state, perhaps a few states away. But it didn't offer her a clear glimpse of his origin; had he traveled a lot, so that his accent became muted over years of work? He didn't look that old, no more than thirty. He had a few extra lines around his eyes than she might have expected to see, a small scar on his left cheek that had to be a few years old. His skin showed signs of being cared for, but was weatherworn at the same time.

So he worked outdoors a lot of the time, but then tried to repair any damage his work caused. Would others have called him handsome? Maybe not, but she could see the energy in his gaze, a sense of humor suggested by crinkles at the corners of his mouth. He wasn't the type of man she would normally look at, but there was something compelling about him.

"Did I do something wrong—coming out here, I mean? I didn't see any signs marking the area as off-limits." He set the camera back on his shoulder, stepping away from the edge of the river.

"No, you're fine out here. I just needed to check that you were alright." She smiled, nodding towards the ridge above them. "I spotted the light shining from your camera when I was up there. Part of what I do is check in on new visitors to the area. There tend to be a lot of hidden dangers out here for those who don't know what to look for."

"Ah, and you think I am one of those weekend wanderers from the city, walking into the area without knowing what to look for?" As he asked, the humor remained in his eyes. Many would have taken offence at her question—more than a few hikers certainly had. Men more than women tended to look at her, giving her that "what-would-you-know" look before proceeding to tell her how they had been to the best store for their gear. She'd pulled a couple of those "dollars-buy-everything-I-need-to-know" types out of sinkholes, away from ridges and cliff faces, and out of a fast-flowing river before. Worst of all, she'd seen several carried away by emergency staff.

"I couldn't be certain from what I had seen earlier, but looking over you now..."

Her gaze lingered; it wasn't just what he wore or how he had his gear stowed—there was something about him that continued to draw her attention.

"Yes?" he pressed.

"Well, you have your equipment stowed correctly." She forced her gaze back to his face. Shorts, hiking boots, a cotton shirt—he looked good. Damn, those shorts showed off well-molded thighs; what did the rest of his clothing hide?

She swallowed hard and tried to focus on the reason she had walked down from the ridge. It wasn't like her to feel so attracted to someone she had only just met. Yet here she was, already wondering what this stranger would look like in less clothing, or no clothes at all. She had to shake herself free of the images her mind seemed all to willing to offer.

"Normally, even the store-coached hikers don't remember to keep their canteen on them at all times. They see the river and assume everything will be alright."

"River water doesn't mean drinkable." He smiled, tapping the canteen with one hand, the other resting on the camera. "I learned that some years ago. One mistake, and I ended up in the ER for a weekend. Now I carry my canteen on my hip, and the purification tablets in a waterproof wrapping in my top pocket."

That admission was a rare one—few would explain if they had learned something the hard way. Especially to a complete stranger.

"Nice to see someone willing to learn. So what brings you out here—did you come here on a weekend trip, just needing to shake off the city for a while?" As long as she looked at his face, it would be easier to keep the heat from rushing to her own face. This wasn't like her; she saw a lot of good-looking men out here. Bear had been handsome by anyone's standards, but even he hadn't drawn her attention the way this one did.

"Well...what is your name, by the way?" He walked towards the small backpack.

"Danielle Wind Dancer. I'm one of the four Park Rangers assigned out here. Most people just call me Dani."

"Nice to meet you, Dani. I'm Steven Black, and it's my work that brings me out here." He set the camera down on top of the pack. "That camera is my source of income. I'm a professional photographer, and my new assignment requires me working out here. The rest of the team should be arriving later on today, though I believe they are coming into town to meet me at the hotel."

Her stomach knotted. Photographer, team—he had to be a part of the group that she had been assigned to look over. "You're from *Blue Skies Photography*?"

"That's the one." He nodded. "Heard of us, then?"

"Yes. My boss asked me to look after you and the models with you when you arrived. He didn't want one of the women falling off the edge of a cliff." She tried to keep the distaste from her tone. "They are arriving this afternoon, or later this evening?"

"That would depend on how many coffee breaks they stopped for on the way out." He smiled, only half-joking. "More than likely sometime this evening, which is why I am out here now, finding some good places to start off in a day or so."

"A day or so?" That long? She had been expecting them to be gone within a few days at most.

"Well if I know this bunch, they will spend a day recovering from the trip out, another day complaining about the area, and then I might be able to get some work done. Don't get me wrong—they are good people, this just isn't what they are used to. Most of them have never done a shoot outside of a studio, or they've done city shoots, not something like this." He looked out over the river as he explained. White horses swirled against the rocks in the middle of the river as sunlight danced specks of color across the churning surface. "If I thought I could get them out here, I'd use the river for a backdrop for a couple of shots."

"I can see why. I might be able to show you an area that would work just as well, if you wanted?"

"I'd love that, if you have the time to spare?" His eyes brightened, an eagerness appearing within his gaze. The love of his work, or of exploring—she couldn't be sure which it was just yet. Either way, she didn't mind. "I could spend all day exploring this place and never find what I need, so if you would help out that way, I'd be grateful."

She turned, nodding toward the river. "It's part of my job. We follow the river east for a short time. Think you can keep up with me?"

"If I can't, I'll holler," he said, shouldering his pack before falling in behind her. "I can't think of a guide I would prefer following."

Just what did he mean by that? Heat rose along her cheeks, flushing quickly across her body as she realized he was giving her ass a long, hard look. No one had looked at her like that in over a year, not since Bear. She wasn't sure how to handle it just yet and opted for the safest path. "You might change your mind after a few hours."

"I can't see that happening, unless you plan on nudging me off a cliff," he said, unaware of how tempting that thought had been to her when she had first found out about the assignment. Now, as she glanced back at Steven, she realized her viewpoint had already changed after meeting the enigmatic photographer, even if he did have an unhealthy interest in her ass.

"This is amazing." His voice was little more than a whisper as he spoke. The walk along the river had taken well over an hour of scrambling across the rocks and through brush. Finally, they had reached a wider track that led back to a smoother path.

There, at the end of the track, they came to a large, flat rock bank on the edge of the river. Behind the ledge the water rushed past in swirls of white, bouncing from the rocks with a low rushing sound. Like the ridge, this was one of the park areas she loved; and with the uneven pathway, it was far easier for people to reach if they knew what to look for.

"I could set up the entire first shoot out here. Does the river flood over this area at all?"

"Not very often—the rocks normally stay dry, except during a storm. Then it might flood, but we'd get a decent enough warning so we'd be able to get you, the models and your equipment back to a pick-up point." She gestured to the path behind them. "We'd only have to follow that trail back about fifteen minutes to reach one of the designated parking areas."

"Good. They'll be able to walk down here, then. I'll still hear a few complaints, but as long as the weather holds off, I should be able to get the first shoot done by Friday." He turned to look back at her. "I can't thank you enough. Can you imagine the way the shoot will turn out, the reception the pictures will receive?"

"Not really, but I'll take your word for it." She sat down on the edge of a rock, looking out over the river. Cool air brushed over the rocks, caressing her skin, pulling through the loose strands of hair that had tugged free from her braid.

"You've never taken a look at really good photography, have you?" He gave her a curious look, then walked to the edge of the rock outcrop. Small beads of spray carried by the breeze clung to his skin, slowly soaking into the shirt he wore. "I'll have to show you some of what I've done over the years. Maybe I'm not the best in the world, but I like to think I know what I'm doing. I can take something like this and show it to people who would never dream of stepping foot outside of their safe apartments."

"Do you work mainly with models, like for this shoot?" She could hear the passion in his voice, a drive she had heard in others when they spoke of something they really believed in.

"No, normally I do still life, panoramic shoots. You should see how a change in lens can alter a picture, or the angle of the sun can turn a simple shot into something spectacular. Though I admit that working with models tends to pay better. I've been taking photographs for years, started back in high school, and I've been lucky enough to turn it into a career."

She shivered, watching him closely as he spoke of a career that had brought this man into her park. What had promised to be a thankless task for her had turned into something more—she knew that just by seeing the gleam in his eyes. "You enjoy what you do—I can see that."

"Yes, I do. Not many people get the chance to work in a job they enjoy. What about you, though? Do you do this because it pays the bills, or because you love the area?" His voice carried easily on the damp air.

"I love the park, always have." She walked towards the edge of the river, moving closer to him as she did so. Her sex tightened under the soft cotton she wore, a moistness forming within her panties. Though she knew it was the breeze that tangled in her hair, she couldn't help but wonder what it would feel like to replace the wind with his fingers. She was tempted to stand next to him, but instead, she kept what she hoped would be a safe distance.

She didn't know why her body reacted this way. It wasn't like her—perhaps her Gramps had been right, and she needed to get out more. Find herself a date now and then. A man in her bed would be better than just a man in her dreams.

"I've spent most of my life wandering in and out of the area, so when I got the chance to work here, I jumped at the job."

"I can see why," he said. "In many ways, I think what we do is alike."

"How so?"

"We each find a way to help protect and promote the beauty around us." He closed the distance between them, reaching out to cup her face in his hand. "You suit this place, Dani. There's a wild beauty about you, a grace in how you move. Would you mind if, when we both have time, I took some pictures of you out here?"

His hand felt strange against her cheek. Not unpleasant, but rather, his touch felt *right*. Without thinking she leaned against his hand, a shiver running through her body as she found herself meeting his gaze. "I would like that."

She didn't move away, not even when he moved closer, his lips brushing against hers in a light kiss. Her breath caught in her throat, the soft kiss sending a tingle through her body, tightening her nipples under the thin cotton. A rush of sensation that caught her off guard as it surged down between her thighs into her now damp cunt.

She should have stopped him, slapped him, done something that would have made it clear she wasn't part of the tour package. Except she didn't feel as though she were being treated that way. He smelt of soap, honest sweat and fresh water, a combination that only added to the deep quiver claiming her core.

"I'm sorry, I shouldn't have done that," he murmured as he broke the kiss. "I don't normally go around kissing women I have only just met. It's just that...I let myself be caught up in this place."

"Well, it certainly wasn't something I expected to happen." She spoke quietly, holding his gaze, her cheeks burning hot enough that he had to notice the blush. "I'm not exactly complaining, Steve."

"And if I wanted to kiss you again?"

"I don't think I would try and stop you," she admitted.

His hand slipped into her hair, tangling into the base of her braid even as his lips covered hers. With a soft cry she gave up trying to hold back, wrapping her arms about his neck, her lips parting to welcome him within her mouth.

Whatever had brought him into the park, she wasn't going to argue. Her body wanted him, needed him—even if all they shared now was a kiss she would accept it willingly. His grip tightened, holding her against him, the edges of his canteen catching her hip, a swelling beneath his shorts catching her off guard. Did he want this as much as she did?

A soft moan vibrated from the back of her throat, his tongue stroking hers, reaching deeper into her mouth, seeking a pleasure she freely returned. Foolish—he had the chance to work with models, women whose beauty far surpassed her own, so why would he choose her?

"I have to get back to town soon. They'll be arriving in a while, and if I'm not there, I'll never hear the end of it," he whispered against her lips as he broke the kiss. "I don't want to go, but work..."

"I know." An excuse, it had to be. She should have expected it, even if the kiss had gone well.

"Tonight—would you meet me for dinner tonight?" His lips brushed over her neck, sparking new shivers of delight, his hand remaining in her hair. The grip should have frightened her, warned her off; instead, she welcomed it. He offered an odd strength mixed with kindness and compassion. Just the short conversation they had shared on the walk had shown her some of the depths within him. The very way he saw the beauty of her world spoke volumes to her. He could have been born out here, shared the same life she had, judging from the passion in his gaze as he had looked out over the river.

"I'll go one better than that—I'll cook dinner for you. I have a small cabin on the outskirts of town where you'd be welcome to join me." Cook; most of her meals were open a can and dump it in a pot or grab something from the diner. She hadn't cooked a meal for a man other than her Gramps in several years. Did she even remember how to?

"I'd love to." She didn't want to wait, though—if work hadn't called him away then who knows what they would have done.

High above the river, a cry echoed out over the park, one she had heard before only that morning, the same sound that had blessed her dream: a bald eagle. Only then did she remember the other details of the images she had woken to. The light from the river, and a blond-haired man...

Chapter Three

Dani's mind raced as she pulled up in front of the wooden structure that made up the Rangers' post. Steve had followed her back to the main path before they had parted ways with another soft, if brief, kiss. She could still feel his touch against her lips, that gentle play over her skin; her neck tingled from where he had held her hair so tight and close, yet never once seeming to threaten her.

She'd come so close to just tugging him down to the ground there and then. Not caring of what would have happened if they had been discovered on the main path. What had she been thinking of? Letting him kiss her, not once or twice, but three times? Then arranging to meet him for dinner?

She'd been date-less too long to act so quickly—it wasn't like her, not in the slightest. She'd been careful not to jump into bed or relationships with anyone. Even with Bear, they had known each other for years before they'd begun anything intimate together. She'd been out in the sun too long—that had to be the answer.

Bear. Her stomach knotted as she recalled the letter. She had to get that damn man out of her mind. He had left her for someone else, someone who would never care for him as anything except a meal ticket.

"Everything look alright out there?" Henry inquired as she walked into the office. Routine; at least walking back into the office had her settled back into routine. Work had a way of calming her down, pushing away any thoughts that would have remained to unsettle her.

"Looking good, though I spotted a couple of paths that need repairing." She pulled out a pen to mark them on the plastic-protected map pinned against the wall. "Here out at Salmon Leap, and also here, the ridge." She circled the two areas in bright red. A damaged path could be a minor inconvenience to someone who knew the area, but a health risk to a stranger.

"No doubt there are a few others as well, but I'll add them to the list. We should be able to get those seen to in the next few days. Was there anything else?" He looked over the map.

"I heard a bald eagle this morning, just about here." She tapped the plastic. "Just the one, but he looked like he was in a hunting pattern."

"Well, now, that's a bonus. I don't think we've had any out here in some years," Henry replied, smiling. "I'll keep an eye out for him and any others that might have followed in. If they have finally returned to the park, that will be something to celebrate."

She nodded and sat down on the edge of the lone desk. Silver Fox would also want to know about the eagle, and the dream she had woken to that morning. The dream would raise questions, especially when he met Steven. She'd talk to her grandfather tomorrow—doing it today might spoil her evening with the photographer. "Any word from town yet, about the models?"

"Not yet, but I figure they will be here before the end of the day," Henry explained. "I hear they called ahead to demand bottled water, some special sheets and deliveries of some weird food combinations."

"It doesn't surprise me, to be honest. I've heard some very odd things about models in the past." Dani laughed. "Have you seen those magazine covers?"

"Stick insects. That's what a lot of them remind me of. I'm not saying a woman has to be huge, but I like a little meat on the bone. Half of them look like walking skeletons or kids. Sorry, that's not something I want to wake up next to." He shook his head as they spoke.

"I'm sure your wife is very pleased to hear that."

"You betcha. I like my lady with a good handful to hold onto." He grinned. Henry was a down-to-earth man, and that was one thing Dani loved about being out here. The majority of the people she knew had a very sensible attitude to life. "Well, maybe you'll be lucky and this group will have some sense. If they aren't a healthy bunch, then you'll be dealing with complaints the entire time—a stiff breeze could knock one of them into the river."

"Wishful thinking," she commented.

"Which part?" Henry asked. A question she was wise enough not to answer—and luck prevented him from pressing further when the phone rang. Her thoughts drifted back to the moment at the river with Steve, barely taking notice of the phone conversation. Only when Henry spoke again did she turn to look back at the older man. "Well, it appears our model team has arrived, so time for you to head into town and introduce yourself."

"Great. Wish me luck," she grumbled, tugging her hair back into its braid.

"Already have."

The three luxury SUV's parked outside of the small hotel would have been ample warning of their arrival even if the call hadn't been placed. By the time Danielle had stepped out of her truck, she could already hear one cultured female voice giving life to an unreasonable demand.

"I made it very clear what I expected when we arrived, and you've been unable to provide even the simplest of necessities. Just how you expect me to survive out here without water, I really do not understand." Tall, leggy, with long blond hair caught in a velvet scrunchie, the woman spoke with a cold tone that instantly had Dani's hackles rising. She wore an expensive pair of shades; her clothing implied that she spemt more money on appearance per year than it cost for Dani to buy her cabin. "I won't put up with this kind of treatment."

"There is water in your room, Karol," the dark-eyed man she was berating replied in a calm voice. "It's even the right brand."

"This time, but I asked for twelve ounce bottles, not sixteen. Any fool can tell the difference. Any fool but you, or so it seems.

Of course, what else would I expect from a man who can only find employment through someone else's connections or their charity?" There was a cold hatred in the woman's eyes, something Dani had not expected to see openly displayed in front of a stranger. "Now get me what I asked you for, Aaron."

"You'll have to wait a few days for anything else to arrive," he replied. "Everything else is exactly how you wanted it to be. The sheets, the fruit, everything else you asked for…so I have the size of the bottles wrong. Sue me. You'll live with it, or you can explain to Steven just why you won't work this shoot. I am sure he can work around you."

"You're intolerable." She turned, stalking towards the open door of the hotel, leaving the man standing in the parking lot as both he and Dani tried not to laugh.

"You handled that well." She spoke softly in case the woman returned.

"I've had a lot of experience with demands like that," he explained, turning to look at her as she walked over. "You must be Dani. Steven mentioned you would be working with us. I'm Aaron, the main driver, gopher, and target for models throwing temper tantrums whenever the need arises."

"Nice to meet you, Aaron." She glanced towards the cars. "There are two other drivers; where are they?"

"Yes, each model has their own car and driver. Lyon and Pete have already crashed for the night, and I had the luxury of bringing that sweet piece of work in today." He nodded back towards the door Karol had vanished through. "The other lads pulled in Anna and Diana, sweet kids for the most part, but they tend to take their lead from Karol." Which meant her possible nightmare had just turned into a full-fledged one, if what she had just witnessed was anything to go by. "So you got landed with acting as the tour guide?"

"Yes, and I met Steven earlier on." The thought of the photographer brought a flush of heat to life between her thighs.

"He mentioned that, and the location you showed him. Sounds like it would be a nice area to do some of the shoot. As for Steve, he's good with people—demanding at times, but not unreasonable the way some others can be." He leaned against the side of the nearest car. Like Steven, there was an intensity to his gaze, but the way it lingered on her uniformed body left her feeling almost uncomfortable. "So when do I get to see this special place you introduced him too?"

"When we head out there for the shoot," she replied. "Where's Steve?"

"Inside, more than likely dealing with Karol and her little spat." He grinned. "Come on, I'll show you his room."

"No, tell him I'll meet him and the others at the diner. They might as well get to see the only place in town where you can get a good cup of coffee." Walking into Steven's room during an argument with Karol or anyone else was the last thing she wanted to deal with. After the kiss, it might make him think she was running after him. No, she wasn't going to risk that, no matter how tempting it felt. "It's just a block down the high street."

"Yes, I saw it when we came in. I'll let him know," Aaron agreed. He seemed to be a good man, the sort that might have stood in on occasions in a shoot. Unlike Steve, he had that more acceptable rugged appearance that seemed to be so popular amongst male models. So he sported a day's growth across his chin—not surprising with the driving he'd done—but whatever it was about Steve that caught her attention was missing in Aaron.

"Thanks." She saw no point in driving that short a distance, not when it was an easy walk that would only take a few minutes. Besides, by the time she started the truck and backed out onto the street, she could have already been there.

Her legs ached after the walk through the park, but she was used to that—it had been a while since she had done that amount of walking in one day. Normally she would have visited the ridge, then headed back to her truck and then done a drive through the main areas. Over the next few days, the checks she'd done today would have taken place anyway; instead, she'd fitted them all into one day. By the time she collapsed for the night, she would be feeling every extra step she had taken—but it would be a welcome weariness to hold her through the night.

"Coffee?" Darcy asked before Dani even had the chance to sit down.

"Sounds good to me." She slipped into the chair, resting her elbows on the smooth table.

"Be there in a minute." Darcy smiled as she moved through the quiet diner. Another hour or so, and the place would be busy with the early supper rush. It didn't matter what day of the week it was—some things didn't change. Breakfast, late lunch and supper were the busiest times of the day. The rest of the time, you were lucky if you found more than two people in the small building.

Darcy returned just as she had promised, setting the mug down. "There you go."

"Thanks. A quiet day?" she asked, pulling the mug close.

"Pretty normal, to be honest—I'm expecting the rush in about an hour or so. Your Gramps might stop by—he normally does this time of week." Darcy eased into the seat opposite, taking a moment to rest her feet. "I hear we have visitors in town?"

"Models, photographer and all the hangers-on that go with them. Henry put me in charge of their group for the duration." Steam curled up from the mug.

"Sounds... interesting," Darcy commented dryly.

"One way of putting it. It's not what I would have preferred to spend my time on, but sometimes you don't get to do exactly what you wanted."

"I can't imagine they will the easiest bunch to get along with. High heels, makeup...they won't like how we are out here. Is that the bunch that pulled up at the hotel earlier?"

"That's the one." She nodded, sipping the coffee. "Steve seems decent; not so sure about the rest of them, though."

"Steve?" Darcy gave her a curious look.

"The photographer working with them." The man she had let kiss her, the man she wanted much more from, and the man she planned on cooking supper for.

"Ah, first name basis already?" Darcy teased.

"Something like that—I stumbled into him in the park. He's been checking the area out for some locations." It wasn't like Dani to offer explanations, and she could feel the heat forming twin spots in her cheeks. "I showed him flat rock before heading back to the office, thought it might work out pretty well for a shoot."

"Flat rock; I can see that. Nice area, easy to get to—but unless you know the area, you won't go looking for it. So it should be fairly quiet down there. I can't imagine they would want to be disturbed by curious walkers." The older woman smiled. "So what's he like?"

"Who?"

"This Steve, of course. Don't think I didn't see that blush," Darcy pried.

"He's a photographer—decent looks, energetic, easygoing." She wasn't sure what Darcy wanted to know. "I think it's going to be interesting working with him, and he's certainly open to ideas."

"Ah, so you're working with him now. And here I thought you were just acting as a guide and making sure they didn't get themselves into any sort of trouble out there." Darcy glanced around the diner before looking back at her. "It sounds to me as though this Steve has caught your attention—and in more ways than one."

"Maybe; he's an interesting man." She shrugged. "It looks like the first of your supper crowd has arrived." Three middle-aged men had walked into the diner, heading straight for what Dani presumed was their normal table.

"So it seems—early, but that can happen. Enjoy your coffee." Darcy pulled the notepad from her apron and headed over to the small group.

Had she worn a sign saying "I'm interested in the photographer?" No, it had been her own fault—if she had just called him by his last name or as the photographer, then Darcy wouldn't have picked up on her interest.

What was his last name, anyway? He had told her and for a moment she couldn't remember it, but it had to be listed on the paperwork somewhere. That was, if he had been the one who'd filed it. He might have, or it might have been the company that hired him. Except hadn't Henry mentioned the name of the photography studio, and the name of the photographer would have been on the paperwork, wouldn't it? She frowned, trying to recall the details when she'd caught a brief glimpse of them. Black, that had been it—a simple name for a man who told tales in color.

"So this is where I find you, instead of out working?" Silver Fox rested his hand on her shoulder. She hadn't even heard the old man walk into the diner. Her grandfather settled down in the chair, looking around before he spoke. "I hear they have all arrived, though, taken over the place, demands for some strange bottled water. Do they think we have illnesses in our pipes they are going to catch?"

"Some people prefer bottled water, Gramps." And some people also had very bad manners.

"Well now, they are going to find out a lot of people around here won't pamper to them." He smiled, waving to Darcy so the easygoing waitress would bring over his coffee when she had a moment. "Big shiny SUV's, fancy clothing, makeup, and no doubt afraid of bugs. Better hope they don't decide to use some of the caves for their work—I can just imagine the screams if they came across a bear."

"Bats would do the same thing." A tempting thought; she could take them all into the one set of caves she knew was home to a colony of bats, but that might put her in Steven's bad books.

"Some of the work won't be so bad, though."

"How so?" He nodded his thanks to Darcy, taking the steaming mug of coffee.

"Just a feeling I have, Gramps." She wasn't quite in the mood to start answering uncomfortable questions from her grandfather. Especially about a man she barely knew. He'd find out about the supper invitation soon enough, but hopefully not until after the fact. That at least might make it easier.

"They can stay away from me." He grunted. "Last thing I need to end up dealing with is a bunch of…" His words trailed off, the door to the diner opening at the same time. "Spoke too soon."

She turned, looking towards the door as the three models, Aaron and Steven all walked into the diner. The two blondes and a brunette looked less than impressed with the diner, and each woman wore shoes that would have crippled Dani in minutes. Just why some women tormented themselves by wearing those things was beyond her.

"That's them."

"Well, I didn't think they were aliens," he commented in a deadpan voice.

"Gramps." She hissed at him, hoping the group hadn't heard.

"Aliens would be more useful—a tourist attraction." At least he didn't speak loudly enough that they could hear. "Just count the days until they are gone, smile, nod politely and do your job. If things go well, then they'll be here less than a week. Unless the weather changes."

Dani glanced up, her gaze narrowing as she watched the three women, and two men approach the table. The distinct click, click, sound of their heels announced their approach even before Steven spoke.

"Dani, I'd like you to meet the ladies working with me today, and my brother, Aaron." Brother; how could two men who looked so different be related? Still the smile that reflected in Steven's gaze had her hoping for rain. "Anna, Diana and Karol, I'd like you to meet Danielle Wind Dancer. Dani is going to be helping us out on the shoot, finding locations with me, making sure we don't stumble into places that wouldn't be so safe."

Two out of the three women at least offered the attempt at a smile, but nothing of the sort even pretended to form on Karol's lips. "It's a pleasure to meet you all," Dani said, attempting to at least be polite. "I hope we will be able to work well together over the coming days. Steve, this is my Grandfather, Silver Fox. He knows as much if not more about the area than I do."

"Nice to…"

"Is there somewhere around here that I can get a decent espresso?" Karol interjected. "I can't imagine this place serves them."

"It doesn't, but unless you plan on traveling back to the city, you'll be without one for a while. Though if you're lucky, the hotel might know where you can buy a small machine," Dani replied. Espresso; who around here would want one? Coffee, good strong coffee, and very occasionally one of those instant-package type cappuccinos were far more common. At most, Dani would order a hot chocolate with whipped cream—but only on a cold day when she felt like treating herself.

"I don't know why they insisted in dragging us out here, not even a place to buy an espresso? Backwards little town. We could have done the same type of shoot in a studio—all they would have needed was to use some backdrops. Or a blue screen. Anyone can use a blue screen for special effects work," Karol complained, glancing around the diner with a cold gaze. "I'm going back to the hotel to pack, and I expect to be able to leave within the hour."

Dani stared at the woman, uncertain how anyone could possibly speak in that manner, especially in public. To expect that everyone would pack up and leave just because she wanted them to was outrageous.

"You can demand that all you want to, Karol. It's not going to happen. The contract includes the area, the description of the location types required and the express desire of the designer that her work be featured against real backgrounds. No screen shots, blue screens, or any other wonderful little trick of the trade," Steven replied calmly.

"And how would she know the difference?"

"You expect me to lie?" Steven kept his gaze fixed on Karol.

"I expect you to do whatever you need to in order to get us back to civilization," Karol said, her gaze sweeping over the diner. "I have no desire to remain here. I don't wish to work under these types of conditions, and I know that both Anna and Diana will back me on this."

He turned, looking at the other two women. "Is that correct—you both wish to break contract and risk not being signed for further work with this company and others?"

"Break contract, Karol, you never said anything about breaking the damn contract. Have you any idea what that would do to me?" demanded Diana, her jaw clenching as she continued. "It's one thing for someone like you to try that stunt, but Anna and I don't have the presence in the trade that you have. Something like this could ruin the pair of us."

"Calm down. My Steven wouldn't report us, and we'd be able to do the shoot back in a studio. We all know how he doesn't like to see me upset. Tell them, Steven." Karol moved closer to him, slipping her arm into one of his before leaning against his shoulder. "Now stop being such a baby over this and give the word."

"Possessive" was the word that came to mind as Dani watched the scene unfold. For whatever reason, Karol thought that Steven would do exactly what she wanted him to do. Even if it meant lying and potentially ruining his career. Steven didn't answer, not at first. "We could make it home in time to still grab a table at Miguel's if we left now."

"No," said Steven.

"What?" Karol looked at him, stunned.

"I said no. I am not going to lie for you, and I am not going to put Diana or Anna in a situation where they might never work again." He pulled free of her grip. "We're staying. The first of the shoots will take place tomorrow morning, and you can deal with it."

"You don't mean that." Karol traced one slender finger over Steve's arm, leaning in closer as she continued. "Think about it… ,just you, me and a bottle of wine after dinner."

"I've given you my answer. Keep this up, Karol, and I'll be making a call in the morning to report your actions to the agency. I am very sure they will not be as impressed with this as you believe they might be. There are hundreds of women in their books who would jump at the chance to take your place out here."

"You wouldn't dare." Dani had to wonder just what had been or was still between the two of them. Just a work relationship, or something deeper? She wasn't used to seeing women touch men that intimately without there being a connection between them.

"Try me," Steven replied, his voice cold and hard.

Karol's gaze hardened. "Bastard." She hissed. "I don't know who you think you've become, Steven; but without my contribution to your work, you'd still be doing bit jobs and struggling to pay the rent." Karol turned, stalking out of the diner, her passage marked by the distinct sound of her heels stopping at the doorway. "I hope you enjoy working with women like that one." She nodded towards Dani. "Because after we get back into town, I'll be making sure that you never get the chance to work an assignment like this one again. You can go back to taking stupid pictures of trees for all I care, Steven Black. You're on your own after this one." With that she was gone, the door left swinging wildly after her exit.

"Steve, I'm sorry," Anna offered even as she turned to hurry after Karol. Diana fell into place after the other two, discomfort and embarrassment clear on both their young faces. They were far younger than Karol, barely twenty—though, as Dani understood such things, they were already old for the trade.

Silence settled on the diner for several awkward moments until her Gramps finally spoke up. "Well now, that was interesting. Do they often pull stunts like that?"

"Some do, some don't. I've worked with more than a few wonderful men and women in this trade, people willing to go that extra mile in order to get the right shot. Karol has been in the business since she was a kid and likes to think that her track record will protect her when she throws a fit, or makes some outrageous demand." Steven turned his focus back to the table where the older man sat. The tone her grandfather had used made it clear his impression of the photographer had been a good one. "I'm sorry she lashed out at your hometown, though. That was uncalled for."

"Can she cause trouble for you, after this shoot is over?" Dani asked. The last thing she wanted to hear was that Karol had ruined things for him over not getting her way.

"No, not really, not as much as she thinks she can. Karol is losing favor with the agency. I'm not sure if she's really angry about the location, or just the fact that someone else was given the assignment she really wanted." Steven leaned back against the counter. He looked comfortable there; even with the cut of his clothes that marked him as an out-of-towner, he seemed at ease. "I'll talk to the agency when I get back and make it clear that I really don't want to work with her again. Now Diana, she's a good one, goes that extra step, puts up with a lot of the fallout from people like Karol. I'd like to be able to help her career with this shoot."

"Rotten apples, you find them in every bag." Silver Fox nodded. "Well, I will leave you in Dani's capable hands. If you two do decide you need some advice come and look me up. I'll be fixing the roof over the next day or so."

"Gramps," Dani protested.

"We've had this conversation. Pick your battles, Wind

Dancer—this is one you aren't going to win with me. You'd have more luck taking on a summer storm." He was right; when *had* she managed to win one against the older man? "A pleasure meeting you, Steven, and I am sure we will talk again soon."

Dani watched as Silver Fox left the diner, smiling as she heard Steven speak again. "So, are we still on for that dinner?"

Her only answer came in the form of a slip of paper she pressed into his hand as she headed for the door.

Chapter Four

"You're not picking up all of this for just yourself, are you, Dani?" the merry-eyed woman inquired as she helped pack up the groceries into a brown paper bag. "It's not like you to grab more than the basics."

"I just thought I'd do something a little different tonight." Telling Stacy about her date would be as good as taking out a notice in the town paper. Better. She'd tell half the population by the end of the day, and the rest would be discussing it over morning coffee. "I've got a long few days ahead; no harm in giving myself a little treat, is there?"

"If you say so. I'm not sure I'd want to cook up something special just for myself. Why don't you give your Gramps a call instead and see if you can have supper with him?" Stacy folded over the top of the sack. "I've had some odd requests in the past day. Water, special coffees and some strange fruit teas. I've never seen a day like it. I'm not complaining about the extra business, though—don't get me wrong there—just the odd orders they seem to think I can fill."

"There are some strange people in the world," Dani agreed.

"So, are you going to ask your Gramps to come out for supper?"

"I'll think about it." She pocketed her change, picking up the sack before heading for the door. "The other orders must have come from the models—I wouldn't worry about it, Stacy. They'll only be here a few days."

The door closed behind Dani with the sound of the small bell attached to the door frame. Those women were going to drive her nuts. Muttering under her breath, she packed the small bag away in the truck, catching a glimpse of movement out of the corner of her eye. There, on the other side of the street, was one of the women who'd come in for the shoot. She couldn't be sure which one, as she was out of sight by the time Dani turned around. No doubt the visitor had been taking a walk to get a feel for the layout of the town. Even if they had come across as slightly stuffy, the models probably wanted to know a little more about the place where they were staying.

The short trip out of town and back to her cabin gave Dani ample time to replay the events in the diner. Karol, whomever she thought she was, obviously believed she had some sort of hold on Steve. Dani couldn't stand women like that. No, that wasn't fair either; *people* like that left her gritting her teeth. It wouldn't have mattered if it had been a man or woman who had attempted to manipulate another in front of Dani—her reaction would have been the same.

Her hand itched as she recalled how Karol had clung to Steven in the middle of the diner. Maybe Karol would settle down and the work would become a little easier to handle. But somehow, she doubted it—women like Karol didn't drop their complaints. She'd find another way to cause trouble for everyone during the shoot, including Dani.

She pulled up in front of her cabin, hurrying inside with the groceries. What had she been thinking of, inviting a man she barely knew over for supper like this? Now she had to try to figure out what to throw together. As long as he wasn't expecting something fancy, it shouldn't be that hard for her to come up with something. So why was her stomach knotting at the idea of cooking for him?

It wasn't just the cooking that left her unsettled, but Steve's arrival in her cabin. They would have the chance of some time alone together, which they both appeared to want—or so she thought. Had she just imagined the depth behind the kiss they had shared? No; even the memory of his lips against hers left her shivering in the warm summer sun.

What would he think of her home? It wouldn't match up with

some slick apartment or townhouse—not that she believed he was someone who would look down on her for where she lived. It shouldn't have even bothered her, not the way she was now letting it affect her. She hadn't been this nervous about a date in years. Did she have time for a shower? Maybe if she put the dinner on first, she could dive in and out of one before he was due to arrive.

The next twenty minutes found Danielle rushing about her small cabin, washing up, getting the meal prepared and in the oven. She'd decided on a basic casserole-type dish that she hoped he would enjoy; then came the mad rush to tidy up. She'd barely pulled on some clean clothes, pulled a brush through her hair, and braided it before she heard the sound of a vehicle arriving. He was early, or she was late, she couldn't be sure which was right now. Without waiting for him to tap on the door, she opened it up.

Steve smiled, holding what looked like a bottle of wine in one hand. "I wasn't sure what you liked to drink, but I didn't want to turn up empty-handed." He tugged the bottle from the brown paper bag. "It's nothing special, just a domestic chardonnay."

"Thanks. I'll get it in the ice box to do a quick chill on it, unless you want to wait until supper is ready. I'm afraid it will be a while yet." She stepped out of the doorway, letting him inside.

"Nice place. Just you living out here?" He looked around as she headed towards the fridge. "Waiting until supper is ready works for me. Though I wouldn't mind a glass of water until then."

"Yes. Gramps lives about thirteen miles away in his own place." How often had she been grateful for the small distance between the two cabins? At least she knew he was unlikely to just turn up without announcing it first. "I can put some coffee on, if you'd like?"

"Thanks, I'd appreciate that." She could feel him watching her as she moved across the small kitchen. Now the wine was safely out of the way, it didn't take her that long to get the coffeepot on. "I am sorry—about earlier in the diner, I mean."

"It's not your fault. You can't be responsible for what others say or do, Steve." She smiled, turning back to look at him as the water began to bubble through into the coffeepot. "I'm glad you're staying out here, though. I think I'm going to enjoy working with you."

"Somehow I get the feeling that was not how you felt about the assignment when you first heard about it," he teased, sitting down on the couch when they walked back into the living room. "Not that I would blame you—you probably had images of high-heel wearing, standoffish women invading your park, complaining at every breath. Wait...that's exactly what you got."

His smile reflected within the deep blue of his gaze. There weren't many men who could make fun of the situations their work might cause for others, but she'd learned earlier in the day that he wasn't like most people she had come across.

"Well, it could have been worse than it has been so far." So far—that was the key. If Karol behaved, than the work would be easy enough; if she went back to complaining over anything she didn't agree with, then it would be a long week. "You're only here for a week, according to the paperwork?"

"That's all the time they set aside for the assignment. Normally a shoot like this would take a couple of days, but they added on extra time due to weather and other disruptions." He moved a little on the sofa before speaking again. "You can sit with me if you want, I don't bite." She hadn't even realized she'd still been standing until he spoke. Heat rose in her cheeks even as she moved to sit next to him, her blush increasing with the touch of his arm about her shoulders. "If you don't want me to, I'll stop."

Stop; stop what? His squeezed her shoulder gently enough that she realized he was talking about where he had placed his arm. "No, I'm fine with this. Honestly."

He nodded, keeping his hand on her shoulder. "You're nervous."

"Yes."

"Why?" he asked. "I'm not going to do anything you don't want me to do. Even if I might want otherwise."

"I know; it's just I haven't dated in a while, and when I was, I stayed with the same man for years." Why was she explaining this to him? "Bear left about a year ago."

He nodded, watching her closely, trailing a pattern with his fingertips over her skin. "And what happened between you?"

"Work—he headed into the city for work. School first, then becoming a doctor—or so he told me."

"Why didn't you go with him?" He spoke quietly. Probing for information in small bites.

"It's not something I wanted. I like living out here. Besides, as I told Bear, I promised Gramps." There was more, though—it just wasn't the right time to tell him.

"Ah. Well, I wouldn't want to leave here either." He moved closer to her. "I've only been out here a day, and I already feel at home."

"What would you want to do that I might say no to?" That question had been fighting to gain a voice since he had mentioned it.

"This." His hand moved into her hair, curling his fingers within the still damp braid, pulling her closer. His breath caressed her face, lips covering hers with a kiss softer than the grip that remained tangled in her hair. With a soft moan her lips parted under his, welcoming the feel of his tongue as it slipped within her mouth, seeking out the delights he offered. She shouldn't let him do this, but already her ability to care had left the cabin in a huff of disgust.

With a growl, he pulled her across the sofa into his lap, deepening the kiss, tasting her as he if she were the rarest of delicacies. Her nipples hardened against the soft shift dress she had pulled on. Being small-built meant she seldom had to wear a bra when not working, something she took advantage of at home—but now it left her breasts barely covered by the thin material. "All you have to do is tell me to stop." He growled, breaking the kiss long enough to speak. "I don't want to push you somewhere you don't want to go."

"I want this." If that made her a slut, so be it. She didn't care; who would know anyway, once he left? Even if this turned out to be nothing more than a fling, then at least she could enjoy it. He left her shivering inside and out, her pussy lined with a liquid heat that already moistened her panties.

Still, it didn't make sense that she'd be willing to risk becoming the talk of the town by sleeping with a stranger. No, not a stranger—she at least knew his name, which was far more than some of the girls she had known back in community college could claim. "I want this more than I can explain."

"Good." His lips reclaimed hers as he pushed her back against the couch fully, covering her body with his own. She arched into him, thighs parting as he pushed her dress up over her hips. A hunger burned within his gaze. "I don't normally do this."

"Nor do I." She moaned, his teeth nipping a rapid path across her neck, that one strong hand still holding her hair. That should have felt threatening, but it didn't. She didn't understand, didn't want to understand; her mind wanted to release all claim on her body and just give in to the wicked delight his teeth brought to life. Gods, this was insane. One hand moved slowly up from her hip, cupping her still-covered breast, massaging it firmly. "Please, I want to do this, need to."

"Good." He rolled from the couch, pulling her with him to the floor until she lay beneath him on the lone, thick rug that decorated the living room. "You're beautiful."

She pulled back from the kiss, meeting his gaze fully. "I've seen the women you work with, Steven. I'm not like them. I don't have the looks magazines seek, so how can you say that?"

Her body didn't want to talk, or to question him. It just wanted to find a way to strip off his clothing so she could feel his cock pressing against the entrance of her cunt.

"Because it's true. You have a real beauty, one that shines through in everything you do. So maybe you wouldn't be picked out for a fashion shoot, but that's based on just that...fashion. Not what I find attractive."

He smiled, speaking softly as he looked down at her, reaching out to cup her cheek when he continued "You're...you. You don't try and be something other than who you are. I don't know how else to explain it."

It didn't make sense to her right now, but the way his eyes almost glowed as he spoke, the pressure and rising heat between her thighs as he leaned down for a new kiss pushed the last of her questions away. Her nails dug into his back, catching on his shirt, her hips raising, meeting the soft rock of his groin between her thighs.

Clothing, there was too much in the way of clothing between them. With a low moan she sought the buttons on his shirt, tugging them open. Hair caught beneath her fingers, something new. Bear had lacked hair there, just as he had been unable to grow a beard; his skin had always been smooth, but now silken blond curls played under her touch. "Soft," she murmured, moving down over his chest. In a moment his pants and shirt were kicked to one side, her dress joining the small but growing pile of discarded clothing.

He pressed between her thighs, cupping her panty-covered mound firmly. "So warm and damp; you do want this, don't you?"

"Yes." She rocked down into his touch, rubbing herself against his fingers. It wouldn't take much for him to pull away her panties or tug down his briefs. Yet she waited, let him set the pace as he had been all along—she, for whatever reason, was willing to let him continue doing just that. Bear, on the other hand, she'd had to almost lead by the hand.

She had to stop comparing him to Bear; it wasn't fair to either of them. "Please. I want this, need it."

"I know." She almost stopped at that, searching for a hint of smugness in his smile. A search that revealed nothing but the desire she returned. His fingers hooked into her panties, slipping down over her thighs, one hand returning to cup her now naked pussy. "I can feel it, Dani." She ground down against his hand, arching as she felt one finger push between her damp lips, seeking within her sex. A second finger moved within her cunt, pressing upwards against a spot she had rarely felt touched before now. A cry, guttural, one she barely knew to be her own, broke free at the sudden double tap against that hidden point.

Feel it; how could he do anything but feel it with the way her pussy rippled on his fingers, as if it sought to hold them within her core. His free hand moved back into her hair, holding her by it, his fingers beginning a slow dance into her sex, pressing, tapping, urging low cries from between her now-parted lips. Her thighs clamped on his hand, her grip digging further into his arms, holding tightly to him with each thrust of his fingers.

Slow, fast, slow again; he didn't keep to one pace, never giving her body chance to settle into a rhythm. He kept her off-balance, her desire growing with the soft and slick sounds of his fingers rocking into her cunt. Even then she couldn't wait, didn't want to wait any longer for him to replace his fingers with his cock. "Please."

"Please what, Dani?" He caught her bottom lip between his teeth, nipping softly, sucking it into his mouth. "What do you want? Tell me."

"Fuck me; I want you to fuck me." She tugged at his briefs. "Now."

"Wait." His grip in her hair tightened, almost enough to hurt but not quite. "Almost time, but not just yet."

Time, time for what? She wanted him now, not later. Well, maybe later as well.

"It's not time for me to fuck you yet; almost, but not quite yet." His teeth scraped gently over her throat. "I won't do it until you crave it more than you crave air." He grip on her throat closed, a rush of fear mixed with delight. She knew, without a doubt, that he would not bite into her throat.

"Gods, please. Now."

"Yes, now." His teeth lifted from her throat, fingers slipping free from her tightening cunt with a soft slick sound. He shifted, pushing back between her thighs, his cock nudging at her swollen vulva, meeting her gaze to hold it a long moment. Only when she whimpered, arching to him, did he finally push within her body, seeking to drive himself into her core. "Such a hot, willing woman with a wet cunt that feels so good around my cock." He groaned.

She should have felt embarrassed. Instead, his words only served to drive her down onto his cock. Before now, she had never been this eager to feel a man's flesh driving into her body. Her thighs tightened, ankles raising to lock behind the small of his back, her groans matching his thrusts as the small hairs on his chest brushed over her swollen nipples. Harder, faster, his rocks drove her body back against the rug, his hand tight in her hair, pulling back to bare her throat to him further. His lips found her pulse point, suckling deeply on sensitive skin, his breath heated as it forced against her flesh in low groans.

"Harder?" He lifted from her throat, looking down at her, soft strands of hair sweeping down from the now-loose ponytail.

"Yes," she grunted, her nails digging into his arms, heels pressed to his ass, her hips raised with each claim into her body. His cock throbbed, seeking to push deeper, stretching the walls of her clenching cunt. The grip on her hair ceased, his hands pressing to the rug, arms straightening out as he took his weight upon them.

With a growl of need, he thrust harder into her sex, rocking her against the rug hard enough that she felt the fibers scrape at her back, knew they would leave a burn, knew the painful reminder she would be left with. Knew and accepted all of that without complaint.

Perspiration beaded across her breasts, each thrust rocking

them hard, her nipples small points aching to be touched. This time he hadn't reached for them; next time. Would there be a next time?

Gods now, she needed to cum now. A scream broke free, her body tightening on his cock. Heat, wet, clinging heat rushed down over his flesh, coating her inner thighs, mingling between them as she heard it, his growl, his release in a word that burned into her mind.

"Dani!"

"I think supper might be ready by now." She smiled shyly at him, her head resting against his shoulder as they lay on the rug.

"We should eat. I don't want to let your hard work go to waste." He brushed his fingers over her cheek, then cupped it gently. "I never thought that coming here would mean I'd meet a woman like you. You're at peace with working in the park, yet so very much a woman in all things."

"I'm not sure what you mean?" She moved reluctantly from his arms, her hair loose from the braid. He'd unbound it when they had collapsed to the floor, playing his fingers through the waist-length strands.

It didn't matter that she walked through her cabin naked, save for the flimsy shield her own dark mane provided. There was something sensual about the way he watched, as if he were replacing the soft touch of dark hair with his own fingers.

"I see a lot of different kinds of women in my work. I've talked to wives, mothers, career women, women who aren't sure what they want to do in life. Women who try to be men, but don't accept that that is what they are doing. Then there are those rare, beautiful women who don't try to hide their gender; they just work harder to do their jobs. They don't act as though every man in the world is out to get them, or presume they have to sleep their way through life, never marry, never seriously date in order to be taken seriously.

Focused on Love

"I've not known you long, but I can see it. You're a dreamer; you work for what you believe in, but don't sacrifice who you are inside in order to get it." He rose, looking around the cabin. His gaze lingered on a large dream catcher that hung on one wall.

"Take your home, for instance. You don't hide your heritage—you embrace it, but you balance it with other things."

"It's just what works for me. I'll be right out, just need to clean up a little first before I start dishing out supper."

He followed her into the bathroom. "I might as well do the same thing, though I am a little reluctant to get fully dressed again. Would you mind if I just left the shirt off?" He leaned against the doorframe as she washed up quickly.

"No, why would I?" She had this odd desire to walk back out into the room and claim his shirt. "It's not as though I haven't seen and, well, felt...what you have to offer." She could feel the blush as it crept over her cheeks and down her throat.

"True enough." He took her place at the basin, brushing against her ass with one hand when she walked past. "Damn, that's one.... Sorry, that would have been uncalled for."

She stopped in the doorway, looking back at him. "What were you going to say?"

"You'll slap me and have every right to." He smiled.

"No, I won't." Curiosity had the better of her. "Even if I want to, you have my word that I won't try and slap you."

"Well." He turned, looking her straight in the eyes. "I was going to say that you have one damn fine ass." For a moment, though it was little more than a fleeting thought, her hand clenched with the desire to do just what she had promised she wouldn't. But the warmth in his eyes stopped her from acting—that and her given word.

"A lot of women want to slap a man who says that, even if they are being offered a compliment. Besides, it's true. All that walking you do has left you very tight. And not just on the outside."

Any chance she might have had at hiding her blush vanished

with those words...

61

Chapter Five

The supper dishes lay draining at the side of the sink, while an almost empty wine bottle sat on the bedside table along with two still half-full wine glasses. For a meal that had been thrown together at the last moment, it hadn't turned out too badly, even if she did say so herself. Now, with the night drawing in, she found herself not wanting to think about him leaving. Both of them danced around the subject, or avoided it entirely, during the hours that passed by after supper. A meal she had enjoyed while wearing nothing more than his shirt.

"I need a bath." She traced her fingers over the rim of the glass. "It's been a long day, for both of us."

"Indeed." He nodded. "Do you want me to leave so you can get some rest?"

"No, I don't." There, she'd said it. "I don't want you to leave tonight." She didn't want him to leave at all, but it was too soon to say something like that to him. It was too soon to even admit it to herself.

"Well then, I suppose I could stay—that's if you don't mind a stranger sleeping on your coach?" he teased.

"Who said anything about the coach?" She smiled, shaking her head. Stranger indeed, how could she look on him as a stranger after what they had shared before supper? Her cunt tightened at the idea of him spending the night with her. A deep shiver ran the length of her spine in memory of his hands over her skin, within her hair. There'd been a strength in his touch that she already craved to experience again. "I have a double bed, and I don't think you're going to turn into an axe murderer overnight, are you?"

"No, though I might decide to see how deeply I can taste you again," he replied, walking towards the bathroom as he spoke.

"So, since we are going to share a bed tonight, do you have any problem sharing a bath as well? It looks large enough to accommodate both of us."

It was—the size of the bath was one of the many things she loved about her cabin. A tub that others might have torn out to replace with a modern plastic-coated one, she'd had it repaired, reinforced, and then installed in her bathroom. Even by hot-tub standards, it would have been classed as comfortable. Now, as a way to end the night, the thought of slipping into the warm water to lean back against Steven's arms appealed to her greatly. "I would enjoy that a great deal." She followed him into the bathroom, watching with interest as he turned the faucet on, sending a mix of hot and cold water sloshing into the tub. Her delight doubled when he reached for a bottle of soap, spilling it into the tub. Bubbles erupted into life, climbing the smooth sides, filling the air with lavender and chamomile.

"Nice choice--it seems to fit you," he commented, scooping a small handful of the bubbles. "Soft, natural, but a hardiness in both plants that matches the strength of will I've seen in you."

Heat touched her cheeks, a blush that seemed to readily answer his words. "I like scents like this. It just feels nice to be able to relax to them. I wouldn't have thought you'd want to be in a bath smelling of flowers, though." She tugged at the shirt, slipping it from her body. Steam curled upwards, clouding the mirror, clinging to her form. Even if she hadn't undressed, she would have felt near-naked with him in moments; the steam would have soaked through the material until it clung to her like a second skin.

"When it's a bath shared with you? I can't think of something I would enjoy more." His pants slid to the floor, falling near the shirt she had discarded. "Shall we?" He held out a hand to her, offering to help her into the tub as he reached to turn off the faucet. Neither of them spoke any further as they stepped into the warm water that filled the old tub. She'd never shared her tub with a man before it had become her place of refuge. Like some of the newer homes, she had both a tub and a shower. Mornings she would dive into the shower, wash off before heading to work. Evenings were her time, a moment to relax and forget the world beyond the cabin. His arms wrapped around her as he settled down behind her within the water, pulling her close. The bubbles smoothed over her skin beneath his gentle caress, covering her stomach, creeping to cup her breasts as he pulled her back to lean against him.

"That feels good," she murmured, resting back against his chest. Neither of them moved now, content at least for the moment to do nothing more than enjoy the warmth. Her eyes drifted closed, the rhythm of his heartbeat echoed through his chest, and small damp curls pressed to her back. She had never imagined being held like this; now she didn't want to think about stepping out of the bath and losing the gentle intimacy the moment offered.

He was an enigma. One moment he would hold her hair in a grip that left her torn between pulling away and sinking against him. The next he was discussing sharing baths with her and offering her the chance to relax.

"I'm glad." He nibbled softly against along her neck. "I like quiet times; you'd think with my work I'd get a lot of quiet times, but I don't. It's often a case of dashing from one assignment to another, working in the dark room, hanging pictures, talking to new clients or dealing with old ones." He brushed along her sides, then wrapped his arms back about her waist.

"Alone is something I am used to. Most of the Rangers I know or have known spend the majority of their time alone. We always have a radio with us, and one in the truck, but the checks, walks, looking over the fire points—it's all done alone."

She loved it, though—there was no denying that. "Don't get me wrong—I enjoy my work. Coming home means grabbing a meal and a bath and collapsing into bed, especially during the tourist season. It's something I always wanted to do, ever since I was a kid."

"And your Gramps?" His grip shifted, cupping her breasts, his cock twitching against the crack of her ass.

"He's always been there. Mom died years back, but even when she was alive she left me in his care." Her ass cheeks clenched on his cock, a mischievous smile tugging at the corners of her lips as she wriggled back against him. "He taught me about my heritage but didn't push it on me as the only way to live. I think maybe that was the mistake he made with my mom, so he wasn't going to repeat it with me."

His thumbs brushed over her nipples, interrupting her train of thought—not that she was complaining. Talking about her family could wait until they had more time. If they had the chance for further time together.

She moaned, pressing back against the swell of his cock, his hands massaging her breasts in slow, firm strokes. Maybe just relaxing wouldn't be the only thing they would do. His teeth grazed over her shoulder, his fingers capturing her nipples, pulling on them, his nipping kisses following the line of her body. Hard, soft, they changed at random moments, stoking a need within her body.

She rocked back against him, tracing her nails across his thighs, groaning softly as one hand moved from her breasts to press between her legs, cupping her sex. Her clit throbbed, the memory of their time in the living room still fresh enough that even the suggestion of a touch was enough to trigger a deep, rippling spasm through her cunt. She didn't have to ask him for more; his fingers slipped through between her lips, trapping her clit in a firm grip. She arched into his touch, unable to fight the soft jerk that played through her body.

Reactions like this were something she had only read about, or heard being discussed by her peers. Conversations she had tried to stay away from, having never understood how they could be anything more than just a dream, or exaggeration of those talking.

Focused on Love

Now she knew better. Now her own body craved the touch of
another, wanted to feel his cock throbbing, stretching the tight
walls of her pussy until she groaned.

"I want you." He groaned against her ear, nipping into the soft
lobe. "Now. I don't want to wait, but I don't want to leave the bath
just yet."

Nor did she. A wicked thought sprung to life as she slipped
from his grasp, moving to her hands and knees within the tub.
Warm water clung to her breasts, tugging at her nipples, soaking
through the ends of her hair as she settled before him, parting her
thighs within the confines of the bath. His growl alone was enough
to spur her on, encouraging her to wriggle her ass towards him.
"Who says we have to leave the bath?"

He grasped her hips, settling behind her sending the water
sloshing around the bath, nudging between her thighs without
hesitation. His grip tightened, not enough to hurt but still firm, a
demand, a need she answered with a desire that turned her cunt
slick before his cock even began to enter her offered body.

She wanted it as much as he did. With a groan of her own, she
pressed back against him, forcing herself back onto his cock in a
harsh thrust. Water surged in the tub, washing over the edge in a
loud splash, but she didn't care. Her clit throbbed, teased by the
tugging bubbles, adding a dozen extra fingers against her skin—
and all she could do was give into the drive he urged to life.

Small, sharp waves slapped against the sides of the tub,
rippling back against her breasts, stinging her nipples. Her cunt
clenched on his cock; the harder he thrust, the more she pressed
back to him, and the greater her desire for him became.

She groaned, lowering her head towards the water, bubbles
caressing her cheeks, barely aware of the now-constant splashing
sound that echoed after each thrust. His body, hers, his cock
buried in her cunt, her clit throbbing, nipples taut beads, water
coating her skin, blocking her vision. More, she needed more,
wanted to cum, wanted to feel him bury himself so deep that they

became one person.

"I'm going to cum," he declared, his fingers digging into her hips, his thighs pressing against her ass. "Going to…" The words were lost in a low gasp as he stiffened behind her, his cock sinking fully within her pussy, throbbing against her moist confines. That was all it took, the last spur she needed to find her own release.

Her scream vibrated into the remaining water, her arms threatening to give way fully and send her face first into the bath. Even with his own orgasm still rocking through his system he reacted, wrapping his arms about her waist, pulling her back to sit on his lap in the tub, sending yet more water out onto the floor, his cock still deep in her aching cunt. They shuddered, almost as one, her legs throbbing, vision blurred as she tried to catch her breath. He'd known she would fall, known she would have hurt herself by doing so, known and found a way to catch her.

"I think we have something of a mess to clean up." His arms remained wrapped about her body, holding her to him through the last of the spasms that worked through her pussy. She sighed, content in a way she could not remember experiencing before. "Not that I am complaining about the work."

Nor would she—for the first time in her life, she didn't begrudge having to clean the bathroom.

A low ringing sound pulled Danie from the haze of sleep, her hand almost knocking the handset from the cradle instead of bringing it to her ear. "Hello?" She yawned more than spoke, trying to focus as she looked at the clock. Early, not even six yet, though her alarm would have woken her within the next thirty minutes or so.

"Dani?" Henry sounded far more awake than anyone had the right to be. "Sorry to call so early, did I wake you?"

"Yes, it's okay." It wasn't the first time he had called before she had been out of bed, but normally it meant something was wrong. "What's going on?"

"It seems we have some vandals to be on the watch for." He replied. "Some kids, I think. They were up at Parking lot A. They kicked over the garbage cans and started a small fire. We caught a lucky break, though—it burned itself out before the alarm sounded."

"Fire? Just great. Kids or not, they need to learn not to do things like that. We could have had a major forest fire on our hands." Even with the rain of the previous month, forest fires could all too easily rage out of control. "I just don't understand people who pull stunts like that. Are we sure kids are behind this?" She sat up in the bed, aware of Steven's presence next to her.

"No, but it's likely. Whoever it was didn't know enough to pour the water out of the cans. They just tipped them on their side, spilled the garbage out and set light to it. They didn't even use any accelerant." Henry sounded calmer than she might have been. "But I wanted to bring you up to date in case I didn't see you until later. I know you are taking that group out to the river today."

"That's the plan," she agreed, smiling as she rested her hands on Steven's arm. "But I'll keep an eye out for any trouble."

"I'll contact you on the radio if I come across anything else, and the copy of the report will be on the desk in the office. I just need to finish going over the findings," Henry continued.

"Sounds good to me. Talk to you later, Henry."

"Henry? Someone I should know about?" Steven mumbled, pulling her closer in a possessive grip once she'd returned the phone to the stand.

"Someone you already know about—he's the senior Ranger." She curled back against him. They wouldn't be able to linger for much longer, not with both of them having work to do. "He was just filling me in on a small incident."

"What time is it?" he asked, pulling his fingers through her hair, tugging through the small tangles with care.

"Nearly six—time we were both up. What did you arrange for

the morning?"

"To meet up with Aaron in the diner, then head out to the park once we've rounded up the others." He said. "And I am supposed to be there by seven, so you're right—we need to be up." He didn't want to move from the bed, she could see that. Nor did she. It had felt right, spending the night in his arms, listening to his breathing as he had fallen asleep. She'd been awake for an hour or so after he had drifted off, content to do nothing more than rest against him, feeling the rise of his chest under her head.

"Staying here all morning won't get the work done, and I can't imagine that Karol would wait quietly." She rolled from the bed, her bare feet hitting the floor.

"That's an understatement," he agreed, following her lead and reaching for his pants. "She'd make the remainder of the day a living hell in any way she could. Don't get me wrong—she can be a dream to work with, but only when things are going her way. I don't like heading off before you, but I'm going to have to dash to the hotel for some clean clothing, my pack and kit."

"I know, and I'll meet you at the diner. I normally stop by there in the morning anyway." She watched as he dressed. He wasn't trying to avoid being seen with her, she knew that; but neither of them would be ready to face explaining their situation to the models or any others.

"See you in about an hour?" He brushed a kiss against her lips, heading towards the door before she even had the chance to reply.

"I'll be there." A frown creased her brow at the speed of his exit. Work; his focus had shifted from her towards his work. That had to be the reason for how he had rushed out. He had work, and so did she. At the end of the day, they would have the chance to talk more; or so she hoped....

"Where in Hell's name where you?" Karol demanded before Steven had even walked into the diner. In the twenty minutes since Dani had arrived, she had tried not to be drawn into the blonde model's snide remarks. Instead, she had relaxed with her morning cup of coffee and talked to Diana. Anna hadn't said a word, but had visibly squirmed once Karol had shot her allegation at the photographer. "I tried calling your room a dozen times last night, and you never replied."

"I was busy last night," Steven replied.

"Too busy to return my calls?" She crossed the diner, her heels clicking over the floor. "I kept calling past midnight, and you still didn't answer. You didn't even answer this morning when I tried again."

"Obviously; so what was so important you needed to talk to me last night?" He nodded a greeting to Darcy, passing her a large travel mug.

"I want to know just where you went," Karol pressed.

"And I would like to know just when I was under any obligation to inform you of my every move?" He spoke calmly. "The last that I checked, you and I stopped dating over a year ago."

Dating? Dani's stomach knotted. They had been an item? That explained a lot—and Karol didn't appear to be a woman who let men go when she thought they could still be of use to her. Now Dani understood the way Karol had molded herself to Steven the previous day.

"What has that got to do with me wanting to talk to you?" Karol refused to drop the topic.

"It means you lost the right to expect me to be at your beck and call, and I stopped having to fill you in on my movements long before we broke up. You saw to that when you decided to vanish for a weekend with, what was his name again... ah yes, Philip." His voice never changed. That, more than his words, seemed to anger Karol further. Better still, the shocked look seemed to given Diana reason to smile. Even if the other woman tried to hide it.

"Now, if we are quite finished with your tirade, the rest of us do have work to do. Or have you also forgotten that we are out here on a shoot, not to rehash some less-than-pleasant moments of our mutual past?"

"You can't treat me like this," Karol protested, oblivious to the amused glances Aaron shot towards his brother.

"I'm not treating you as anything other than a person I am working with, Karol. And your actions are holding up the rest of us." Steven smiled as he took the now-full travel mug from the bemused Darcy. "Dani, if you would fill the rest of the team in on the location we will be using today, I would appreciate it."

She waited a moment in case Karol planned to interrupt further, but the blonde merely slumped into a seat, glaring at anyone who glanced her way. The only interruption came from Aaron, who slid into the seat next to Dani. Strange, there were plenty of other seats in the diner, but there was a good chance he just wanted to get a better look at the map, especially with him being one of the drivers.

"Well, the rock flat is easy enough to reach—it's a fifteen-minute walk from parking area A, just off county road thirty-three. The path is easy to walk as long as sensible shoes are worn. The rest of the Rangers know where we will be, and I will have my radio with me in case any help is needed." She unfolded the map she had brought into the diner, smoothing it open on the table, pointing out the location for all to see.

"When we get there, I want you to listen out for me. If I tell you to move, do it. Ask questions later. Hesitating should something go wrong could cost you your lives."

"What sort of dangers are you talking about?" Anna inquired, looking over the map. "You mean snakes and that type of thing? Are there snakes out there? No one told me I would have to deal with that."

"There are some snakes, but the odds of you seeing them are slim. For the most part the animals in the park will stay out of your way. Most animals, including snakes, are far more afraid of people than we might be of them."

Focused on Love

"So what should we be on the lookout for?" Anna trailed her finger over the map.

"Manmade dangers. Don't leave any garbage behind—that includes cigarette butts, soda cans, bottles. Bottles and cigarettes offer the greatest problem. Light can reflect through the glass of a bottle and cause a fire; a burning butt is also a fire risk. The dangers I will be on the lookout for come mostly from the weather, or someone in the party not realizing where they are walking." She and her coworkers normally handed out the same information a dozen times a day to walkers and picnicgoers. It was also posted on notices around the park, but she doubted the models had taken the time to learn just what they could walk into. "Your best bet is to remember to do what I tell you, listen for my warning, and not go wandering off. You'll also need to forget about wearing your normal shoes. Even deck shoes would be safer than the ones all three of you are wearing right now."

"She has got to be joking." Karol snorted. "She wants me to change a five-hundred dollar pair of shoes for ten-dollar deck shoes?"

"She has a name, and Dani knows what she is talking about. Unless you like the idea of ruining your shoes and perhaps breaking an ankle in the process, I suggest you listen to her," Aaron spoke up, looking around the diner. "Take a good look at the men and women in here and their shoes. Most of them have lived in the area for the majority of their lives. They know the terrain; they know what to wear."

"They're ugly. I will not wear something like those boots that woman has on." Karol folded her arms across her chest, giving Dani the impression that the model was a seven-year-old rather than in her twenties.

"You'll be wearing hiking boots for part of the shoot; why not use them to walk to the location? It might make an interesting selling point," Aaron suggested. "What about it, bro?"

"It makes sense to me. And you'll need to change in the SUV's or go back to the motel before we head to the park and change into the main clothing needed for the shoot. The area doesn't exactly have the facilities to change in." He seemed to take delight in Karol's growing frustration, and Dani wasn't sure she liked this side of him.

"Are there even rest rooms out there?" Diana spoke up. "If there are, maybe we could change out there?"

"Yes, in the parking area. Nothing fancy, but they are clean. I'm not sure the lighting would be good enough for what you three might need, though. So my suggestion is to change at the hotel and use the restrooms to touch up before the shoot if needed."

One thing she had made certain of was having the restrooms checked earlier in the day. Normally they were looked over once a day as it was, but if there was one thing likely to set off the models, it was a dirty restroom.

"Anything else we need to be aware of?" Steven asked as she folded up the map.

"Not that I can think of. You were given the list of equipment that would be allowed, and it's my job to make sure this goes off without any park-related problems."

"Then let's get this day started." His fingers brushed against her hand, that momentary touch the only sign they had shared something special the previous night....

Chapter Six

Over three hours after the meeting in the diner, the work out at the rock finally began. Three changes of shoes, different complaints that had varied from lighting, bugs and the sun in the models' eyes had finally been put to rest a little before noon. Through the majority of it Dani had sat on a rock, watching the team set up for the shoot. It had been an eye-opener in many ways. Even the clean restrooms had given rise to a complaint from Karol. They were too small, the lighting poor, the tissue paper something that a one-stay motel would use...and then she had seen a bug.

Screams of outrage had faded into grumbling complaints when the women were slowly ushered away from the cars. Karol had been the hardest of all the women to move down the pathway—instead of following when she had been told to, she had lingered near Steven's car. Whatever she'd been thinking, she had given up her wait after it became clear that the shoot would start with or without Karol's presence. Now Dani was finally able to relax, as Steven had taken over the work.

Aaron had taken a seat next to her, his job of setting up the battery-run lights, cooler, and extra bags over for the time being. "Well, I have to admit this is a great location. Have you ever worked with companies like this before?"

"No, this is my first." Aaron was an easygoing man, far more relaxed than his brother now appeared to be. Steven appeared focused on the women as they moved across the rocks under his directions. The complaints had silenced fully once Steven pulled his camera from its waterproof bag; instead of arguments, there were now smiles, the women positioning themselves around the rocky area with little more than the occasional word or nod.

"A virgin, then?" His dark eyes sparkled with an easygoing humor. Without that humor, the intensity of the way he'd looked at her during the shoot and the set-up would have left her feeling uncomfortable. Everywhere she had moved, his gaze had seemed to follow her. Perhaps it was nothing more than her imagination, though, or just the fact she was someone new to him.

"Something like that," She finally responded to his virgin jibe. The teasing made a welcome change after the stress of the morning. "How long have you been doing this?"

"Five years. I started working with Steve on his shoots when he needed an extra set of hands. It beats flipping burgers—pay is better, and the scenery certainly is, though I wouldn't mind being deaf some mornings. This morning being one of them."

"Karol?" She nodded towards the women.

"Yep. Don't get me wrong—she's a star in her own right, but she could do with learning how to treat people. She and Steven dated for a couple of months and took another year to break up fully." He answered her unspoken question. "Every now and then, she tries to make it seem as though they are still an item. Normally so she can get her own way over something."

"Not the first time she's pulled a temper fit, then?" She kept her voice pitched low, not wanting it to carry towards the working the group.

"No. And it won't be the last, either. Not just with Steve—she's tried it with me and Johnson, another photographer she works with on occasions. She'll do whatever she thinks will work best in order to make her the focus of attention." He pulled a bottle of water from the nearby cooler.

"Are most like her? Models, I mean?" She refused the bottle he offered.

"No. The majority of models are hardworking people, a breeze to do shoots with, willing to work from dusk until dawn. The hangers-on at a shoot can be the real problem. Boyfriends, girlfriends, agents, parents or appointed guardians with the younger models, those people who think they know the business and try to force the photographer into making their 'darling' the focus of the shoot." He slipped the second bottle back into the cooler. "Diana and Anna are both a dream to work with. Quiet, attentive, they take directions easily and they turn up on times for shoots. I'm not even sure if either of them date. They are both determined to make it in this business."

"I'm guessing you have to be determined to get somewhere as a model." She might not like the way a lot of models were used to portray the "ideal woman," but the more she listened to Steve and Aaron, the more she realized it wasn't exactly their fault.

"Very much so. There are photographer's who insist on weigh-ins; they won't use a model if she's gained even a pound. Steve's not like that. He tends to do shoots like this one, using locations that will make people just sit back and go, *wow*. That way, if the woman is less than picture-perfect by whatever the current standards are, then the shoot will still work."

"He sounds like a good man." Her gaze drifted back to Steve as he moved across the rock, snapping pictures.

"He is," Aaron agreed. "One of the few who will stop a shoot if he thinks the model is at risk. It's lost him a couple of contracts when he demanded a drug test on one woman a few years back. Some agencies aren't so protective of those they have on the books. Meat factories, Steve calls them—places that just shuffle bodies through the door. Some of those even encourage the models to take drugs, or turn a deliberate blind eye to the ones they know are popping pills."

She listened as Aaron spoke of a world she'd had no dealings with until Steve had walked into her life. A few articles in magazines, the occasional passing comment on the news, but none of it had really sunk in over the years. Now she found herself trying to piece together half-heard comments as she watched Steve work. "So who's the older one out of you both?"

"I am. Steve is the dreamer. He's always been the one to look for the next shoot, that next ideal location. He's never taken the time to settle down because of it, not with the way his work takes him all over the world. Or at least that's the excuse he uses. Personally, I don't believe him. He's afraid of committing to just one woman," he finished, tracing a slow line over the knee of his jeans.

"And you?" She listened closely to what he had to say, wondering what had prompted his less-than-subtle warning about his brother.

"I'm the practical one, worked as a cook, driver, even did over the road trucking for a time. What I did was about money to pay the rent, keep a roof over my head, food on the table for my kids." He shrugged.

She glanced towards his hands. "You're married?"

"I was—two kids living with the ex-wife." He turned his hands over. "It's been six years now since the divorce; not a mistake I will make again. Some people aren't supposed to get married." He looked back at her, smiling. "I'm guessing you agree, as you aren't married."

"I guess you're right; not everyone is cut out to be married. I'm not sure if I am or not. It's not something I've really thought out. Some Rangers marry, others don't; it's not as though we get guidelines on this when we take on the job." It felt odd to be discussing the sort of things you normally didn't talk about with Rangers, but there was an ease about him. The sort of feeling she normally experienced when talking to someone she had known for years.

What about Steve—was he like that? She had that same sense of him being comfortable to be around, but there was an edge to him that Aaron lacked. If the more easygoing of the brothers felt as though marriage was a mistake then the odds of Steven being the right one – no, she didn't need to think about that right now. "Some people just don't belong in a relationships at all, marriage or otherwise."

"So, how do you think it went?" Steven asked as they walked back towards the parking area. The three women walked ahead of them, carrying nothing but their own bottles of water. Everyone else had taken the time to clear the area after the shoot, carrying a mix of bags and equipment with them.

"It looked like it went well, but I'm not really one to ask about it." She smiled, the heavy cooler swinging in her hand with each step.

"Aaron mentioned that you were a virgin—well, in this sense, at least." He held her gaze for a moment.

"I, erm… yes ,well, your brother and I had the chance to talk when you guys were working." Her thighs tightened as she walked, a moist heat seeping through into her panties. What was it about this man that had her squirming at simple comments? "He seems like a good man."

"He is," Steven agreed. The path widened as they approached the parking area ahead. She could make out the shapes of the cars ahead and the now-familiar voice of Karol voicing a new round of complaints. This time, they seemed to be about the length of the walk back to the cars.

"We have fallings out; most families do, and working together doesn't help there, but we talk them out. For the majority of the time, we work well together."

"What about the rest of the week—do you have any ideas on what sort of locations you'll need?" They rounded the last corner, breaking free of the cover offered by the trees.

"A few ideas, notes and suggestions made by the company. Perhaps we could go over the suggestions they provided later on today? I trust your judgment on finding suitable places, especially after how well this spot worked out." His praise brought a smile to her lips. "Once we get back to town and I've had the chance to develop the film, then we could meet up for supper?"

How had he planned to develop the film? "Will you be sending them back to the city by courier?"

"What? The pictures? Oh, the film—no I have a mobile lab with me. It doesn't take that much work these days to develop film, as long as you have the right set-up. Didn't you see the trailer parked at the back of the hotel?" He paused to set down his pack before digging out the keys to his SUV.

"No, but it makes sense that you would bring the equipment with you. Having to travel back into the city to check it, only to find you needed to do some extra shots, wouldn't make a lot of sense." All that traveling to correct a mistake would work out to be quite expensive after the first few times.

It didn't take long for the small group to pack up their cars, work that continued in a comfortable silence. Even Karol had given up on her complaints for the time being, no doubt relieved that they would be heading back into town. They weren't the only ones—despite her love for the area, Dani was tired and wanted to catch up with her Gramps before sitting down with Steven.

"Fuck's sake!" The swearing caught her off guard, especially from Steven. "Two flats; how in hell's name did I end up with two flat tires?" He kicked the nearside back tire in disgust.

"Easy enough to pick up nails, or hit a piece of glass on the way up." She set the cooler in the back, then crouched to look at the flat. "You have a spare?"

"One, yes, but not two. I might be able to scrounge another one from Aaron's ride—the tires should be interchangeable, so I can at least get back to town—but this is ridiculous." The odds of two flats on the same car at the same time were rare, but not unheard of. "This is going to take a while." He grunted, tugging the jack and first tire from the back of the car. "Aaron, I'm going to need your spare—two flats over here."

"Be right over," Aaron called out, already heading for the back of his own vehicle. "Just your luck, right?"

"Luck? Annoyance would be more realistic." Steve grunted, setting the jack in place, cranking it up. "Two damn flats; who would have guessed the odds."

"No bookie I would visit." Aaron set the second tire down. "Looks like you picked up a nail in that one." He tapped the edge of a piece of metal still sticking out of the tire. "Is there a local garage where we can replace the spares?"

"Two, but the one I prefer is just a couple of blocks from the diner." Dani took the nuts from Steven as he worked at changing the tire, catching sight of Karol leaning against Aaron's car. Why did Karol seem so smug? She couldn't be sure, but it almost seemed as though the woman was pleased about what had happened to Steven's car.

"I'll head back into town, drop the diva off." Aaron glanced back towards the three women. "Unless you need my help?"

"No, I should be fine. And I can't see Dani abandoning me to the wilds—can you?" Steven looked up from his work, sliding the new tire into place.

"Agreed; for some reason, I think she's quite taken with you, Bro." He headed out to the other car before Dani had the chance to form a reply. "Keep an eye on him, Dani. He has this odd habit of finding trouble without even looking for it. I'll catch up with you both in town."

Finding trouble, like the flat tires; was that what Aaron had meant? She would have to talk to him about it when the chance arrived. "Here, I'll get it into the car." She had turned back to Steven in time to see him rolling the first of the damaged tires towards the back of the car. Together, they managed to complete the changeover in half the time it might have taken him to finish alone. Whatever had caused both flats, only one of the tires showed any sign of metal or glass; the other one offered no visible clues as to the cause.

"We should be able to pick up new tires for you easily enough," Dani commented as she hauled the second flat into the back of the car. If there was one thing the garage was likely to have on hand, it was a supply of various tires.

"I hope so. Even a minor setback like this can be annoying to deal with." He wiped off his hands. "Thanks, for the help, I mean. It's appreciated."

"I wasn't about to stand back and just watch. I'm not like that." I'm not like Karol—that was what she had wanted to say, but had chosen the more diplomatic route. "I'll follow you back into town, in case one of the spares has a blow, or we missed something with the other tires."

She didn't wait for his reply but headed straight for her truck. The tires, how both of them had been flat when they had returned to the parking lot—it didn't make sense that he had run over something on the way out. She slid into her seat, starting the truck as she sorted through the random thoughts, images of what they had seen on the drive up.

Steven had been behind her truck, and in front of Aaron; so if there had been a bad patch on the road, surely she would have hit it first. No, it wasn't that simple—nails, glass, they could be anywhere on the track. She was overanalyzing the situation. A fault of hers her Gramps had warned her about more than once. There were times a cracked glass was nothing more than a cracked glass.

"Looks like someone slashed the tires." Warren ran his fingers over the re-inflated tire, then used a pair of pliers to pull the metal shard from the rubber. "This was jammed in at the end of a tear, and I 'm betting the same thing was used to slice the other tire, but I won't know until I inflate it again."

"Are you sure? Maybe I just hit something on the trip up?" Steven frowned, looking at the piece of metal held within the grip of the pliers.

"Very; this looks like it's the tip of something else, and there is a tear in the tire, not a single puncture." Warren let the piece fall from the pliers' grip into Dani's hand.

"Nail file?" She turned it in her fingers; the small ridges on either side of the metal were familiar. She didn't use files often, but still recognized what it appeared to be. Karol—it had to be Karol behind this. Her smug look, the way the woman had lingered around Steven's vehicle before the shoot had begun, and her obvious problems with Steven refusing to be at her beck and call.

"That bloody woman. If she thinks I'm going to take this lying down, she is out of her mind," Steven growled, his gaze darkening.

"You've no proof it was Karol." Even if Dani also believed the model was behind it, they needed proof and not just supposition before anything could be done.

"Who else could it have been? She's trying to get back at me for not being around last night and not treating her as if she were made of glass." Steven shook his head, looking at the metal in Dani's grasp. "It would be just like that woman to pull something this petty." The same passion and fire she had seen focused during his work with the camera now reflected in his gaze in an unfettered form.

"Well, whomever was behind this, it doesn't matter. It will cost a few extra dollars to replace the tires, but no long-term damage has been done. If she had thought before doing this, she would have slashed the tires *before* we headed out to the shoot and not after we arrived," Dani pointed out, handing the metal shard to Steven. "That way, she might have had the chance to stop you from using the location you wanted and to force you to give into her."

"She doesn't know me as well as she thinks she does," he muttered, pocketing the piece. "I doubt anything short of an all-out forest fire would have changed my mind."

"Steven?" Diana called out from beyond the doors of the workshop. "Are you in there?"

"Yes. Hold on, we'll be right out." He glanced over at Dani. "Do you mind if we postpone our talk until tomorrow, say breakfast at the diner around eight? I'm sorry, but after this, I wouldn't be very good company. Might be best if I just retreat into the trailer for the night, work on getting the film developed."

"That works for me." She tried not to let her disappointment show. "It will give me time to sort through some ideas myself. Now I've seen some of the clothing you want to feature in the pictures, I should be able to make a few suggestions."

"Steven, is everything alright?" Diana asked the moment they both stepped out of the workshop. "Aaron told me what happened with the car. You weren't hurt, were you?"

"No. I spotted it before I got in the car," Steven explained, giving the woman a warm smile. "No harm done; nothing to worry about there."

"Good. Sorry, I shouldn't overreact like this; I just worry." Diana took a step closer, then stopped as if seeing Dani for the first time. "Sorry. I didn't want to make it look like I was ignoring you, and I meant to thank you earlier for helping us find such a wonderful location for the shoot. I can't wait to see how the pictures turn out—Steven does such a wonderful job with any assignment he takes on. I've been lucky—this is my fourth shoot with him now. You'll be helping Steven track down some more possible areas?"

"Yes, though not until tomorrow." She smiled; Diana had an easygoing personality, at least from what she had seen so far. Even if she gushed about the photographer's talents. "Right now, though, I should go and look over my maps. My Gramps might have a few ideas as well. So I'll see you both tomorrow?"

"I look forward to it," Diana replied, her gaze firmly fixed on Steven. "Can I give you a ride back to the hotel?"

"No need—my car is fine."

"You might want to get the rest of your vehicle checked out, just in case," Dani suggested as she opened the truck door.

"Just in case of what?" She heard Diana ask; but if anything further was said, it was lost behind the now-closed door—a door, however, that didn't block her view. There, as she watched from the truck, she saw Steven slip his arm about Diana's waist as they walked towards her car. With the model he made an offer of public intimacy, when he had done everything possible to avoid even touching the Ranger throughout the day.

"So he's caught your eye, Wind Dancer?" Silver Fox reached out to touch her hand across the table of the diner. "Or didn't you think I would see what has already formed between you two? I'm old, not blind, you know."

"He's an interesting man," she protested. The short drive to the diner had given her no chance to think things through, and she'd only stopped because she had seen her grandfather's truck parked outside. If she'd known, however, that walking in would have meant another discussion about her love life, she'd have headed straight for home.

"And he is interesting enough that he spent the night at your place." The words were a statement rather than a question.

"How did you know?" She pulled back her hand from his grip. Had he been snooping through the cabin? It wasn't like him to invade her privacy like that.

"I drove up to your place last night, on a suggestion that I might like to join you for dinner, but you already had company." He smiled, tapping the table as he watched her. "The rest I didn't know until you told me just now. You have to learn to put on a better poker face than that."

"Damnit, Gramps." She leaned back in her chair. "I suppose I get the lecture now?"

"I could save it until later; or you could just tell me yourself why what you let happen last night might not have been a good idea." He folded his hands on the table.

A hundred answers sprung to life at the back of her mind. "I never claimed it was a wise idea, Gramps, but I'm not expecting it to last. Besides, you said yourself that I needed to start dating again."

"Dating, yes; falling into bed with a stranger is not the same thing. It's something I would have expected from your mother, not you."

Her jaw clenched at his words. "I am not my mother."

"Maybe not, but if word of this gets out, then you will have the entire town thinking you've become her. All the work you've done will be for nothing." He spoke far more calmly than his words suggested he felt. "I love you, Dancer; ever since your mother placed you in my care, I have loved you as much as I did her. I don't want to see you following her path, making her mistakes. The people of this town have very long memories."

She was nothing like her mother. "He's a good man."

"And one who will leave when his work is done out here," he replied. "I'm no fool—his world is beyond here, and you belong in this area. It's as much a part of you as the color of your hair. I saw how it tore at you when Bear left, but this man...this Steven, he's reached in to touch a part of you that you've kept protected. You've let him into your life and your heart, even if you won't admit it to yourself. When he leaves, you'll crumble for a time, or shut off again like you did before."

"Or maybe I will just accept that all he and I can be is a moment in time?" She didn't want to give her grandfather's concerns too much credence. Bear's leaving had hurt her, even though they had both known it was coming; but Steven? They hardly knew each other. So she had enjoyed one night in bed with him; so what? It didn't mean she had fallen in love with him, just that they both shared some common interests. "All I wanted to do was enjoy a few hour's company with him."

"I can see it in your face, all those modern excuses you're trying to cling to. You're not like that, Dancer. You may look almost like one of them, like a woman of the city, but you've an older soul in your body. And that soul wants to believe in walking with someone for the rest of your life." He met her gaze fully, refusing to let her tear away. "He's not the one, Granddaughter. Don't believe he is. Don't let those false hopes force you into the mistakes of the past."

Focused on Love

Her gaze lowered to the table as she tried to control the
anger that threatened to gain life. A rage that, if given even a slim
chance to speak, would result in her throwing hurtful words at
the old man who wanted nothing more than for her to be happy
in her life. "I don't know who he is yet, Gramps, but I know things
are not as they seem. The eagle is back in the park. I saw him
when I met Steven down there, and he called out to me just as he
had done that morning in my dream."

"An eagle? Well, now, that makes things interesting. Maybe
I should take with the spirits." He smiled as he spoke. He didn't
often talk of the traditions he had tried to enforce on her mother,
but an eagle returning to an area where there had been none if
close to fifty years was a sign. Even if that sign had nothing to do
with what had happened between Steven and Dani.

"Maybe you should." She reached out and touched his hand,
feeling the soft wrinkles beneath her fingers. He had seen so
many years, experienced things she would never have the chance
to. That he loved her, wanted to protect her from harm, was
something she did not doubt. He had to learn, though, to give
her the chance to see things for herself. "I don't know what I'm
going to do, Gramps, but this is something I need to let play out
between him and me."

"Come to me if you need help, Dani. That's all I am asking—
that you come and seek me out if you find yourself in need." His
hands closed on both of hers. "I won't turn you away or make
fun of you. I'll even try not to say 'I told you' so if things work out
badly."

"You'll try, Gramps, but you'll still say it." He was right, as much
as she did not want to think about it. A week; they had a week
or less, and then Steven would leave to return to his city, and she
would remain behind once again.

"Of course, I'm human after all." His smile softened the words,
as did the wink that followed. "Though don't tell Darcy that—I
have her believing I am a spirit walker."

"Gramps!" she protested, laughter bubbling up within her. "You are a wicked, wicked man."

"So all the ladies keep telling me. Now, since you cooked that new one a meal, I expect a supper invitation from you next week." His hands slipped away from hers, the tension lines around his eyes easing. "And I will come prepared with some of that herb tea they keep trying to get me to take when I've eaten spicy food. If it works against that, it should work with whatever you cook for me."

"My cooking isn't that bad."

"Tell that to the mice who were avoiding the remains of your supper pot last night."

Chapter Seven

The sheets tangled about her legs as dream images claimed her closed eyes. Unwanted and desired visions mixed as one, leaving her squirming on the bed. He was there, watching her through the shadows of the night. She knew his presence, felt it, sensed it; smelt her own desire rising as he stepped towards the bed.

It was a dream; he wasn't truly there; he'd turned down the chance to spend an evening with her thanks to the anger and childish behavior of another. But her mind didn't care, and her body clung to the idea of his presence, her thighs parting on the bed in anticipation of his touch. She wanted him, craved the pressure of his presence between her thighs, ached to feel his touch as his cock slid within the depths of her moist cunt. Her hips pressed forward, desire prickling to life in her breasts, tightening her nipples into twin points, each breath carrying the unspoken plea of his name.

She groaned, turning on the bed, seeking out his hands. It was just a dream, nothing more than a dream that tormented her mind when she wanted the real man in her bed. Strange how sleeping without him, even after just one night with his arms about her, left her shaking as she awoke from the restless sleep. It had been his choice, though; he had other things he had needed to take care of. Work, film to develop, notes to read through—a hundred small tasks he needed to finish before they could spend some time together again.

Coffee and a shower would chase the remains of the dream away, or so she hoped. The last thing she needed would be to face Steven still clouded by the affects of an unwanted night of tossing on the bed that still smelt of his presence. She had to find a way to ignore the suggestions her mind offered

He was an odd man, not like most she had met. Their night together had been followed by a day where he hadn't so much as attempted to kiss her. Had he been afraid that someone would discover what they had done?

No, Aaron had guessed that there had been something, as had her Gramps. So if he was worried about discovery, then it was from a narrower source, not the world in general. Karol, perhaps? Not that the model could do anything to her. Still, if that had been the reason, it was one she could both understand and respect. Karol set her teeth on edge just by looking at her.

Her maps and notes lay scattered across the kitchen table, ideas to show Steven, places within the park that offered a beauty she believed he would appreciate. Amongst the notes lay two reports from Henry. One of the fire the other day, and the second, more troubling, one the older man had hand-delivered late last night.

She'd seldom seen Henry so disturbed before then, and the report had explained why. Sometime late in the afternoon, there had been a break-in at the small cabin the Rangers used as an office; petty vandalism, but it had left her boss shaken. Locals would never have been behind something like that. Paint had been splashed over the inside of the cabin and the radio set smashed. The damaged radio, which would have to be replaced immediately, was the greatest concern. Without it, the ability to contact Rangers out in the field was reduced. Calls for help could go out, but the chances of being heard were reduced. People had died because of a call not being heard. Nothing had been stolen, not even the spare truck parked at the back of the cabin, or the bottle of whisky that Henry had kept out there. Everything pointed to someone who had a grudge against the Rangers themselves. The idea alone left Henry unsettled, and it didn't do much for Dani either.

Her gaze lingered on the empty wine bottle she had left by the sink. Why she hadn't thrown it out or taken it down to the recycle bins in town, she didn't know. A reminder of a pleasant night, or a hope for something more at a later time? Her gramps had been right—she was an old soul in a modern body. He would leave in a few days time, a week at most, and she doubted he would ever return. She knew it would have been better if she had not allowed that night to occur. If she had found the strength to say no, the ability to ignore his touch, she would not now be facing the painful reality of him leaving. Would it have been a strength she needed to ignore his touch, or a weakness in trying to pretend she didn't crave the company of a man like him?

Blond hair, blue eyes, a youthful look about him mixed with a darkness that she had seen, even felt. He wasn't abusive, she was sure of that, but he needed to be with a woman who would let him take charge during their intimate moments. Someone who wasn't afraid to be a real woman with him.

Real woman; that term turned her stomach. Everywhere she looked in life, she could see images that portrayed what a real woman was supposed to be,--a confusion of lies and conflicting messages that he was part of providing to the world. How could he even imply she was a "real" woman, a woman he wanted to be with, when he worked with the likes of Karol every day?

"Just another quick turn in the sack." She growled, sweeping the papers to the floor in the wave of anger that sprang to life. "That's all I am to him—a pleasant pastime during his visit."

How could she have been so foolish to think otherwise? With the anger came a determination as she replayed the small clues she had seen since his arrival. The way Karol reacted to him, how the other models looked at him, even how Aaron spoke about Steven. It was so clear to see, now that she allowed herself to. Steven was a wonderful, sensual man whose presence turned her cunt into a rolling wave of liquid desire. A man she would want to spend the rest of her life with, if he had been anything other than the smooth, momentary-pleasure-seeking man she now recognized him to be. "No more. Once, but no more."

A light rain had begun before Dani'd left her home and showed no signs of letting up as she drove into town. At least with the change in the weather, the models could not expect any work to be done that involved them. Steven, on the other hand, would be willing to go and look over the locations she had marked on her map. She could feel her teeth grinding at the thought of the photographer. After the anger he had caused for her this morning, she tried to tell herself she wasn't looking forward to spending time with the man. Yet her body tingled at the thought he might look her way again, the slim chance that maybe, just maybe, he would ask for forgiveness, sweep her into his arms, and...behave like a bad romance novel. She growled; what had gotten into her?

He had, in more ways than one.

By the time she pulled into the parking lot of the hotel, she was fighting for control on her anger, struggling to find a way to keep it locked down so no one would realize the depth of her fury that threatened to break free. Her hands gripped the steering wheel, knuckles turning white, nails digging into the covering. Only when one of her short nails threatened to crack did Dani finally take a long breath and release her grip on the wheel. She had to control this, to stop him from taking that level of control over her emotions. He was a stranger, a man she had shared a bed with once, and in a few days he would be gone, out of her life for good. All she had to do was look at this as nothing more than work.

If only it were that easy. She waited for several minutes in the truck, steadying her breathing, making sure she thought of nothing more than the work, the places in the park she needed to show him. Would the lighting work; what was the access to the areas; what dangers did she need to be aware of before suggesting them to him?

Only when she felt calm enough did she leave the truck and walk into the hotel. It had been years since she had stepped inside the warm building. Unlike so many motels that had sprung up over the years, the town hotel didn't sprawl out on one level, but rose above as a three-story building. It was older than a lot of the buildings in the area, close to a hundred and fifty years old, and many of the original features of the hotel remained in place.

Though the town was a small one, the hotel was built by a couple who had taken cues from larger businesses in the cities of the time. An ornate chandelier hung from the ceiling in the entrance hall, warm wood panels lined the room, and a desk that had been loving polished over years sat within reach of an open fireplace. The hotel lobby was a cross between a traditional lobby and a comfortable living room.

She already knew from the talk within the town that the men and women who'd traveled in for the shoot were on the ground floor. The old hotel only had one small elevator, and if the models had been given rooms on an upper level

"Hey, Dani, are you looking for someone?" Aaron called out as he walked into the lobby. Raised voices filtered down the hallway after him, one male, one female in an argument she couldn't fully make out.

"Steven—is he about? I'm supposed to be going over new locations with him today to set up the rest of the shooting schedule."

"He mentioned something like that. He should be in his room—if you want, I can show you where that is." Aaron glanced back towards the corridor as he spoke. The argument appeared to be growing more heated by the moment, and it didn't take much for her to realize that the male voice belonged to Steven. "Or maybe not—might be best to wait until those two have finished their spat. I could keep you company while you wait, if you'd like."

"Steven and Karol?" she asked.

"Yeah. She started in on him this morning again. I swear, those two act like a married couple at times. Always making up and breaking up." Aaron shrugged as he walked over to the coffee stand in the lobby. "I don't know why they don't admit what might exist between them and save the rest of us a lot of trouble."

"I thought they just had a working relationship now?" She could feel her hands clenching. "At least that's the impression I had after the other day in the diner."

"They do, I think. You'd have to ask Steven for the details. Sometimes, I just think they fight far too much for it to have been a real break-up. You know how women are, Dani. She wouldn't be so clingy with him if there wasn't still something between them. He has to be giving her some form of come-on, doesn't he?" He looked back at her, then flinched. "Sorry, I know you kinda like him, but my brother can be a pain when it comes to women. If you two are thinking about hooking up for a time, I would rather you be aware of what you're letting yourself in for."

She didn't know what to say. Everything she had seen of Steven and Karol had suggested their relationship had been over for some time, yet here was Steven's brother claiming otherwise. Why would Aaron do that unless he knew something about the situation? Doors slammed at the far end of the hallway.

"Maybe it would be best if I waited at the diner. If you'd let him know where I will be, I'd appreciate it." Doubt; everywhere she turned, she found more things to help raise the doubt in her mind about Steven.

"Sure, I'll let him know," Aaron agreed. "Just think about what I've said though, will you? We can talk about it tonight if you have the time."

"Morning, Dani; sleep well, I hope?" Steven smiled as he pulled up outside the diner. She hadn't bothered going inside but had waited for him in the morning sun, the maps folded away into a waterproof clear folder that protected them from the light rain. "I haven't kept you waiting, have I? I thought you'd be inside, so I let myself get delayed this morning. Diana had some questions about the shoot, and then Karol started off again. I swear, out of the entire group, only Anna seems to know I don't have the answers to everything off the top of my head."

"No, I haven't been waiting long. I had a feeling you would be late." She tapped the folder in her hand. "You might want to leave your car behind and come with me in the truck—it will make this easier if you don't have to follow me down unfamiliar tracks." That, and it would be practice in avoiding the reactions her body had allowed free reign the last time they had been fully alone.

"Sure. Didn't you get wet waiting for me out here?" He locked the car door and followed her to the bright red truck.

"Yes—it's just rain, though. It's not going to hurt me." Heavy storms had a way of sneaking up on the area, but the light mist that had soaked slowly through her hair and coated the paint of her Ford could be just as worrying to deal with. Unless people knew the area, they seldom realized a light shower still turned the pathways slick, still added water to the rivers, still wore away soil and turned it into a thick mud. Hidden dangers; she lived in a world of hidden dangers.

"I don't think I'll ever get used to being out here. I keep thinking I can; then I see you standing out in the rain, welcoming it, and I think about how Karol almost screamed at the suggestion of taking some shots in this." He smiled as she started the truck up. "So what have you got in mind to show me today?" He reached across, tracing a light touch over her thigh.

She tensed, but tried not to react to his hand, refraining from even mentioning what he was doing. "There's a glade I think will work well for one set of shots, and then there are also some caves I want to show you, Mr. Black."

His hand froze on her thigh. "Mr. Black, is it now?"

"Yes—that is your name, after all." Maybe that would get the message through to him. "And you are out here on business, just as I am supposed to be working with you in order to make your show go off without a hitch." She didn't look his way, not even when his hand left her thigh. "So which did you want to see first?

The glade or the caves?"

"Have I done something to upset you?" That was a question she had not expected him to ask.

"I'm not sure what you mean." She kept her eyes on the road.

"You're cool, almost cold. I've been around women long enough to know that means something is wrong." He was watching her, she could feel it, the way his gaze moved over her form but lingered on her face. "So what did I do?"

She didn't reply, not at first. Not for ten minutes or more as they traveled through the edge of the park. Her focus was on the road, watching for any signs that the dirt track she turned off onto had been affected by the light storm. A heavier vehicle had been used on some of the roads recently, an SUV perhaps—maybe Aaron had been getting some practice driving in. Strange, she hadn't seen any signs of mud on the cars; but with the way Karol complained, it made sense he would have had the car cleaned off.

"So, are you planning on keeping me in the dark for the rest of the day?" he pressed after the truck had stopped in a small parking area. Unlike the place they had used the day before, this one had little in the way of facilities. Not even a restroom, however basic, existed here. "It's going to make life a little difficult if you don't even speak to me, Dani."

"Perhaps I don't believe there is anything we need to speak about." She grabbed her radio and the small pack she had prepared before heading out that morning.

"Bullshit." He snorted. "What is going on with you, Dani?"

"I could ask the same of you. We spend a night together, then you make it clear you don't want to be seen even touching me in public the following day, but you're very willing to put your arm around one of the other women you work with. She a better lay than I am, or is that strictly a business matter between the two of you?" Her temper snapped into life. "I don't take kindly to being brushed off like that."

"I did not brush you off." He growled, taking a step towards her. "I would never do something like that to you, or anyone else. But especially to you."

"Especially me? You treated me as if I didn't exist as a woman to you." Her hands tightened into fists; that anger she had spent so many years learning to control demanded far more life than mere snapped words. It wasn't her imagination; she was certain of it. He had ignored her—not so much as a touch to her hand, or a brush of a kiss against her cheeks, even when she had stayed to help change the tires over. "Were you afraid that someone would see you slumming with a local woman?"

"Slumming? Is that what you believe you are, a way to slum around?" He grabbed her arm, pulling her tight to him with a growl of fury that matched her own rage of emotions. Despite the sudden pain in his grip and the moment of fear that threatened within her, she felt it, that deep unwanted yet desired reaction at his touch. Her panties moistened, nipples hardening under her shirt, a soft whimper pulling from her lips in the need to meld closer to his body.

"Let me go." The protest sounded weak even to her. This wasn't right, to be held so tightly by him, forcing her to take in the musky smell that clung to his skin.

"No," he replied, his gaze fixed on her face. "You don't want me to let you go any more than I want to release you. There's something between us, Dani. I know you feel it. I know you want to be with me."

She barely knew what she was doing when her free hand slapped across his face. "You arrogant bastard!"

"Yes, I am; so just what would be your point?" He could have struck back at her, lashed out or shoved her to the ground with what she had just done. Yet, despite the reddening skin left behind from the slap, he did nothing more than continue to hold her tight within his grip.

"What makes you think I want to be with a man like you? You brushed me off, Steven. Publicly ignore me, then privately, you expect more from me now?" Her hand stung from the force of the blow. Her cheeks flushed with embarrassment. It had been years since she had lost control on her temper that way; now he had pushed her into striking him. If he reported the incident to Henry, she would lose her job, or at least end up with a notation in her file. Far worse, she was certain he could file charges against her for assault. More than that, his own brother had warned her against him, tried to let her know of the potential problems he could bring if she refused to be aware of the relationship with Karol.

"It's simple—if you didn't want me, you wouldn't have become so anger, Dani." His full lips tugged upwards in a self assured smile. "If I meant nothing to you, then what I failed to do would not have you so upset. Neither of us spoke about what the other night meant to us, or could mean. Why would we just yet? I didn't think you would want your private life splashed all over your town, and you assumed I was brushing you off. We both made mistakes there."

"And that gives you the right to hold me like this?" She couldn't deny his arguments, not without blatantly lying, and that was something that sat ill at ease with her. Avoiding questions, misdirection—those were things she did do and felt comfortable with her. But openly lying made her feel sick.

"You want it, I want it; isn't that reason enough?" He grasped her other arm to pull her closer. "I want you, Dani—maybe that is foolish after just one night together and a few days of talking, but I want you in my life."

"My life is here," she tried to explain. "Your life is in the city, or traveling around the world with your work."

"That doesn't mean there can't be something between us. Maybe it will work out, maybe it won't; but don't we have the right to explore that?"

His lips brushed over hers, a light touch that sent tingles down her spine, curling along her buttocks and into her sex. One light kiss, and she was almost ready to forget her anger.

Focused on Love

"Give it a chance; that's all I ask for. Just give me this day to show you I'm worth exploring a life with." His grip loosened on her arms, tracing along her sides before cupping her ass.

"What about Karol?" she murmured against his lips. She couldn't help the doubts that lingered in the back of her mind.

"There is nothing between Karol and me anymore," he replied, his hands sliding along her body, following the taut curves that lay beneath her uniform. "I have told you that, and I will tell you every day for the rest of my life, if that's what it takes. We just work together—she might want there to be more between us, but there isn't."

She leaned into his touch, closing her eyes as his fingers tangled into her hair. "I want to believe you."

"Give me this one day, Dani. Just twenty-four hours to show you I can be the man you need." His breath caressed her lips, teasing her with the promise of a kiss.

"Yes." Her answer barely gained life before he kissed her, her lips parting beneath his with a low groan. She wanted him, needed him; all the doubts about Karol slipped away under his touch. He had to be telling the truth—Aaron had to be mistaken. And she was going to give him the chance he deserved.

Her body melded to his, her arms wrapping about his neck, the light rain slowly soaking them both despite the shelter of the forest canopy.

"Show me the park first, Dani." He broke the kiss, his grip easing in her hair though he didn't pull away fully. "We have all day, and I want to see this place through your eyes and show you how I see it—how I see the beauty of the world you live in."

Chapter Eight

"There are a couple of places I want to show you." She slipped back from his grasp reluctantly, her heart torn in two at putting off the contact she craved from him. He was addictive in a way she had never imagined a man could be. If a friend had come to her, speaking of falling for someone so fast they were willing to risk everything of importance in their lives, she'd have told them to snap out of it.

Yet he had done the right thing, telling her they would explore first, take care of work, give themselves a little breathing space before doing anything more than kiss . His words had silenced most of the doubts about Karol. If she truly had been nothing more than a fling on the side, then he would have pushed for sex right now, wouldn't he?

"Well, I'm ready if you are," he replied, shouldering his pack.

More than ready, she wanted to say. Had she turned into some sort of slut overnight? All she could think of around him was how it had felt to have his skin pressed against hers.

"The glade is about a twenty-minute walk from here, but I'm not sure if the rest of your team will be happy taking the walk down here." The path wasn't the easiest to walk along, but the glade at the end of it was well worth the hassle—at least as far as she was concerned.

"Well, only one way to find out." He smiled, following her onto the small walkway. "If I haven't said so before, I do appreciate the work you're putting in for us. That has to be a lot more than you had originally expected to take part in." Forest debris crunched under their boots. "I can't believe no one has thought to use this area for a shoot before."

"With the way some would complain about the walking involved, I can understand why, though it is a pity—they are missing out on some of the most beautiful locations in the world." Perhaps that was an exaggeration, but she loved the park and the surrounding area. "My gramps started bringing me down here when I was a kid, and there's a ridge I want to show you later on in the day. It's fairly close to where you were the other day."

"When you spotted me at the river?" They could barely feel the rain under the thicker canopy.

"Yes—I was up there when I saw the light playing off your camera." She pushed through a slightly overgrown spot on the path. "If you do want to use this area, I'll have to make sure this part of the trail is cleared."

"Agreed—we'd never hear the end of it if one of them ended up scratched up." Steven smiled as he spoke. "Did you know some models have insurance to cover them from injuries? I don't mean the standard type of accident insurance, but the type that provides compensation should they become scarred."

"That doesn't surprise me—their looks are their livelihoods." It felt odd to be discussing work to this level; but they had to learn about each other, their lives, the differences there, if they could even be able to give each other a chance. "I couldn't live that way, always worrying about my appearance being damaged, or watching every last thing I eat in case some photographer decided I was a pound or two overweight."

"Ah, you've been talking to Aaron about the meat factories." He laughed, ducking under a low branch. The path widened out a little more now, becoming easier to walk along. "He knows how I feel about people who do that. It's not that I don't understand why it's done; it's how some people handle it."

"So why do you do this line of work if you don't agree with others in the trade?" She glanced back at him as she spoke. It had to be strange for him, to work in an industry where so many acted in ways he didn't approve of. Not that she blamed him for disliking some of the tactics she had been told about. "Don't you find yourself biting your tongue with some people?"

"Yes and no. I don't always manage to keep quiet, and that's why I end up doing shoots like this instead of the big cover shoots others do. I'm not interested in yelling at some kid who should still be in school just to get the picture I think will get me that next big paycheck. Dani, I take pictures because I love doing it. I do work like this because it gives me the money to do the shoots I really want to do. Oh..." His voice trailed off as they entered the glade.

Shafts of light played down through the canopy, spears of brilliance lingering on the granite rocks at the far end of the glade. A shelter of maple leaves protected them from the worst of the rain—ancient trees that had begun their lives perhaps hundreds of years ago circled the natural clearing, reaching out towards each other. There was a simple, elegant beauty about the place, a sense of peace she had been drawn too on countless occasions.

Here, she had said goodbye to Bear; and not until she looked back at the stunned expression on Steven's face did she remember she hadn't been here since that day.

"This is ideal—if we can get them to agree to the walk," he exclaimed, moving further into the glade. "Just a few small places on that path that may cause problems for them, but if we can get the path cleared off, then I think it will work wonderfully. Can we get clearance to do a mock picnic set-up here?"

"Shouldn't be a problem, just as long as the clean-up afterwards is done properly." She watched as he explored the small glade, the delight evident on his face. "So you really think this will work?"

"Yes, yes I do." He turned, grinning. "I love it. I can imagine it's been used for picnics, campouts, romantic liaisons and more over the years."

Heat flushed across her face. "Well, yes—more than once."

"By you?" He set his pack down, turning his full attention on her. "With Bear, wasn't it?"

"Yes." She spoke quietly, shifting her weight from foot to foot. "We used to come out here once or twice a month." They'd enjoyed more than a few liaisons out here, and now she could feel the embarrassment growing as they spoke of the past.

"You're blushing," he murmured, brushing his fingers over her cheeks. "It doesn't show quite as much with you, but I can see it in the way your eyes move, the creasing at the corners of your eyes. You almost glow when you blush; did you know that?"

His touch fed into the blush he spoke of. He might not be able to see it, but she could feel it spread down across her face and beneath her shirt. "You're a beautiful woman, Dani."

"No, I'm..." she began to protest.

"Yes, you are. I told you that the other night, and I still mean it." His hand cupped her cheek. "I could look at you all day, take a thousand pictures of you, and still not be able to look at you enough."

She leaned into his touch, her voice quiet. "I'm not used to people saying that about me." She didn't know if she refused to accept his words because he wasn't of the People, or because of the work he did; neither were options she wanted to look too closely at right now.

"Just because it's not often said doesn't mean it isn't true." He slid his fingers down her face to hold her chin, lifting her gaze upwards to meet his. "I want to take some pictures of you, Dani. Will you let me do that?"

"You want to photograph me?" She trembled, high-school memories of the one boy who had used his camera to get naked pictures of the girls in his year came to mind. Dozens of them had ended up all over the campus, pinned up on notice boards, or mailed to family members. He'd tried that line with Dani—*you're beautiful, would you let me take some pictures of you?*—and when she'd refused, the insults had started. The jabs that she was too ugly anyway, that no one would want to look at a picture of her. Even though she'd known he was just lashing out, it had hurt. For three months before the pictures had begun appearing across the town, he had bullied her in an attempt to get her to agree.

"Yes, will you let me do that?" he asked again. "Just a few shots here in the glade, I can stop anytime you want me to."

"Yes." She tried to hide the fear that attempted to surface. He wasn't the boy from school. Her pictures weren't going to end up all over the town, and she doubted he would try and sell them. Not that there would be a market for pictures of a woman in a ranger's uniform, unless he tried selling it to one of the trade magazines. "Just a couple of pictures, though—I do have some other locations I need to show you."

"Sure." He looked around the glade, reaching for the camera from its protective bag. "What about over by that small group of rocks—they should still be dry enough for you to sit on, shouldn't they?"

The damp mist had coated the glade, but the rocks didn't seem to be that wet—nothing that would affect her too badly, at least. "Still damp, but it won't matter if I'm just going to be sitting there for a few moments." An odd excitement rose within her at the idea of having her picture taken, the fear pulling back as she walked over to the group of three large boulders. "This shouldn't take long, should it?"

"No—not unless I get on a roll." He smiled, waiting until she had settled on the largest rock. "You might want to take your jacket off for this." He nodded towards the dark, heavy jacket she had pulled on when she'd left the truck. "Not that I mind you wearing it, but it hides a lot of your figure."

"It's not designed to be flattering," she teased, but slipped it off, laying it next to her. "Anything else you want me to do?"

"Well, you could strip down completely," he joked, the crinkles about his eyes making that clear. "No? Well, then let's continue, if you're ready?"

"As I'll ever be." She rested one heel on the nearby rock, leaning on her knee as she looked at him. Small wisps of dark hair had pulled from the braid, brushing over her cheeks in the light breeze, her gaze fixed on the camera in his hands. "I still don't understand why you want to do this, but it's your film."

"I should spank you for comments like that," he muttered, moving the lens cap from the camera. "You have this habit of putting yourself down a lot—did you know that? Don't frown, it will spoil the shot."

The soft click of the camera reached her ears. Did she put herself down? She hadn't really thought of it that way. To her, it was just a form of self-honesty. "No I don't."

"Yes, you do. You don't want me to take pictures because you think that will be a waste of my time and my film, right?" Another click followed his question.

"Yes, that's true." What was he getting at?

"And you think it would be a waste because you don't believe you are beautiful." Two swift clicks echoed through the glade.

"Well, yes." She didn't like where he was going with this.

"That's putting yourself down, Dani." He snapped two more quick shots before reaching for the lens cap. "Every time you say something like that, you're telling me you think yourself to be less than other women. You're telling me you believe that you're not worth my time, or someone else's time or attention. I don't understand that about you. You're a strong, confident woman, working in a place most of the women I know could never handle. They'd run screaming for help at the first sign of a snake, or panic at the idea of changing a tire alongside of me; yet you don't have the courage to look in the mirror and see what I see."

Her hands tightened in her coat as she snagged it from the rock. He was wrong, and this was just another line being spun her way. One of dozens she had heard over the years. Though she didn't know what he thought he would gain by saying it. He'd already got what most men seemed to want from women. "I just think you're wrong, that's all."

"Dani, you need to take a good long look at yourself," he said, closing the distance between them. "I don't know who did this to you, who turned you into a woman afraid to admit what she looks like; but whoever did this has me wanting to strangle them. I hate seeing women put themselves down; every woman in the world has a beauty of their own. For some it's internal, a glow that might show when they are working with something they love, or when they hold their children. Others have a beauty of heart, when they give a thousand times more to others than they will ever receive in return. There are women who have an external beauty that catches the eye of any man who walks past. No, you aren't a model, you aren't a film star, but you have an internal and external beauty—one of heart, soul and body. If I can do nothing else but show you how I see you before this assignment is over, I will be a happier man than I was when I arrived."

She scowled at his words. "You like taking charge of situations *and* women, don't you?"

"It's part of my work. Not just women, but anyone I am taking pictures of—but I also like to be in charge in other things, as I am sure you remember." He smiled. "I don't remember you objecting about that either."

No, she hadn't; nor had her body. Her cunt clenched, her nipples hardening into firm points beneath her shirt. "No, no I didn't—at least not that time."

"Or any other time with me to come, I think. You know I won't hurt you, however tight my fingers might be in your hair, or how demanding I might appear in the moment. You know you are always safe with me."

She swallowed hard, meeting his gaze. "I don't know about that." The fear was part of the attraction, wasn't it? That momentary belief that maybe he wasn't as safe as she hoped he would be. What if he did grasp her tighter, or refuse to release her? Hadn't he already done that out by the truck? Even then, when she hadn't been really afraid of what he would do, there had been doubt; a moment of hope, desire, and that slight hint of what if fear. What if he...

"Yes, you do—it's just another thing you aren't ready to admit yet." He picked up his pack. "I won't deny that I want to push you to the ground, strip the clothes from your body, and explore every inch of you here beneath the trees. I want to hear you moan and cry out my name as my cock sinks into your tight cunt."

He spoke so casually that for a moment, she didn't believe she had heard him correctly. Her body knew better, though—her thighs pressed tightly together, fighting to hide the jerk that tried to push through her hips.

"You're a strange man, Steven. One minute you're rushing me, seeking to make love to me before we even have dinner; the next you're talking about waiting, not doing what you want to do. Do you think I would turn you away?"

"Maybe you would. I wouldn't blame you for saying no, or hitting me again. You've got quite a powerful blow there, by the way." He reached out, tracing a finger down her throat. "I want you, Dani. If I thought it wouldn't upset you right now, I would do just that—take you to the ground, I mean."

She cleared the small gap between them, growling as she wrapped her hands about his neck, her jacket dropping to the ground. "Then maybe I should be the one to do the pushing this time." She didn't give him the chance to reply before kissing him. Her lips pressed tight to his, her tongue seeking entrance into his mouth, demanding entrance with a force of passion that surprised even her.

She'd never done that before, never taken the first step with a man. But no matter how much he liked being able to take charge, she wanted to show him she could match him there. He didn't stop her; instead of the expected demand to take charge, or the delicious tight grip in her hair that she had almost grown used to, he accepted the kiss with a low growl.

Steven wrapped his arms about her waist, half-lifting her from the ground in the depth of the kiss they shared. Her tongue danced within his mouth, only to be suckled hungrily in return as he set her back onto the ground, letting her continue with her aggressive explorations. The growing bulge in his pants made it clear how much he'd welcomed her sudden assault on his senses.

She pressed her hands to his hips, urging him to the ground, ignoring the fact it would be damp from the light rain that still fell in its soft haze. He didn't fight her suggestion but moved back onto the ground as she followed him down. With a low moan, her lips sought out his neck, nipping lightly over his skin, her fingers tugging his shirt free from his waistband. She had no intention of taking things slow, or easy—the pace her body demanded was hard, fast, and on her terms. A spirit now possessed her that she had never experienced before.

"I think I like this side of you," Steven growled, arching his hips from the ground as she tugged his pants down about his thighs. "Something I hadn't expected…." His words trailed off, his shorts missing down with his pants, anything else he might have said lost in a low groan as her lips captured the end of his hard cock. She hadn't planned this, and had seldom used her mouth on any man before—but as his cock sprung into view, the urge to take it into her mouth was overpowering.

"Gods!"

She smiled, a wicked delight urging her on at his cry. Her tongue wrapped about his cock, suckling it into her mouth, licking over the soft skin, teasing around his swollen head. She could do this, wanted to do this; wanted to hear him moan in a need to bury himself within her tight, damp sex.

Her lips slid down the length of his already throbbing cock, suckling as she lowered, soft strands of hair brushing over his stomach, hiding his face from her view. He moaned, arching up towards her as she reached beneath him, cupping his sac in a gentle grip.

Slowly at first, she worked her suckling lips over his cock, growling as she moved back to hold only the head, sending a deep sound in vibrating waves through his throbbing member. No words were needed to know she was doing the right thing— his sac tightened in her hand, a deep, salty taste forming on the head of his cock with that first few beads of pre-cum.

She'd always pulled back at that first taste, but now determination drove her further. With a soft whimper, she pressed back down over his cock, taking him deeply, wrapping and un-wrapping her tongue about his thickening form until her lips nuzzled at the base of his shaft.

Steven groaned, arching further, his cock nudging deeper within her tightening throat. Panic gripped her yet she stayed in place, suckling on his cock, trying not to pull away even though she could feel her breathing becoming challenged. That deep, almost sensual, choking sensation overtook senses as she pushed herself further to tease him with her tongue, holding him in place until she could stand it no longer.

With a cry for breath, she pulled back from his cock, gasping for air, tugging at her own belt. She needed him now; she wanted to feel his swollen shaft sink into her cunt instead of her throat.

"Dani," he gasped her name, his eyes glazed as he watched her strip off her boots and pants. The damp grass soaked through her socks, forming a clinging wrap about her body, a chill that should have warned her of the foolishness of what they were doing. It didn't matter, not right now. She straddled his body before her clothes even hit the ground, pressing down over his straining cock, one hand grasping his flesh, guiding it to the entrance of her slick lips.

His hands settled on her hips, but didn't dig in. He didn't claim her, or seek to take over; instead he watched, waiting only to cry out in pure delight as she thrust down onto his cock. She arched, dancing her hips down onto his cock, the walls of her sex gripping him with a hunger, a drive she had no choice but to obey. His hands reached under her shirt, cupping her breasts, rubbing his thumbs over her nipples. "Dance for me, Dani."

She rocked, her pussy rippling along his cock, pressing down onto him, arching back as her hips tipped. She could feel it, feel the way her cunt tightened on him, squeezing and releasing on his length, matching a pulse they both seemed to share. He arched beneath her, pushing up into her sex, one hand leaving her breasts to seek out her clit, rubbing in quick light circles.

The rain fell harder, soaking them both, turning from a mist into a downpour the glade offered no shelter from. They should have left, grabbed their clothing and run for the truck, but neither of them suggested it. She wasn't sure she could have stopped if she had wanted to—and she didn't want to. Her body set the pace, her cunt clenching on his cock, squeezing harder, faster with each hard rock that drove them both.

"I need you," Steven groaned, but she wasn't at a point where words made any sense. Her pussy tightened, hips thrusting forward, pressing against the seeking touch at her clit. She couldn't hold much longer; his fingers slid over her clit, urging her further, higher; her pulse throbbed into her nipples, vibrating in her clit, pulsating into her sex as she danced on him.

"Need to cum, have to cum. Gods!" he screamed out into the rain, arching beneath her until her knees left the ground. That was all she needed—her own body matched his release, her cry mingling with his, gaining fresh life as his hand tightened on her breast. "Dani!"

Her hands sought out his chest, resting there as her body slumped back down, slackening her grip on his cock as her release passed. Rain-soaked strands of hair clung to her cheeks. Her breath ragged, she shivered as she lay down on him, his cock still buried within her cunt. Slowly he wrapped his arms around her, holding him against his chest as they both eased down from the unexpected moment in the glade.

Neither cared that the now-heavy rain pelted down onto their forms, soaking them to the skin, dirt turning into mud beneath him. His lips pressed a soft kiss to her neck, nibbling slowly as they rode out the soft jerks playing through both their bodies, his cock twitching against the walls of her cunt.

Focused on Love

"I think I've fallen in love with you, Steven," she admitted to herself as well as to him. "I don't know why, I don't want to know why, and I know you will more than likely leave me, never to return, at the end of this assignment. I only know that you've touched something in me I didn't know existed." For a moment he didn't reply, and that doubt, the fear of rejection she knew had been there all the way through her life, gained a voice in the back of her mind.

"Then I think we have a problem, Danielle Wind Dancer, because I've fallen in love with you as well."

Chapter Nine

"What on earth happened to you two out there?" Aaron demanded as they ran into the hotel lobby. "You look like you went mud wrestling instead of scoping out locations." The middle-aged receptionist had already hurried off in search of towels for them both, leaving them to explain to the almost-laughing Aaron just what had happened.

"We slipped—when the rain started coming down heavier than expected, we were already on the way back to the truck. I slipped and took Dani with me when I tried to steady myself," Steven explained, taking one of the towels from the curious receptionist and handing the second to Dani. "She warned me not to run, but like a fool, I didn't listen to her."

Dani tried not to look at Aaron when Steven offered his excuse, concentrating instead on rubbing the muddy water from her hair. They had darted to the truck and nearly slipped in their rush to get out of the rain. Neither of them had fallen, but at least Steven's story wasn't a complete lie.

They'd barely spoken on the way back into town—a comfortable silence had settled in the truck for the short trip, one that neither had seemed willing to break until they had entered the hotel. Half the work they had intended to get done had been left untouched, thanks to their intimate time in the glade. What made things worse was the odd intensity in Aaron's gaze when he looked towards her. It lacked the humor she had seen before; now, she found herself trying to avoid the look he gave her. "We were lucky we didn't get caught in a flash flood. If we'd tried going back down to the river, it would have been a real probability"

"Is that common around here?" Aaron inquired.

"Do you two need some hot drinks, coffee, tea or maybe some hot chocolate?" the receptionist inquired, holding out the rest of the towels.

"Hot chocolate, please," she replied before looking back at Aaron. Steven echoed her choice to the older woman. "Yes, it can be—it all depends on the weather patterns. Flash floods can be dangerous, I've seen hikers killed by one if they didn't take into account what they were doing. I'm glad the shoot at the river was completed yesterday, as I don't think the rock would be accessible right now."

"How badly will this weather affect the rest of the locations?" Steven pulled off his shirt, much to the amusement of Gladys, the receptionist returning with the hot chocolate.

"We might have to hold off another day," Dani admitted, sitting down on the edge of the couch. "Though now I think about it the old logging station could be an option. It's about three miles outside of town and might work with those lumberjack-style shirts you mentioned. I'll drive out there tomorrow morning and check it out, if you want? We would need to get permission from the owners, but I can't see that being a problem. The station's not been used for a few years now—close to ten, I believe."

The old building was huge, and very well-built, but with the conservation program that had been put in place, the local logging industry had all but ceased to exist. She was old enough to remember the outrage the announcement had raised. In time, the town had accepted it, and new options for employment had followed the demise of the logging industry.

A deep shiver ran through her body; even with the towel, she was still chilled to the core.

"We need to get you out of those clothes, Dani. You'll catch your death of cold standing around in them." Aaron's gaze lingered on her damp form. "I'll see if Diana has some sweatpants or something you can borrow."

"Thanks, I'd appreciate that." She tried to rub some of the water from her hair. Now why a model would have clothing like that, she didn't know.

Her cheeks flushed; that had been a bitchy thought, and she was glad it hadn't gained a voice. Diana hadn't been sharp with her in any way. In fact, though they hadn't really spoken much, she seemed to be a nice-enough woman.

Of course a model might have some looser clothing, or downtime slacks, something to just relax in. There was a fair chance that Diana and others in that line of work would really enjoy the change of pace from high-end clothing into sweats, slacks and jeans. She just hoped Diana wouldn't mind loaning her the clothing.

"Not a problem, I'll just be a few," Aaron replied, giving her a lingering look before heading out of sight.

"I should have insisted we turned back for the truck earlier." She spoke directly to Steven as they both took the hot chocolate. "Now we both look like muddy, drowned rats."

"You don't hear me complaining." He smiled, glancing over her damp form. Strange how he and Aaron could both look at her in the same way, yet Aaron left her feeling a little uncomfortable. "You look good wet."

The play on words doubled the size of her blush. "You're a wicked man, Steven," she murmured, keeping her voice low in the hopes that Gladys wouldn't pick up on the conversation. It wouldn't be long before someone else realized what was going between them.

"Yes, I am." He settled down on the edge of a chair. "But I don't hear you complaining."

What could she say to that? She wasn't complaining at all about that wicked streak she had seen in him—not just seen, actually, but experienced on several occasions. Being around him had become an adventure, a delight in more ways than she had ever expected. "Tomorrow we can go and look over the Logging Mill. I should be able to call the owner tonight to arrange a viewing."

He nodded, looking up as Aaron and Diana returned to the

Lobby. "You might want to use Diana's room to shower off before you pull on those dry clothes."

"Would you mind me doing that?" she asked Diana as the woman came into view, holding the clean clothing. "I don't want to impose, but he's right—it's either shower here, or head for home and hope I get there before the chill settles into my bones."

"Sure. Come on, I'll show you the way." Diana's smile was a natural, easygoing one. "You two really do look like you went mud wrestling." Her gaze moved over them both, lingering on Steven— or so it seemed. Well, that made sense; she worked with the photographer and no doubt worried about him. "Steve, you do need a shower yourself before you end up ill."

"Yeah, I know." He got to his feet, still holding the cup. "I'll meet you back out here in a few?" Steve addressed his question to Dani.

"Sure. It shouldn't take too long." She wanted to talk to Steven before heading back home. There were things she wanted to discuss, ideas forming in her mind for possible shoots, locations— anything that would allow her to spend further time with him. Yes, she was acting like a high-school girl with a crush, but she no longer cared.

Steven looked at her in a way she had never expected. He wasn't using her—what did she have that could further his career? Even if she tried to explain it as him taking advantage of her local knowledge, that didn't work—she would have shown him the same places regardless. He had to know that, considering how she'd taken him to the rock shelf at the edge of the river before their first kiss. So no, he wasn't trying to use her.

"What on earth were you two doing out there?" Diana asked as she pushed open the door to her room. "Sliding down the side of a mountain?"

"No—I was showing him a glade, and we got caught in the heavier rain."

Diana's hotel room was simple but comforting. A thick

comforter covered the bed, heavy furniture with an aura of age decorated the room, and rugs lay scattered across the floor, offering a sense of welcome to those would use the room. She'd visited the hotel on several occasions, but had never stepped foot into one of the guest rooms before.

"I should have insisted we returned to the truck earlier than we headed back, but even an experienced walker can make a mistake." She set the dirty towel down on the open-weave wicker hamper. It looked as though she hadn't been the only one out and about in the rain—on top of the hamper, now hidden under the towel she had set there, lay a pair of mud-splashed jeans.

"I guess so. It's not something I know much about." Diana sat down on the edge of the bed. "This is only the second time I've taken part in a shoot outside of the city. Though I am glad I was picked for this one—working with Steve is a dream." Her voice took on a wistful tone.

"He seems to be a good man," Dani agreed, looking towards the shower. "Are you sure you don't mind?"

"No, go ahead. You have to be frozen." Diana scooped up two towels, sweatpants and a t-shirt. "Hope these will work for you. Enjoy the shower—you do need it." She tossed the clean clothing at Dani.

"Thanks." With a grateful smile, Dani caught the clothing and headed into the bathroom. At least Diana had been generous enough to lend her the clothing and the use of the shower; she seriously doubted Karol would have done the same thing. If the blond had seen her this way, it would have just provided the cold-faced woman with another source of amusement.

The warm water pelted against Dani's now-bare skin, washing off the traces of mud and dirt from her form. She'd pulled the remains of the braid free, washing through her dark hair with firm fingers. Mud spilled down, pooling about her feet before being washed away.

She wanted to linger in the shower, enjoy the warmth the

water offered her, but stayed only long enough to clean off and chase the chill from her body. It had been worth it, even if she hadn't yet said so openly. Despite the rain, the mud, and the cold that now tickled a warning at the back of her throat, it had all been worth it to feel him groan beneath her body.

Once she was dried off and dressed, they could talk again; perhaps she could arrange to visit the city on occasions. It would take months, even years to work things out between them. But it could work; it would work. They wanted to be with each other, even if that meant making some compromises. That was a part of being in love—a little give, a little take.

Her hands clenched in her own hair as she realized for the first time she had never really loved Bear. There hadn't been that compromise between them, from either end. Bear hadn't offered one, nor had she; and now she knew why. Their relationship had been a comfort thing for them both. It provided a support system for Bearl and as long as she had been dating Bear, there had been no expectations for her to be involved with anyone else.

Had she really been that afraid of dating?

All the beliefs she'd had about herself—about her strength of purpose, her belief in doing the right thing, in why she had made the choices she had—they all washed away along with the mud. Why had she been that way? She needed to talk to her gramps in the next few days, sort out the doubts this had raised about herself.

"Dani?" Diana called out from the other side of the door moments after Dani had stepped out of the shower.

"Yes, just getting dried off now, I'll be out in a few." She rubbed the towel through her hair.

"Good, because there's someone here to see you. Says his name is Henry."

Henry; what would her boss be doing out here? She grumbled under her breath as she tugged on the sweatpants and t-shirt. "Coming right out. Don't worry about him. He's a good man—my boss, actually."

"Well, I didn't think he would be an axe murderer." She could hear the smile in Diana's voice.

"There you go spoiling my reputation again," Henry quipped as Dani walked back into the bedroom. "So you two got caught out in the storm. That's not like you to be so careless."

"We all make mistakes. So what had you looking for me?" She took a brush from Diana as she sat down on the edge of the bed. "Nothing serious, I hope."

"Unfortunately, yes; Diana would you mind if I spoke to Dani alone? It's business, and I hate to ask, but I need to be able to talk to her in confidence." That wasn't like Henry either. Wery little was kept secret out here; what did a Ranger have to hide anyway?

"Sure, I'll be in the lobby," Diana replied, snatching up her purse before disappearing from the room.

"Why do I have a bad feeling about this?" Dani asked once the model had left the room.

"It's about Steven Black." He began to explain. "Has he shown any signs of being violent towards you or others? A temper that can't be controlled, intimidation tactics used with the models, anything of that nature that has left you feeling uncomfortable?"

"No; well, not in the way you mean. He's certainly a dedicated man, gets very focused when he is working and the women working on the shoot seem very comfortable with him. Why?" A knot formed in the pit of her stomach.

"I started doing a couple of background checks after I found this in the station." He pulled a form from his jacket, a piece of paper he had placed in a clear plastic cover.

"It's one of the permission forms." She made no attempt to keep the confusion from her voice. "Why is that so surprising?"

"Because it's one of the copies his company should have had, and it shouldn't have been in the station unless someone had dropped it there. I think the person responsible for the damage of the station is part of the team here." He pointed out the stamp on the bottom of the paper, the approval stamp that had granted them permission to use the park for their assignment. "So I talked to Nigel and asked him to run a background check, and the information he passed on to me was disturbing. Steven black has a criminal record for assault on another photographer."

"So?" She looked from the paper to Henry. "Are you suggesting he is behind the damage done to the station?"

"If he is capable of hitting another human being, of course he's capable of damaging property," Henry replied.

"It doesn't make sense. I don't think Steven could have done that. Besides, he's not like that. I can see him striking someone to defend a friend, or protect someone he was working with; but not damage like this. Besides, someone slashed his tires with a nail file, and I am certain Steven was nowhere near the station when the vandalism took place."

She couldn't bring herself to say just where he had been during that time. That would have caused too many problems right now, and she wanted to talk to her gramps before the rest of the town found out.

"Maybe not, but I want you to be careful, Dani. Keep an eye on him—we don't know what else he has kept secret, and you're spending a lot of time alone with him."

Henry was worried, she could understand that; but Steven wasn't the violent man that the charges suggested he might be. "The rest of the checks should be done soon. But until then, I want you to keep a watch on this Mr. Black."

Henry's warning still had her unsettled by the time she walked back into the lobby. No matter how much she tried to convince herself Steven was not the danger Henry thought him to be, she couldn't shake the uncomfortable knot in the pit of her stomach.

A fire had been started in the lobby, flames dancing over the small logs, the smoke sucked up the chimney as the welcoming heat bathed the couches around the room. There was no sign of

Steven, but Aaron and Diana had settled down near the fire.

"You look a lot better there." Aaron smiled, waving towards one of the chairs. "Steven should be back in a few, but you might as well take a seat. We've got some beer here if you want one."

"Thanks, but no thanks. I really shouldn't, as I do need to drive back home soon." She slipped into one of the overstuffed chairs. "Thanks for the clothing, Diana."

"You're welcome. I can't imagine it was very pleasant to stand around in that damp clothing." Diana had curled up on a couch, her bare feet tucked out of sight. Even without makeup and the trappings of a shoot, she was an attractive woman, with long brown hair and hazel eyes. "I'll be glad when this weather eases up again. Steve has to be itching to get the rest of the work done. I know he likes it out here, though—he's more relaxed in some ways, but he can be a bug bear about getting his work done on time."

That didn't surprise her to hear. There was something compelling about Steven, a drive that shone through in what little she had seen of his work. "I am sure we'll be able to figure out a way to get the rest of the shoot done even if the weather doesn't let up."

"I hope so—he has a lot riding on this job." Aaron spoke quietly, glancing up towards the hallway as he did so. "If this one doesn't work out, the agency might not hire him again."

Both women gave him a sharp look. "What do you mean?" Diana spoke first.

"Karol—between her and a few other complaints, the agency is very seriously talking about never using him again." He shrugged, twisting the top from a bottle of beer. "I'm not entirely sure of everything going on, but I know there's some pressure on him over this. I overheard the last conversation he had with them, just before we headed out here. It didn't look good for him."

"I won't work with any other photographer. All the others are just...well, they make me feel stupid. As if no matter what

I do, I still can't do anything right. Steve's different. He listens, works with me, he lets me try to follow the flow of things. And he doesn't yell at me if I mess things up," Diana said, her hands twisting in her lap. "I can't imagine doing a shoot with anyone else now. Not after he's shown me how things can work." Her bottom lip caught between her teeth. The young woman's face contorted with the obvious dilema that she now faced. "I won't let them fire him."

"You might not have any choice," Aaron commented. "It's not in your hands, but Karol's and those like her."

"Should my ears be burning?" Karol walked into the lobby just as Aaron mentioned her name. "Ah, yes, the evil Karol who screams and shouts if she doesn't get her way. So what? I throw a tantrum to get what I want, and it works, so I keep doing it." The smug look on the blondes' face irritated Dani.

"There are other ways of getting what you want—you could try just asking," Diana suggested.

"What? And end up like you—a no-name wannabe on her way out before she's even begun." Karol smirked. "If that was what I'd wanted, then I would be happy flipping burgers—which is exactly where you're going to end up at the end of this shoot."

Dani had never met a woman prior to Karol whom she could quite happily imagine strangling. Malicious was the only word that fit her—she might have looked beautiful on the outside, but inside, under that perfect skin, she was ugly to the core.

"I don't want to be like you." Diana spoke far more calmly that she obviously felt. "I just want to enjoy working with Steven."

"Enjoy it whilst you can, because if he doesn't start doing what he needs to do, I will make sure he never works again." Karol tapped her all-too-perfect nails against the back of one of the couches. "He just has to learn to see things my way, like he used to. Ah, but of course he's slumming it now, enjoying the diversions that small towns like this offer. Just as he has done in the past—hasn't he, Aaron?"

Diversions? She didn't like what that implicated. A look passed between Karol and Aaron as Diana fell silent. Whatever was going on here, the fact she had not been told about it before left her with an uncomfortable feeling. Those doubts that had been silenced during their time in the glade resurfaced. She didn't want to believe that Steven used her, but the implications were clearly laid out by Karol's words.

"He's changed, Karol," Aaron replied, glancing towards Dani for a moment. "He's made some mistakes—haven't we all—but you're the biggest mistake he ever made."

"My my, ever your brother's defender...well, almost ever." Karol shook her head, looking up as Steven finally returned to the lobby. "There you are, darling. Don't you think it's time you and I had a little chat about your dalliances here and how that seems to be affecting your judgment?"

Steven stopped in his tracks at her words, his gaze narrowing on the arrogant woman, shutting out the presence of everyone else within the room—or so it seemed. "What are you talking about?"

"I'm talking about you and your time wandering off with our little Ranger here. Has she been showing you the sites, or have you been getting her to pose for you?"

Karol folded her arms under her breasts. Unlike Diana, Karol still wore her good clothing, appearing as if she had stepped right off the cover of a magazine. "You will either start listening to me again, or I will make sure the agency is made well aware of just what you've been spending your time doing."

"And what have I been doing?" He didn't make a move towards her, but his voice had dropped into a low whisper. A coldness entering his tone, an edge there that left Dani shifting uneasily in her seat. "This is a pattern for you, Karol. If you don't get what you want, you threaten, attempt to intimidate, push for some way to get me or whomever your target is to do what you want.

"Well, it's not going to work this time. Maybe a year ago I would have bowed down to you, but I have something I really want just within reach."

"Something or someone?" Karol didn't back down.

"It's got nothing to do with you, and you can either accept that or go screaming back to the agency. Frankly I don't care either way. After this shoot, I am going back to doing the work I enjoy, scenic photography where I don't have to deal with whiny, hard-nosed bitches like you." Despite the anger in his words, his voice never rose, remaining little more than a low whisper.

"Steven!" Diana protested.

"I don't mean women like you, Diana, but people like Karol," he explained, finally shifting his gaze away from the now-stuttering blonde. "I'm sorry this means I won't be working with you again, but I've had enough of bowing down to Karol and those like her."

"But I like working with you. You can't really mean that, about giving up working with me," Diana pleaded with him, pushing out of her chair to clear the distance between then. "You can't...I mean this is important, we're important, I don't want to work with anyone but you."

"He's a selfish bastard, Diana. He might rant and rave about meat markets, but he's no better than the rest of them. He just hides it under a veneer of concern," Karol finally spoke up again. "Don't lose your heart to him. You wouldn't be the first, won't be the last, and he moves on the minute a new one catches his attention. Or haven't you learned that much about him? It was that Lucinda woman in Canada, and what was her name on the New York shoot...ah, yes, Rachel the makeup artist. Who do you think he has his heart set on now?"

An uncomfortable silence settled in the lobby as Karol's gaze moved from person to person until it seemed to settle on Dani. Did she know? The smug look said she did. How could she, though, unless Steven had mentioned it?

"That's enough!" Steven growled, taking a step forward.

Without warning he grasped Karol by the arm, marching her out of the lobby and out of sight. He hadn't said a word to Dani—no denials, nothing that offered her a chance of protection from the hinted allegations. He didn't even look at her before vanishing from sight with the stammering woman in his grip.

Chapter Ten

"I can't believe he just did that, just walked out on me like that." Diana sat down hard on the couch next to Dani. "After everything, he just grabbed her and left. I thought I meant something to him." Of all the things Diana could have said, that was the last thing she expected. So it wasn't her Karol thought was involved with Steven, but Diana. How could she have missed it--the small signs of Diana seeming to hang on Steven's every word? Or was she wrong; did the distraught woman simply hope he would look her way one day?

"As Karol said, you're not the first and you won't be the last, Diana," Aaron mumbled under his breath. He cracked open another beer and handed it to the model; a second one he passed to Dani. "Drink. You both need it, and I don't want to hear any excuses about you putting on weight, Diana. There isn't a spare ounce on you." Neither of the two women offered a protest this time, but took the beer instead.

"This will all work out in the end. We'll get the last of the shoot done thanks to Dani's knowledge of the area, Steve will tell Karol where to stick it and go back to what he prefers doing, and then I can continue to help him where I can without driving Miss Bitch around. So it will all work out in the end."

The fire crackled in the hearth, bathing the lobby in a soft warmth that did little to shift the cold hand now gripping her heart. Who was he involved with? Those damn doubts; it only took a small hiccup, and those doubts would appear. If she loved him, the way she had said, then those doubts should never have gained any form of life within her.

No—in order to overcome those doubts, she would have to be nearly inhuman. They were at the start of something—a relationship, a fling, she wasn't sure just what—and they knew so little about each other that there were bound to be doubts.

The beer tasted odd; she didn't often drink, and when she did, it wasn't bottled beer. Now she felt too tired or confused to really care about what she was drinking.

"How does Karol know about the other women?" Diana spoke quietly, cradling the bottle of beer in her hands. "She was one of those women, wasn't she?"

"For a while, yes, she was. Not for as long as she wanted to be, though. And I don't think she likes the idea that he dumped her and not the other way around. Karol doesn't like being walked out on. You've seen how she is—she likes keeping the upper hand." Aaron took a swig from his beer.

"And the others?" Diana pressed for the same information Dani had been reluctant to ask for. They both wanted to know just what was going on—how many women had their really been? Was Karol's threat nothing more than a scare tactic to bring Steven back into her sphere of control.

"There have been others; not hundreds, but in the double figures," Aaron admitted, not looking at either of them. "He had a bit of a playboy reputation for a time—well, as much as he could have without the funds to back it up. Think about this for a moment. He's a decent-looking man, surrounded by women in his everyday life, women who will do almost anything to get their faces on that next magazine cover. Or at least some of them act that way."

He offered an apologetic smile towards Diana. "There are good people in this business. It's just I've seen so many of the bad ones that it's too easy to lump everyone together like that."

"It's okay. I know you didn't mean me, not like that." Diana tried to smile, but it didn't reach her eyes. Though she knew very little about the woman, Dani couldn't help but want to try and ease some of the hurt Diana obviously felt. "I've seen the types of women you're talking about, and the photographers, designers, the people doing the layouts who treat some of us as if we are nothing more than mindless props to be pushed around where ever they see fit. It's a part of the trade; there are good people and bad people, just as there are in any other job."

The double doors of the hotel opened, slamming shut in a gust of wind that sent a shiver through her. What warmth the hot chocolate and shower had provided vanished in that full-body shiver. The rain and time spent in the mud with Steven had hit her in more ways than one.

Her thighs pressed tightly together at the memory of how it had felt to slide over his body, the joy at his cock pressing into her cunt. She had to stop thinking about that. Until she could talk to Steven about Karol, and about everything Aaron had said as well, she could not allow herself to become sexually involved with him again. No matter how badly she wanted to find him, feel his lips pressed against her own, smell that odd mix of sweat and soap that she had come to associate with him.

Damn it, this was wrong. He was a bad boy, and if she didn't admit it, accept it, then she would deserve anything that happened. Her heart was on the line here, and she had to be the one to take action. Maybe she wasn't the full new millennium woman she had tried to be, but she wasn't going to turn into one of the whimpering, whining, it's-all-his-fault-because-I-love-him type of women.

There were choices in life that she could make or ignore; even ignoring what she could do to avoid problems was a choice. Yes, her heart tugged at her, urging her to rise, walk down the hallway to find Steven and talk to him there and then. But she wasn't going to give in to it. Not now; she'd make the mistake of falling into bed with him again, or to the floor, the shower, over a chair...

She barely prevented the low moan that threatened to escape from her lips.

"He won't change, Diana." Aaron set the beer bottle down on the table. "I've known him for far too long to even except that to be an option. He is a good man, don't get me wrong, but don't go looking to him as a possible husband."

Dani drained the bottle, shaking her head at what he'd said. "Aaron, what makes you think he can't change? People change every day; even someone who's been a drug addict can make a change if they really want to. Maybe all it will take with Steven is a reason to alter the way he's been acting."

Privately, though, she wondered, how far had it gone between Steven and Diana? Or had the relationship never even had a chance, considering how Karol kept track of the photographer whenever possible?

"He's too stubborn to even think about it." Aaron grinned. "It runs in the family." His gaze lingered on Dani's form, moving slowly down from her face, resting on her t-shirt-covered breasts. Without a bra, she knew her nipples pressed against the thin cloth, becoming far more visible than usual. "We're both one for the ladies, Dani. I doubt he could change any more than I have."

"It wouldn't be so bad if I didn't enjoy working with him," Diana mumbled, the catch in her voice making it clear she was struggling not to cry. "He's given me a better look at myself. I didn't believe in my ability to do this before I met him. But he stopped me from listening to the others in the business who told me I was fat, or ugly, or that I needed to get plastic surgery in order to make it."

"Diana, I don't really know you, but you're a lovely woman," Dani tried to reassure the model. It felt odd trying to help another woman believe in herself when she struggled with that daily herself. "I don't know many women who can look at themselves and see only the positive. I guess we're all conditioned to believe we need to change something—a nip here, tuck there, wrong hair color, too pale, too tanned—you know how the fashions change almost by the minute."

That, at least, got Diana smiling. "Yes, I know what you mean. I've been on shoots that have stopped halfway through because the designer suddenly realized whatever he or she thought was the next big sensation had already been launched the day before."

"But Steven keeps calm when things like that happen?" Dani asked, trying to help Diana focus on the positive aspects of the conversation.

"Yes—he's even talked some of the designers into continuing with the shoot, even offered suggestions on how to make it look different, give it that flair that will make the line stand out in some way. He's never worked with the top designers, of course, but I don't think he wants to. Nor do I. It's too fast a pace for me, just something I can't imagine facing anymore. Maybe a few years ago I would have jumped at the chance to do that. Now, though, now I just want to work with Steven. Do you think he will need models to work with him sometimes when he does these scenic shoots?" She addressed her question to Aaron, hope shining in her eyes.

"There's always a chance. When we've got the body of this assignment over, that would be the time to talk to him about it." But when Aaron looked over at Dani, she could see the slight shake of head, that small but clear indication that he thought the chance to be a slim one.

"I'll do that." Diana rose, rolling out her shoulders to work out a kink. "I can't just sit here, though. Rain or not, I'm going for a walk."

"Careful out there—the sidewalks can be pretty slick, and some of them are due to be repaired before the end of the year." She couldn't hear the hiss of rain any longer, but it would have been just her luck to get a call saying Diana had slipped and broken something. The state of the sidewalks wasn't really her concern—she had nothing to do with the upkeep of the town itself—but handing out warnings had become second nature. The memory of the muddy jeans returned. Had Diana taken a walk earlier on in the day, or had they been from the night before?

"I'll be fine, I just need to get some fresh air and work a few things out." Diana smiled. "But thank you for looking out for me."

Aaron didn't speak again until Diana had left the lobby, and when he did, it was obvious his thoughts had been drawn to something else. "Steven is right about one thing, though—you're an attractive woman."

"Where did that come from…and what makes you think he has said that to me?" She rose, smoothing down the sweats against her thighs. "I thought you said that was something he said to women he was interested in."

"Mostly, yes, but he's said it to others as well, like Diana." His gaze seemed to bore past her clothing. "In your case, though… well, I know my brother. He's interested in you, and you in him."

She didn't know how to reply to that without giving away what had happened between her and Steven. For a moment she didn't give him an answer, and when she finally could, she took what she hoped was the safest path. "Your brother is a talented man, and I enjoy the park. It makes a pleasant change to be able to show the area to someone who actually appreciates it."

"If that was such a simple statement to make, why did you have to think about it before speaking?" Aaron's gaze met her own squarely, without a hint of compromise in his eyes. "I'm not a fool, Dani. I can see what has been going on between the two of you, even if neither of you want to discuss it. Just remember you are not the first, you won't be the last, and once this shoot is over with, he will leave without ever looking back."

He caught her arm, that same movement Steven had used on her earlier in the day. "He might be offering you sweet words now, hopes, even vague suggestions that there is more between you. But that is all it is, and all it ever will be."

"Let me go." She tried to keep her voice calm.

"Think about what I just said, please." Unlike his brother, he did let her go the first time. "You're a good woman, Dani. It would be different if he had told you upfront that this was just a moment or two for you both to enjoy. But I won't stand by and watch him break another heart."

"If you think he is going to break my heart, Aaron, you are

sorely mistaken. I've not known him long enough to even come close to that." Her stomach knotted as she gave life to the small lie.

"The only person you might fool with that comment is yourself." Aaron shook his head, collecting the empty bottles from the small table. "Take a good long look at yourself and then ask one question—if you've not fallen for him, why are you so ready to look only for the good in him publicly when I know you're tearing yourself up inside with the doubts, the questions he hasn't answered? If he means so little to you, why are you shaking now?"

No matter how tightly she grasped the steering wheel, she still shook. Aaron had been right; she hadn't admitted it to him, but she hadn't needed to. He had known; that look in his eyes, the way a smugness had formed within his smile, it all made it very clear that he was well aware of her feelings for his brother. She couldn't shake the feeling that she had been played, just like many others before. It would stop; even if she decided she wanted to enjoy the rest of the time they might have together, she wouldn't let herself fall any further for him than she already had.

The rain had turned the narrow track leading to her cabin into a slick mud-stream, which pulled her focus back towards driving. At least she could use her anger for something useful, and at least the rain had eased off to nothing more than a few drops here and there. She darted into the cabin, carrying her still dirty uniform with her, the door closing behind her with a soft snap.

Her clothing needed washing, but she had more than one uniform, which was a blessing. With the type of work she did, it made sense to have five sets of work clothes, plus heavier clothing for winter and bad weather. Now all she wanted to do was find a way to keep busy, so she wouldn't end up thinking about Steven and the mistakes she had walked into with open eyes.

Scowling, she headed through the house, gathering up the laundry to get that work done. She was still grumbling under her breath when the washing machine started up in the back of the house and she finally curled up on her couch with a hot drink, in clean clothes that at least belonged to her. She hadn't wanted to return the sweats without washing them and had ended up doing a full load in the machine, sweeping the kitchen and cleaning her boots off before she headed towards the couch.

Hot chocolate with brandy swirled in the large mug, the welcoming smell snaking upwards in soft swirls of steam.

Now, with the drink and in the safety of her own home, Dani was finally able to relax. The rain had faded completely bringing clear skies and a warmth that seeped into the cabin. Within a day, two at most if this kept up, the mud would be dried up and the constant risk of forest fires would return. That also mean that unless a bad weather front moved back in, Steven and the models would finish their work out here and be gone by Monday at the latest. A mix of regret and relief mingled; she didn't want to see him leave, but it was easier to accept that it would happen no matter what she wanted.

The phone ringing pulled her out of her thoughts, Henry's voice on the other end of the line half-expected after the conversation in the hotel. "Dani, I've got the rest of the background checks done. Steven isn't the only one in the group with a record—two of the models each have one as well, as does his brother. All minor infractions for the most part—but there is one I'm concerned about and have asked for further details on."

"Who?" Worry furrowed her brow. What else had Steven kept hidden from her?

"Not Steven, but I can't give you names right now. What I can say is that I believe it's linked to the growth of vandalism that followed this group in. If I'm right, we have to be very aware of the danger you might be in if you continue to work with them. One of them has a record for arson."

Arson; of all the crimes that could affect the park she loved, arson was the most dangerous of all. "How bad?"

Focused on Love

"Burned down a warehouse—they were young, but it's still a concern. I looked back over the trash can fire, and there has been another one this afternoon. Small one at the edge of town. Fortunately it was too wet to go anywhere, but with the way the weather is picking up…" He took a slow breath before continuing. "I can't give you the name, and I shouldn't have told you about Steven's record either. That could have gotten us both in trouble. Maybe legal trouble, local sheriff as well; but if I 'm right on this, then we might have to request that this person leave the park."

"Anything I can look out for?" Sometimes arsonist had scars from the way they were drawn to flames.

"No, I don't think so. Nothing I know about right now. I just want you to be on the lookout. One man with a temper, and now someone working with him who likes to start fires…that's all we need."

Henry's voice was almost a growl, and she didn't blame him at all. Lives could be lost in a forest fire; towns had been wiped out, entire worlds destroyed. The town had come close to experiencing that a few years before, when a high-school boy had raged out of control, lashing out at the world around him. He'd had excuses when he was caught; didn't they always have excuses? Her gramps had had his own words to say about the damage the teenager had been responsible for.

People like that destroy because they have been destroyed within, Wind Dancer. Better to help heal them than simply judge them and cast them out. It is a sickness, and all such sicknesses of body, heart or spirit can be healed if just one person is willing to work with them.

What would he say when he found out about this new source of danger; what illness would he see shining from the perpetrator's eyes?

"I'll keep a lookout, but it would be easier if I had some actual details to watch for." Dani tried to keep the annoyance from her voice; she'd be watching them all because of this.

"I'm sorry, Dani. I'll try and get some more information to you in about two days. It depends on how long it takes for the files to be sent out to me, but for now I daren't pass on anything more unless the Sheriff gives me the clearance." She knew the older man regretted putting her into the situation without a safety rope. "Look, if I can, I'll get clearance to explain the rest to you."

"Thanks, that would help. If I only have one person to watch instead of a dozen, it would be easier." Silence followed her words, then an awkward half-cough.

"I can reduce it by one more; that shouldn't cause any problems. Neither of the Black brothers are behind this."

"That helps, at least lowers it by two." It just left the models and their drivers. Five people to watch instead of six. At least with the shoot being this small, she didn't have to watch for makeup artists. That had been one of the complaints she'd overheard Karol voicing—the primitive settings had forced them to do their own makeup. Steve's counterargument had been fun to listen to: they were shooting outdoor wear, not glamour-wear. The makeup needed was minimal at best, and they were all quite capable of doing that for themselves.

Dani had struggled to keep the smirk from her face at the stuttered protest; next time, she wouldn't try at all. "I've got to get in contact with Jeff, about the logging mill."

"A location?" he said, the interest clear in his tone.

"Yes—they'll need to get some work done tomorrow, and I don't think the park will be dry enough to use." She tugged on her still-damp braid.

"Good idea. I'm meeting Jeff and a couple of others for coffee in an hour or so. I'll check it out with him if you want, save you the trouble."

"Appreciated; thanks, Henry. I need to get some work done here, so I'll talk to you later?"

"Sounds good, you get some rest; it's been a busy few days."

If it wasn't one thing, it was another. Trouble had followed this group in, and she would be glad if it followed them out too, never to return. She could feel a headache growing behind her eyes, tension building on tension, stress growing with every breath she took. Meals had been grabbed between looking over maps, except for one breakfast with Silver Fox and that meal with Steven. A hot meal, long bath, and a good night's sleep might provide some of the answers. It certainly wouldn't hurt her.

She drained the last of the drink, setting the mug down as she pulled herself up from the couch. Her cabin had always been her safe haven—the place had been her mother's for a short time, but it belonged to her now. The small touches of dream catchers, colorful rugs, and the beaded bridle hanging on the wall were just some of the things her mother had refused to display when the cabin belonged to her.

Dani didn't embrace the ways of the People to the extent her gramps did—it took a lot to get her to attend tribal gatherings, and she had been made to feel ashamed more than once at her lack of skill in the tribal language. She was caught between two worlds—the one her gramps lived in, and the one she worked in on a daily basis.

Men; why did anything involving a man have her looking over her life and finding fault with everything she had done, every step that had taken her away from the way her gramps had hoped she would live her life?

Chapter Eleven

She sank into the bath, her eyes closing as she relaxed into the warm water. Dani had bundled her hair up at the back of her head, using pins to keep it in place and out of the bath. She couldn't stay in the water long, as a meal she had grabbed from the freezer was already cooking in the oven. So it wasn't as good a meal as she had prepared earlier in the week; it would fill a hole, allow her to sleep without waking hungry halfway through the night.

She'd even managed to avoid thinking about the night she and Steven had put the bath to another use. Instead, she'd thought only of breathing—taking long slow breaths in through her nose, out through her mouth. That simple trick her gramps had taught her years ago helped calm her nerves, pushing past unwanted distractions so she could relax.

"You look good enough to eat in there." Aaron's voice caught her off guard, sending her reaching for a towel.

"What in hell's name are you doing in here?" Heat flushed her cheeks, the towel clutched to her breasts as she hoped the bubbles covering the surface of the bath would also shield her body from his view. But judging by the way he looked at her, it seemed unlikely.

"I came out to see how you were doing, make sure you'd made it home in one piece. Driving after a beer in bad weather can be dangerous." He leaned against the door frame, making no move to leave her alone. "But it certainly looks like you made it back safe and sound."

"Get out," she snarled, keeping the towel tight to her breasts. "Get out now."

"Is that any way to speak to someone who traveled out all this way in concern for your health?" He moved, but not away from the door frame. Instead, he walked further into the bathroom.

Focused on Love

A darkness touched his gaze, a hunger that tugged between her thighs, tightening her nipples in a wanton manner she had no control over.

He was invading her home, her safety; she couldn't react this way. It wasn't right. He had to leave, get out, leave her alone, get out of her house and never return.

"You don't look that unhappy to see me, I bet if I reached down into your bath, your cunt would welcome my touch just as it did my brothers."

"I told you to get the hell out." She sat up further in the bath, water splashing over the edge to spill onto the floor.

"I don't want to leave, and you don't want me to go." He sat on the edge of the bath, pulling the towel away from her breasts, his free hand tangling in her hair. "You want something else from me, don't you, Danielle?"

She arched under the grip, panic closing her throat. He didn't have the edge of softness to him that Steven did. He lacked the gentleness that tempered the firm grip. Yet her body refused to accept that; her cunt trembled, clenching with the force of his grip. "Let go of me. I want you to let go of me and get out of my house."

His grip tightened in her hair. This didn't make sense. In the lobby, he had complied, left her alone; why would he do this now. Why would he risk trouble with the law? His lips covered hers, claiming her in a kiss she fought to avoid responding to.

Still she arched towards him, her arms wrapping about his neck, water spilling onto the ground as he tumbled into the bath with her. Water sloshed out onto the floor, his body trapping hers in the tub, pushing her further down. She couldn't breathe; his weight, the water, the grip in her hair; she couldn't breathe anymore. Panic surged within her; she clawed, trying to get free, but his weight smothered her, pressing her into the bath until she couldn't move...

A scream tore from her throat, and water slopped over the

edge of the bath as she sat bolt upright, water dripping from her face. Slowly the dream slid away, her gaze taking in the empty room. She was alone—no one in the room or the cabin except herself. A vision, dream, a warning? It didn't matter right now—she was just relieved that the moment was gone. Nothing more than a bad dream, and it was over. What had triggered it, she neither knew nor cared.

With a shudder she pulled out from the water, wrapping the towel about her body. Some parts of the dream had been true—her hair had been pinned up out of the way, and she had put a frozen meal in the oven to cook during her bath—but the rest had been nothing more than stress-produced dream images.

Gramps would have the answer and she'd try and get hold of him in the morning, maybe meet up with him for breakfast the way they normally did. It would help, having someone to lean on as she sorted out the mix of emotions the dream and dealings with Steven had left her with.

Not just Steven now, but also his brother. Had her imagination taken the intense looks Aaron had given her and fed into that? She wrapped the robe tightly about her body, fastening it as she walked back out into her bedroom. The cabin was warm enough now that she could walk through it in bare feet and nothing more than the fluffy blue towel robe. This far away from town, the odds that anyone would drive by and see her like this was slim.

The area around the cabin had been cleared for a fifth of an acre in each direction, but the trees still gave her some shelter from the worst of the weather fronts that could hit. She could have left the growth closer to the cabin, but she liked the small amount of open space. She'd even tried growing herbs over the previous years, but the long hours she put in during the growing season had quickly put an end to that experiment. By the end of a summer's day, all she was normally capable of was grabbing a meal and a bath and slinking into her bed for an exhausted sleep.

Winter brought its own wave of work—her truck had a hitch

on the front for a small plough attachment, and that ended up being used on more than just her driveway. Like Henry, she helped keep the main roads into the park clear, just in case they had that call to help track down some hiker or climber who'd decided a small thing like a winter storm wasn't going to stop him from heading into the park.

She frowned, a sound drawing her attention to the main door of the cabin. Someone had pulled up outside.

Dani darted for her bedroom, pulling on jeans and a sweatshirt just in time; she'd barely tugged the sweatshirt down before the sharp sound of someone knocking on the door rang through the otherwise silent cabin.

"Dani, I'm sorry to disturb you, but I ended up thinking about you doing the drive home after the bad weather, and I started worrying. It wasn't until I pulled up out here that I realized how stupid that was. You have years of experience driving around here, no doubt in far worse weather than we've seen," Aaron explained the moment she opened the door.

Her dream; had that been a warning? No, it couldn't have been. His gaze lacked the threat she had seen in the bathroom—there wasn't anything threatening about him. So he tended to look over her body in a more familiar manner than seemed appropriate; but a threat?

"It's okay. I'm fine, as you can see." She hesitated for a moment, then opened the door fully. "You might as well come on in now. It's not that long of a drive for me, but it would be rude of me to send you away without even a coffee." It would take a short while to put some coffee on. Dani flinched, seeing the muddy tracks leading through her living room. When it was just her, it wouldn't have been so bad; she couldn't remember leaving that much of a mess when she'd come in. Had she been so tired she had forgotten to wipe off her boots first?

"Thank you, I'd enjoy that. I should have found a way to call ahead—that way I wouldn't have disturbed your dinner. That's if the smoke coming from the oven means it's done?" He smiled, nodding towards her kitchen.

"Smoke?" She turned; a thin tail of dark smoke curled up from the closed oven door. "Oh damn it, my dinner." She darted across the kitchen, grabbing a cloth as she yanked open the door. Cursing under her breath, she pulled the now-blackening meal out; dark crusts had formed on the paper dish the meal had come in. Instead of lasagna, she now looked at something pretending to be burned cardboard.

First the mud, now the burned meal; what else could go wrong? She glanced at the temperature the oven had been set to, far too high; her mind must have been slipping to make that basic a mistake. "Well, so much for that idea," she muttered, dropping the meal in the sink to cool off.

"I've done that myself on more than one occasion." Aaron smiled, walking into the kitchen after her. "They always come out either undercooked or burned, and I hate cooking for myself so its frozen meals, tins of something or a sandwich unless I grab a meal from a diner or drive-through."

"Nearest drive-through here is fifteen miles away, and I just wanted to get home." She shook her head, looking at the destroyed meal. "Well, I guess I'll have a tin of soup or a sandwich then; no point me looking for something else from the freezer now." She was too tired and hungry to deal with cooking another meal that would leave her waiting for at least an hour before anything would be ready.

"Go and sit down. I'll fix you something," Aaron said, placing a hand on her shoulder.

"Pardon?" Had she heard him correctly?

"I said go and sit down, I'll fix you something to eat. You're wiped out, Dani. I'm not sure what has brought this on with you, but you are exhausted. Let me fix something for you, even if it's only a sandwich." He turned her back towards her living room, pushing her gently to the couch. "No arguments."

She was too tired to argue even if she wanted to. Instead, she curled up on her couch, watching in stunned silence as Aaron vanished into the kitchen. No one had cooked for her since she had left her Gramp's cabin to live out here. Now a virtual stranger was busy in her barely used kitchen, putting a meal together, or a sandwich at least. Someone attempting to take care of her like this felt strange but comforting at the same time—as long as he didn't think she expected it all the time. If nothing else, being a Ranger had rid of her of the last of her expectations of being pampered.

"It's not going to be anything fancy, but it will be warm, unburned and edible," he called out from the kitchen. She didn't feel that comfortable with him rooting around in there, but calling him back out would have been awkward.

"Thanks." What was he up to in there? Small banging noises filtered into the living room, the fridge door opening, then closing again quickly, the sound of his steps across the floor as he worked. She had no idea what he was putting together and was very tempted to get off the couch and take a wander in, except that she was certain he would frog-march her back into the living room. Apart from that, she was bone-weary, and the idea of getting up again so soon after sitting down almost had her cringing.

"You don't have to do this for me." Maybe if she said that enough, he would change his mind and come back out into the living room?

"I know." He walked back out into the living room, lingering near the entrance to the kitchen. "You look as though you need a little pampering—not that this could be classed as pampering, nothing more than a quick bite to eat for a friend." Aaron looked relaxed, at home despite the fact it was his first time in her cabin.

"It's been a long few days," she admitted, pulling a blanket off the back of the couch and wrapping herself in it. "Longer than I had expected, but it looks like we have the location for the shoot tomorrow sorted out."

Henry had called moments before she had slipped into the bath, clearing the use of the logging mill. The paperwork would be waiting for them at the hotel right about now; all Steven had to do was sign it. "I should call your brother in a few to give him the heads up about that."

"You might want to wait until you've had something to eat first." Aaron didn't look as though he would give in on that statement either. Both brothers had this strength about them—no, not strength—perhaps dominance was closer to what she had witnessed? She didn't see them using the whips and chains she had always associated with the word, but there was an insistent *you-will-do-as-I-say* quality about them a lot of the time, even if it was less obvious with Aaron. "It won't hurt you, or him, to hold off for a little longer. Besides I think this is ready." He vanished into the kitchen; what could he have prepared that would be ready so quickly?

"Alright, I'll wait until I've eaten, but not any longer than that," she called out, watching for him to return. She didn't have to wait long as he stepped back out carrying two small plates with him. Grilled sandwiches—he was right, it wasn't anything special, but she had forgotten she even had some cheese in the fridge.

"A grilled cheese—just enough to do two. Hope you didn't mind me making myself one as well?" He passed her one of the plates and took a seat on the same couch.

"No, that's fine." She yawned before taking a bite to eat. "Strange how something made by another person, no matter how simple, tastes better than anything you can make yourself."

"I've noticed that myself." He smiled, eating his sandwich as he watched her. "Your kitchen is fairly simple—not a lot stocked in there though, would have thought you'd have a lot more with you living outside of town. Just in case you ended up trapped out here during bad weather?"

"I do, in winter, but I haven't had the chance to get a lot of stocking up done recently. I plan on changing that after the shoot is over and done with. I should get the time then." The sandwich vanished quickly; not until she smelled the melted cheese had Dani realized just how hungry she had actually been.

"Sounds like a good idea." He set his plate to one side, watching her. "You are a beautiful woman, Dani. Steven is right about that. I just wish you would look at me with half the interest I know you have in my brother."

She shifted on the couch. "Everyone makes mistakes."

"Ah, so you know it was a mistake now?" he pressed, moving a little closer along the couch.

"Yes—he's leaving next week, along with the rest of you." She tensed for a moment as he moved close enough to touch her. "However, now that I have accepted he is just out for a distraction during his stay here, it is a lot easier." If she kept telling herself the lie, it would be easier when they left.

"So you've no objection to occasional intimate dalliances?" He reached out, tracing a slow line along her shoulder. Her instincts said *move away, tell him to stop*, but just as with the dream image in the bath, her body had other ideas.

"As long as I know that's what they are at the time." Stupid move—she'd never involved herself in anything like that before. Saying it and doing it were two different things. Bear, Steven; she'd come close to being involved with others in the past but had stopped herself, unwilling to go that extra step.

Now she could see what Aaron wanted from her: the chance to explore her body, move between her thighs the way Steven had. Her cunt clenched at the memory, a low moan slipping from her lips in the moment before Aaron moved closer, covering her lips with his.

Wrong, this was wrong and she didn't care. She groaned in delight, her lips parting beneath his seeking kiss, arching closer to him. He tasted like Steven, and in a strange way, he felt like him as well. She couldn't pull away from him, not even when his hand moved over her breasts, cupping them softly, his thumb teasing across her already hard nipples.

"I've wanted to do this since I met you in the diner," he murmured against her lips, scraping a path over her neck with his teeth. "Say no, tell me to leave, I'll do that and never come to bother you again. If you want me, then say nothing and we'll enjoy this together."

Steven; she wanted Steven, not him; so why couldn't she pull away? Anger, hurt, the need to lash out at Steven built slowly inside of her. She needed to prove to herself that she could accept him leaving, even if that meant sleeping with his brother. Would that make her a slut? She didn't care.

She pulled him closer, pressing against his body, her lips nipping along his neck in soft kisses. He shifted on the couch, pulling her sweatshirt up over her head, a low groan sounding out at what he saw. Hungrily he lowered his lips to her breasts, cupping them, kissing, suckling along her skin, capturing a nipple between his teeth.

Under only a small touch she lowered to the couch, her jeans skinned off with a single tug. "No panties." He grinned, cupping her mound, pressing one finger between the lips of her vulva. "I like a woman with no panties." She wanted to tell him the reason she hadn't worn them had been because of the bath, that she hadn't had the chance to dress fully when he arrived, but she lacked the voice to. Instead her thighs clenched on his hand, hips rocking towards him as she felt his finger press deeply into her damp cunt.

"Such a hot, tight little pussy; how would it feel clenching about my cock? Will you rock up to meet me, Dani, or wait eagerly to be fucked? I think you'd be an eager lover, wouldn't you? Not one who would simply lay there waiting for what I would do."

Her only answer came from the low groan that echoed from the back of her throat, her hands clenching into his hair, his lips nipping light kisses across her breasts, going from one nipple to the other, his fingers pressed between her thighs, rocking into her cunt, one finger finding her clit, circling it with each deep thrust into her eager body. She tangled her fingers into his hair, gripping him tight to her breasts, arching upwards as the heat grew between her thighs, grew until her cunt rippled with a need she had no desire to control.

Aaron fumbled at his jeans, tugging them down with one hand, his other remaining pressed against her sex, fingers slipping into the soft depths of her vulva. The slick sound should have embarrassed her, but all she could do was rock against him. She needed to feel him within her; there was no love, no attraction, for the first time she did nothing more but give into her need to be fucked. "I want you, now."

He growled, moving between her, pulling a small silver foil package from his stripped-off jeans. The foil tore under his finger; a moment to smooth the condom over his cock and he was ready, his cock pressing against the lips of her cunt, his grip moving to her hips, half-kneeling on the couch. "Hard and fast or slow and easy?"

"Hard." Her heels wrapped about his body, tugging him closer, feeling the walls of her cunt tighten about his cock. Nothing else needed to be said. His fingers tightened on her hips and her heels locked in the small of his back, her back arching as her shoulders pressed to the couch.

A low moan turned into a whimper with the touch of his fingers as he released his grip on her hips to grasp her breasts, squeezing them, twisting her nipples with each tight rock into her body. She couldn't help but clench about him, arching fully, her thighs slick with the heat that seeped from her willing cunt.

Each twist rippled through her cunt, each ripple had him thrusting deeper into her sex. The soft, slick sounds echoed in her ears, marking how willingly her body responded to his cock driving into her cunt, stretching her walls outwards.

His cock swelled within her cunt, his grunts, his eager thrusts, she could tell how close he was to coming now. Her own body rushed towards that edge, blood roaring in her ears, hips rocking, his fingers twisting at her ripe nipples. Slick, heated, her body needed this, needed this moment of release.

With a groan, her cunt clamped on his cock, arching upwards until only her shoulders rested on the couch. She couldn't hold back any longer. Her lips parted in a cry, liquid heat coating his cock as she rocked fully down against his body, driving him deeper into her sex at that moment of release, his own coming within a heartbeat of hers.

He slumped down against her body, his cock twitching against the tight walls of her sex, his breath coming in hot short gasps against her neck. "Gods, you are... you are wasted out here."

"This is where I belong." She pulled her fingers through his hair, catching her breath, soft tremors playing along the still-heated walls of her cunt. "This is where I've always belonged, Aaron. Nothing changes that."

"One day, something will." He leaned up on his arms, looking down into her eyes. "A part of me hopes that something—or someone—will be me."

Chapter Thirteen

"What makes you think I want to change?" Dani met his gaze calmly, then began to move out from under him, reaching for her clothes. "I like it out here. I don't even feel that comfortable visiting the city, so I doubt I could ever face living in one."

"That's a talk for another day." He wrapped his arms about her, keeping her pinned under him on the couch.

"I thought we'd agreed this was a one-off thing?" She didn't like the way the conversation was going.

"Unless we both decide we want more." He leaned down, pressing a kiss against her lips, his tone softening. "You're a beautiful woman, Dani. A very beautiful woman, and I'd like to spend more time with you. Tonight, maybe tomorrow, whenever you are willing to let me into your life."

She tensed, shaking her head. "I have to get up, Aaron. I still have some calls to make before I call it a night."

"To my brother," he muttered, releasing his hold on her, pushing back up from the couch. "I've come on a little too strong; sorry. I get that way at times—it's one of the reasons my wife and I broke up." He smiled, shaking his head as he sat on the other end of the couch, pulling his jeans back up.

"Yes, amongst others." She tried not to let her mood slip into something darker. "The shoot tomorrow at the logging mill could be interesting, even for me to watch. The lighting in there might need some thinking, through." Talking about his work could help—she didn't want to upset him but the chemistry, the attraction she had felt between her and Steven didn't exist with Aaron. He was a good man, a decent man, but she couldn't force something into life that wasn't there to begin with.

"Well, I'll get these cleared up, and then we can talk a little more." He rose, collecting the plates on his way to the kitchen.

"Sure," she replied, biting back the response she wanted to say instead. Her urge to tell him there wasn't anything to talk about, that she had work to do, that the moment on the couch had been fun but it wasn't the start of something else between them.

She reached for the phone, dialing the number for the hotel as she refastened her jeans, shuddering. It wasn't like her to not wash up after sex and she felt sticky now, uncomfortable as her still-wet cunt molded to her jeans.

"Hello, can you put me through to Steven Black's room, please... sure, I'll hold." Elevator music replaced the cheerful voice of the receptionist. Silence would have been better than the low, grating music she was forced to listen to.

"Hello?" Steven's voice cut in, the music ending in the second before he spoke.

"Steven, I've got some information for a location tomorrow—we can use the logging mill just outside of town." She could hear something in the background—a soft noise at first, like a murmured voice.

"Sounds good. What's the access like? Is the mill still in operation?" He spoke quickly.

"No, the mill closed down a few years ago, but there's a huge parking lot, and the road was built to take the weight of eighteen-wheelers. It should provide easy access for everyone involved." She'd not been out there for a few months but remembered the access well. "We can head out there around ten, if that works for you." Laughter—she wasn't imagining it—she could hear the sound of a woman laughing in the background.

"Sounds good. We could be out there most of the day getting work done. I really need to push this lot to be finished on time. The agency has some new assignments for Karol, so once this is done, we'll need to head off that night. I need at least one more location, though, rock-climbing theme. Any ideas?"

"Yes, one fairly close to the mill. During the set-up or while the models are putting the finishing touches on their makeup, I can show you the area; or when it's time to take a break." There were some caves less than a mile away that would be ideal.

"I've a better idea—what if we meet up around ten and then head to the shoot at noon?" Steven's voice was muffled for a moment, the laughter turning into a low giggle that sounded as though the woman had been told to be quiet.

"Works for me. Did I disturb you?" Her curiosity finally got the better of her.

"I'm just going over some layout ideas with Diana—she dropped by after Karolleft." He didn't hesitate with his answer. "And yes, Karol is pissed off, but there's nothing new about that one. I'll be glad when she's back in the hands of the agency and I don't have to deal with her again."

"I can understand that. Well, I'll let you get back to work and I'll see you tomorrow. Henry said he'll drop the paperwork off for you to sign tonight—that way we don't have to wait another day. He should be there before ten."

Thank heaven for Henry; he had become a mix of her boss and her friend over the past few years. He had never treated her as if she needed protecting, or required extra help because she was a woman, but at the same time had always been there for her to lean on should the need arise.

"Sounds good, I'll see you tomorrow."

"Night." She set the phone back down, only then becoming aware that Aaron had been listening to the conversation.

"Well, that's that sorted out. The logging mill should work well. I imagine it could turn into a fairly dramatic setting with the right lighting. The same with the cave system I should be able to show Steven in the morning."

"Caves? Oh for the climbing gear, that would be cool." Aaron sat back down, smiling. "It's a pity this will be his last job with that agency—they have been a blast to work with, from my point of view."

"But for Steven?" She glanced over; Aaron was making himself far too comfortable in her home.

"He doesn't like the work being sent his way, the changes in demands, the short-notice work but the expectation of high-standard return. He only received a week's notice about this assignment; did he tell you that? That's why he didn't have the area scouted out beforehand." He leaned back on the couch, swinging his legs up.

"No, he didn't...and it's getting a little late, Aaron. I do need to shower and get some sleep." She needed to get him out—her skin now itched from where he had touched her. A mistake; it had definitely been a mistake to let that happen between them.

"I thought you'd just had a shower?" He frowned.

"Yes, but I always wash up after sex." What did she need to do, draw him a diagram? Men; they could go from screwing someone to heading out for a meeting without even thinking to wash up half the time.

"Room in that shower for two?" He grinned, his gaze lingering over her form.

"Aaron, I need to get some sleep soon. I don't mean to be rude, or not appreciate the sandwich, but I do need to wash up and then collapse into bed." She rose, nodding towards the door. "I have a very early start—before I meet Steven I have to stop in by the office, double check paperwork, catch up with any reports, and then head out to the hotel."

"Oh, so you need me to go?"

She was about ready to strangle him by this point. "Yes, I need you to go. Look, maybe we can meet up for a coffee tomorrow evening?" Why had she said that? It didn't matter; whatever her reason, it had been enough to get him to finally move towards the door.

"Sounds like a great idea to me." He headed through the cabin. "Though I wouldn't mind staying overnight—I don't have any objections to getting up early."

"Not tonight." *Not ever,* she wanted to say, but she wasn't vicious in that way. "I sleep a lot better alone, Aaron."

"Well, that's a fair point. I doubt we'd get much sleep sharing the same bed." God's gift to women—that's what he thought he was. Even though she had come quickly, it hadn't been that spectacular to begin with. "Goodnight, Dani."

He leaned in as they reached the door, his arms circling her body, tugging her close for a kiss. She tried not to tense at his touch, parting her lips almost mechanically just to get the moment over with. He didn't notice the lack of enthusiasm, but he had enough for both of them. Then at last he was gone, dashing into his car. She didn't wait to see him pull out before closing the door.

"Stupid, stupid woman," she growled, heading back through her cabin towards the bathroom. The sound of the SUV heading down the driveway reached her ears, her clothing tossed into the laundry basket as she started the shower.

"Of all the dumb things to go and do, you had to sleep with that man." She knew better—ever since she had first met Aaron, the looks he had given her had left her feeling uncomfortable. Now she had made matters worse by sleeping with him. What in hell's name had she been thinking of?

Heated fingers of water pelted against her skin, the soap foaming in her hands as she started scrubbing at her skin, trying to get the feel of him from her memory. She'd have to talk to Steven about this before Aaron did. If she was lucky, he'd understand.

What did she need him to understand?

"You love him, you idiot. Of course you need him to understand," she muttered into the steaming water, scrubbing harder against her skin. She'd talk to Steven when they went to go and look at the caves, before the shoot at the logging mill. Maybe it would work out, maybe it wouldn't, but she'd be honest about the situation. She didn't know how else to be.

The scent of fresh coffee filtered into her bedroom, forcing her to wake up. She'd tossed and turned half the night, her dreams a mixture of violent arguments, lost loves, Steven going off with Diana or Karol, Aaron marrying her, Steven sweeping her up into his arms. One image had faded into the next before her poor confused mind even had a chance to make sense of what she'd seen. The only image that remained clear as she stumbled from the bed was the crow flying through each image.

Now, with the coffee and distant sounds of someone moving around her cabin, she hurried from the bed, grabbing the shotgun she kept under the bed. The first thought on her mind as it cleared was that Aaron had returned, entering the cabin without her permission. She checked the shot in the gun—rock salt, enough to hurt someone without killing them—and snapped the shotgun closed as she headed into the kitchen.

"Now is that anyway to greet your grandfather, Dancer?" Silver Fox smiled, unperturbed by the sight of the shotgun in her hands.

"I'm sorry, I didn't know who it was." She lowered the gun, relaxing. "Give me a moment to put this away and I'll be back out." She turned, heading back into her bedroom. Gramps and his wandering ways; it wasn't often that he came into her cabin without asking her first.

"You might want to put some clothing on as well," he called out after her. Heat burned in twin points on her cheeks and chuckled as she searched through her closet for a clean uniform. Within a few minutes she had dashed into the bathroom, cleaned up and dressed.

By the time she walked back into the kitchen, the coffee was ready and her gramps had already poured two cups out. "Now that looks better. Here, you'll need this—you have another long day ahead of you, as I understand it."

"Yes, but it's been that way since Steven and co. arrived." She settled down, taking the cup from his hand.

"A lot of things have been going on since that man arrived. Some of those, I think we need to talk about; don't you?" His dark gaze met hers, the deep lines about his eyes crinkling with the concern she could feel radiating from his smile.

"What things would those be?" There was no point in dodging the question.

"Steven Black. You and he have become close." He watched her over the rim of the cup. "Closer than you want people to know about, Dancer, but I am afraid it's too late to keep it secret. Half the town already guesses, and maybe more than a few know for certain. That blonde woman, the one with no heart, has spoken loudly enough for the mountains to hear."

"I see." She set the cup down, taking a slow breath, gathering her thoughts before continuing. "And why would it matter what other people think they know?"

"It's because you've been the good girl, Dancer. The one people have watched for, waiting to see you fail, to see you make the mistakes your mother made. Now they have that moment. This Steven, he seems to be a good man, but I know a wind-born spirit when I see one. He has no intention of settling down—it's not a part of him. I can see it, the way he shifts from foot to foot, barely sitting still for any length of time." He spoke calmly. "I don't want to see you hurt."

"It might be a little too late for that, Gramps," she admitted, interlacing her hands on her lap. "I made a mistake, I know that."

"More than one. I saw another car here last night, same type but not the same man." He nodded slightly. "I had meant to talk to you last night, but I didn't stop when I saw the car here. The brother, wasn't it?"

"Yes." She swallowed hard. "Gramps, I've been having some odd dreams. Strange ones that almost come true, glimpses of things that frightened me at one point, that have me looking for answers."

"Is this tied in with the two men?" Silver Fox inquired.

"Yes, I believe so." Slowly, she began to explain about the dreams, piecing together the first once from memory, how she had dreamed of the eagle and a blond-haired man, then run into

Steven the following day and heard an eagle hunting overhead. Then the more disturbing of the dreams, the one she had had in the bath, where Aaron had forced his attentions on her, how she had not been able to fight him. The terrible smothering sensation that had plagued her in the dream, the fear, how she had finally woken in the bath only to find Aaron on her porch moments later.

"Dreams that then come to pass; I have wondered about this since you were a small child, Wind Dancer. Your mother used to be able to do the same thing, but when you passed into womanhood and made no mention of that happening, I assumed it was not something that had touched you."

He nodded towards the old dream catcher that hung from her wall. "I need to make one just for you, one you will use, and not just as decoration. These dreams of yours are not all for the good, and until we have chance to go to the medicine lodge, I want you to be protected."

She was tempted to protest, to say she didn't believe in that; but the way the dreams had come true, each in their own way, had left her shaken. "Thanks, Gramps."

"I'm not just doing this for you, but for both of us. I should have taught you about dreams years ago, what to look for, but I didn't want to repeat the mistakes of the past. I pushed that too much onto your mother, and I do not want to lose you the way I did her." Silver Fox lowered his gaze, hiding the tears she could see already slipping down his silk-creased cheeks.

"Gramps, you could never have pushed me away. I love you too much for that. And I have a tongue in my mouth; there was nothing stopping me from coming and asking you. I just thought that it was nothing more than a dream at first, but that second one had me shaken." Terrified would have been more truthful. "Is there anything else I can do?"

"I need to talk to a few of the elders, to make sure we do this the right way. Sage can be used to purify your home, and as the dark one from your dream has been here, then I will do that whilst you work. Would you let me bring the items I need to make the dream catcher into your home and work on it here? I believe that will help, I can draw on your presence, work what I feel for you into the dream catcher." He spoke softly, looking back up at his granddaughter. "I do not want to push where I am not wanted."

"Gramps, oh Gramps, you've never done that," she protested.

"Yes I have. Every morning of late in the diner. Don't tell me I haven't—I've seen it in your eyes, in the way you've tensed over certain topics. I avoided talking about our people and substituted other topics instead."

He nodded as he spoke; for the first time, or so it seemed, she noticed just how grey he had become. The braids he insisted on wearing were almost completely iron-grey now, with small silver streaks where only a year ago he'd still had touches of raven hair. He'd aged right before her eyes, and she had never noticed.

Yet he was a strong man—under his shirt, she knew his chest still bore the marks of the sun dance. Though many of her age and older didn't take the rite of passage, her Gramps had—a fact she had always been proud of, though she had failed to tell him so.

"Thank you, Gramps." She moved across the room, taking a seat next to him as she wrapped him into a tight hug. He felt thinner, frail, but the energy she had always associated with him remained. "I have to head for work soon. I need to go into town and show Steven the caves before we get that shoot done out at the logging mill."

He cupped her face, turning her so he could look directly into her eyes. "You need to let him know about Aaron as well. Do not hide things from him."

"I didn't think you'd care about him?"

"I care about you, and if you love him—which I think you do—then I can accept that. Just remember he is a wind spirit, a wanderer; it will only work if you can welcome that part of him into your heart. If you believe you can live with him only visiting when his work permits, when the wind blows him this way."

"If the wind blows him this way, I will accept that, Gramps." She pressed a kiss against his cheek, tasting the tears.

"I'll work a butterfly into the catcher." He nodded, looking about her cabin as she stepped away. "You need it...and the sage I will bring also. I'll do the first pass through your home, and then you will need to do one again tonight before you sleep. No more risks on this. I want my granddaughter's spirit to rest when you sleep and not be plagued by ill-fortune."

"What of the crow?" she asked, tucking her shirt into place.

"What crow?" Silver Fox asked quickly. "You dreamed of a crow?"

"Yes, this morning—the rest of the dream didn't make any sense, but I can remember the crow flying through each section of the dream." She tugged her braid tightly until it settled down her back, reaching for her jacket.

"Dancer, if you saw a crow, then you will need help with what is to come. Just as the Eagle brought a time of growth and lessons in your life, the Crow shows betrayal." His voice shook as he spoke. "Be careful today, please. I do not like what this might mean and what dangers you may face. I don't want to lose you."

"You won't, Gramps. Trust me." She smiled, trying to keep her own concerns from growing out of hand. All those years she had wasted by not asking him about their heritage, the stories she had missed out on. Whatever happened in the next few days, Dani was now determined to sit down with her Gramps after the assignment with Steven was over and learn all she could before it was too late.

"I do—it's these others involved I do not trust."

Chapter Fourteen

The drive back into town had given her plenty of time to think. Though she knew her gramps would do everything he needed to in order to clear the dreams and unwanted energy from her home, she didn't want to leave all the work to him. A butterfly; she could recall one being worked into the blanket she still had from childhood, but until he had mentioned it as being associated with dreams, she had all but forgotten. How much else had she forgotten, or shoved to the back of her mind rather than enjoy so she could pass the stories on to her own children?

What children? Even now she doubted they would ever be a part of her life. That still didn't mean she was right to shut out the heritage she had been born into. She pulled up in front of the hotel, smiling as she saw that Steven was already waiting for her—at least they would save time.

"Morning." He smiled, slipping into the passenger seat.

"Did you get the paperwork signed?" She waited for an answer before moving the truck from the parking lot. She'd stopped in at the now-cleaned-up Rangers station on the way into town, checking in on the reports, but Henry had had no more news for her. He had confirmed that the paperwork had been dropped off, though, and they'd spoken for a short while about her gramps.

"Yep, and I have my copy here." He tapped the backpack he had brought with him. "Aaron is going to get the rest of my gear and the team out to the logging mill. I've got everything I need here to go exploring, and I've even had two cups of coffee this morning, so I am well and truly awake."

His good mood was infectious. "Good—we can head out then. The cave system is about an hour away from the mill, so my idea was this: if you need a second day at the mill for any reason, you could do that tomorrow, and then do the last of the shoot at the caves. Karol and co. can change at the mill—there are still working bathrooms there, with better lighting than they had to use at the first shoot."

"How come? I thought the place had been shut down," he asked as she backed the truck up.

"Pipes that are not looked after have a tendency to burst in winter out here, so it's common sense for the owner to keep them in working order. It costs less in the long term." She glanced back towards the hotel, catching a glimpse of a woman watching them leave. "Did you tell the others where we were going?"

"Yes—they weren't too happy, but it needs to be done. Besides, I wanted to spend some time with you again." He glanced towards her, smiling, reaching out to press his hand onto her thigh. "I missed you last night, Dani, and I'm sorry I let Karol disturb our time together."

She tensed, wondering what he would say when she told him about Aaron. She had to tell him before he did. "I wasn't... I mean, I didn't go without company."

His fingers tightened on her thigh, then relaxed. "Your gramps?"

"Aaron came out to see me," she replied quietly, trying to keep her focus on the road ahead. This wasn't the best of situations to be discussing this with him. "I made a mistake last night, a big one, I admit that."

"What type of mistake?" She could feel his fingers squeezing into her thigh, releasing only to squeeze again.

"A big one, with your brother; one I won't let happen again." She hoped he would be able to put the pieces together without her having to go into the details, details that still left her feeling sick at the thought of them.

"You and he....?"

"Yes." She nodded, unable to look towards him.

Silence settled on the truck as he moved his hand away from her thigh. She didn't know what else to say; nor did he, it seemed, as he continued to drive out of town. What else had she expected him to do? Rant and rave perhaps, call her a whore or slut?

That might have been easier than the silence she now faced. She'd made a mistake, and losing him would have been the expected price to pay. Tears stung at her eyes, though she kept silent through the rest of the ride, not even speaking when they pulled onto the small track and finally stopped in what was nothing more than a widening of the dirt road.

"We've got about a thirty-minute walk from here." Her throat felt tight. Swallowing had become a chore, and she fought not to let the tears spill from her eyes. "That's if you're still interested in taking the walk with me."

"Yes, I am." He was quiet still, and said nothing more when he followed her down the narrow path towards the caves. The track was easy to walk along—narrow, but it had been kept clear of overgrowth due to the locals that loved the area. The caves were one of the reasons the park had been an attraction long before it had been officially granted park status. Her Gramps had spoken of young men coming out here on dream quests—here and the ridge were both prime areas for those seeking visions. How many still followed that tradition, she didn't know, but at least a few still came out here. For her gramps the ridge, was his favorite location.

"Why did you do it?" Steven had stopped behind her on the track.

"I don't know, not fully," she said, turning to look at him. "It was a stupid mistake—I knew that when it was happening, but I didn't stop. I guess I was angry that we'd spoken of love but nothing else. You'd not mentioned the others to me either. It was Aaron who told me about your habit of picking up women on a shoot."

"My habit?" He blinked, looking at her ,astounded by her words.

"Yes, he said this was something you did on a regular basis. He warned Diana not to fall for you as she wouldn't be the first, nor would she be the last." She frowned, watching him. "He spent most of yesterday afternoon after we got back from the glade telling Diana and I about your habits, and he'd mentioned some of them before. You'd even mentioned you'd dated a few people in the past, so I thought nothing of it until he went into more details.

"Diana was very upset about the whole thing. I tried to keep it from showing, but I hurt when I heard about it. Stupid, I know—we barely know each other and...." She stopped, seeing how badly he was reacting to the news.

"What...I don't believe he would do something like that to me." He didn't move, staring at her as he spoke. The shock in his eyes, the way the color drained from his face; it wouldn't make sense unless Aaron had been lying or overplaying the situation. "My own damn brother would pull something like this on me?"

"What's going on?"

"I've dated a handful of people over the last seven years, and he makes it sound like I pick up women at every shoot. Sure, I've made a few mistakes—who hasn't?—but I'm not some player working my way through women at every turn. What the fuck does he think he's doing?" he growled, his blue eyes narrowing, turning darker with the anger he had every reason to feel.

"He lied?" she murmured.

"Yes, he damn well lied. Did you really think I did things like that?" He shook his head, his hands clenched into fists. "I would never treat women like that. Yes, I like female company—I'm a man with a heartbeat, and I don't know a straight man alive who doesn't enjoy being with a beautiful and willing woman—but most of us know how to stop pressing our attention where it isn't wanted. Of all the damn things to say about me.... I went out of my way to give that bastard a job and he tries to screw me over with the woman I love."

He still loved her, even after what she had done with Aaron? "I'm sorry, I should have come to find you. Or I could have waited until you had finished with Karol." She'd been tired, upset; there were a dozen excuses she could have offered him ,but none would have been right. She'd screwed up, and blaming him would be wrong.

"I'll kill him." He should no sign of calming down. "I'll tear his lying tongue out and force him to eat it."

"Steven, you can't…." She reached out, catching him by the arm. "Yes, he's an asshole, but he's still your brother."

"Dani, don't you understand—thanks to his lies, I may well have my name blackened in this trade. He might be the reason the agencies have been acting funny with me over the past year." He shook his head, but didn't pull back from her arm. "And you—you slept with him because of his lies?"

"No. I slept with him because I made a mistake and didn't think." She didn't want to lose him; if she did, it was her own fault, and she was willing to accept that. "What I did was wrong. I don't love Aaron; he was nothing more than a man in the right place at the wrong time. I spent an hour in the shower afterwards scrubbing myself down, that's how badly my skin crawled."

"You don't love Aaron, but you do love me?" he said, the anger easing from his voice. "Or am I just another one who is in the right place?"

"Steven Black, until you I had slept with one man, one…in my entire life. Bear, a man I had grown up with, who left over a year ago." He had every right to suggest that to her—she knew that.

"And if he walked back into your life?"

"I'd send him packing with a boot up his ass. He lied to me and is getting married." He was trying to put the pieces together, she understood that. "He cheated on me for some time in the relationship, and I only found out a few days ago thanks to a letter he sent me."

"So I'm a rebound?" A wry smile tugged the corners of his mouth.

"No. If it started that way, I am not aware of it, and even then that never entered my thoughts—not even when we ended up at my cabin." She couldn't bear the thought that he assumed she had used him in some way. "I love you, Steven, even if you are a wind spirit."

"A what?" He frowned, looking at her.

"A wind spirit—it's what my gramps calls a person who isn't ready to settled down. It's a man or woman who is happier traveling the world, exploring instead of staying in one place." She didn't step back from him but remained close, watching him for signs of his anger returning. "That's you, isn't it?"

"Yes. I've never heard the term before, though," he admitted, smiling, the tension easing fully from his shoulders as he curled one arm about her waist to pull her close.

"The only person I've ever heard use it has been my grandfather." She leaned in against him. "I'm sorry, what I did with Aaron...."

"Is over. I don't like what happened, but re-hashing it over and over again won't do either of us any good. You said you'd made a mistake with him, and I agree—it was a mistake, one my brother might not be so willing to let go of. He tends to fixate on a woman. I just hope now he's had... now you two spent some time together last night, he will move on to another."

That didn't sound very comforting. "And if he doesn't?"

"Then we'll deal with that together, and your gramps is right—I am a wanderer, but I have every intention of coming back here as often as I can. I don't want to lose you from my life. Not now, not ever. I've even got some pictures of the park I wanted to show you, brought them with me for you to see." He brushed a soft kiss over her forehead. "But we have some work to do yet, haven't we?"

"Yes, the caves." The light had returned to his eyes, chasing away the darkness of his anger. "We've not got much further to walk, if you're ready to continue?" He was, and this time when they walked down the narrow trail, they did so side by side.

She'd never expected him to be so forgiving, nor would she

risk losing him again. Honesty played a large part in this, of that she was certain; but whatever had been the turning point in the conversation she wasn't about to question it. Now all she needed to do was help her grandfather chase the remaining unwanted presence from her home.

The pathway opened up into the clearing, a rock face climbing out from the ground, clawing its way towards the sky like a jagged hand, with sharp fingers pressed together that shadowed over the clearing. There, at the base of the rock, were two small cave entrances, slivers of darkness beckoning adventurous souls to explore within.

"Wow." Steven finally moved away from her, looking around the clearing, taking in how the light played down over the rock face, they way the entrances into the caves seemed to swallow the sun, denying its existence.

"This is ideal. I've never been in a place that has so many different facets to it. The woodlands here, the maples, they're just turning. If we can get a few shots at the tree line under the maples, the colors in those leaves would be ideal. Then we can do the climbing gear shoot here."

"The ground is still a little damp, but as long as it doesn't rain again, it should be fine for tomorrow's shoot." She pressed the toe of her boot into the dirt, the ground steady though the give was there, showing how damp it still was.

"That I can see. I can't wait to get out here tomorrow." His enthusiasm was contagious. "What about the caves?"

"No way we can get lighting in there for a shoot."

"I didn't mean for the shoot---can we go in there?" He nodded towards the entrance. "Or is it too dangerous?"

"The caves are safe, so yes, we can go in. Why?" She glanced towards him, seeing the smile on his face.

"Because I'd like to explore the caves with you. I know we don't have a lot of time before we have to head out to the mill, but I want a moment with you, discovering a new place with you at my side." His pack remained shouldered as he caught her arm, turning her to face him fully, brushing his lips against her own in a butterfly light kiss.

"I have only a few days left before I have to return to the city, and then it will be weeks before I can head out this way again. Can you blame me for wanting to grab as many private moments with you as possible in the time we have left?"

"No, not at all." She smiled, leaning up into his kiss, reaching up to embrace him. Her body melded against his, nipples hardening under the uniform shirt, the feel of his heartbeat vibrating against her breasts and adding to the closeness she felt in that moment.

She wanted to enjoy any time they had left, and not think about the day only a few days away when he would leave. His word that he would return helped, though it didn't keep the regret at bay completely. She wasn't going to ask him to give up his work, and she wasn't ready to leave the park.

It could work, being with him, as long as they were both honest and made the most of their time together. Didn't the families of truck drivers and those in the armed forces deal with far worse than this? She knew that he would only be a few hours away in the cities, a six-hour drive—that wasn't so bad, really, and when he had to travel for other assignments, she'd know in advance.

"Gramps calls this place the Dreamers' Caves."

"Then maybe they will give us a glimpse into shared dreams of our future," he murmured against her lips; then, with a playful grin, he licked slowly across them. "Shall we?"

Dani felt like a girl again, exploring the caves for the first time as she pulled out the torch from her belt and headed into the darkness, with Steven following her close behind. The entrance was narrow but opened up into a wide cave about five feet into the cliff face. The beam of light from the small torch illuminated the interior of the cave, catching on the small crystals that lined the cave walls. Tiny points of light, no bigger than pinpricks, marked small patterns in the darkness. "This is beautiful. Has anyone taken pictures of the caves?"

"They might have done, but I haven't seen them." The look in his eyes and the sense of wonder around him as he took in the raw beauty of the caves allowed her to see the area in a whole new light. As if she were visiting the caves for the first time all over again.

"I've spent hours in here, wandering through most of the park, if I'm going to be honest. Here and the cabin are where I feel the most at peace. The rest of the world just slips away out here; it might as well not exist." Time was running out on them now—they had barely an hour before they needed to be at the logging mill to begin the shoot.

"We can come back again before you head back to the cities. I'll have a better chance to show you around then. Maybe when we set up to do some of the shoot here, there will be some time then?"

"Your polite way of reminding me I have work to do?" He moved behind her, wrapping his arms about her waist, pulling her close.

"Yes. I don't want to drag you away back to work, but we have to." She leaned back into his arms, relaxing. Even after the tension that had passed between them earlier, she found herself able to just lean back against him, relax, forget about the argument. There would be doubts later on, but she hoped they would ease until they ceased to exist.

"I'd like to show you the pictures I developed last night, the ones I took out at the river and the glade." Her stomach knotted. Did he mean the pictures he had taken of her? "They came out very well indeed. You're a lot more photogenic than think you are."

He headed back out into the sunlight, pulling the large envelope out from his pack once they left the caves. She watched nervously as he tugged the photographs out, laying them out on the back on the envelope in a fan of color and light.

"These are wonderful." She couldn't keep the awe from her voice as she looked at the captured images. Flecks of light danced off the surface of the river; somehow, as she peered at the photograph, it seemed as though the water still moved, still rushed past the flat rock. Shadows cast across another picture, living fingers reaching out towards her in the glade, caressing her skin in an unfelt caress. If she hadn't known for certain that the woman in the pictures had been her, she would have sworn it was someone else. She looked alive, flushed with a spirit, a passion she never dreamt she could lay claim to.

"How did you do this? It's like you captured the heart of the park."

"Having good subjects to work with helps, but it's how I look at the world, how I see you." He reached out, cupping her cheek softly. "This is what I see when I look at you: your life, spirit and beauty."

"I never thought I'd look like this," she whispered, unable to tear her gaze away from the pictures. "You're a magician, Steve."

"No, I'm just a photographer." He smiled, tracing the line of her jaw. "One who has been very lucky to work with some amazing women and locations that even an amateur could not screw up. Well, maybe a few of them could." He leaned in, pressing a soft kiss against her lips, setting the pictures down as he pulled her closer. "I tried telling you that you are a beautiful woman, Dani; now do you believe me?"

"Yes." Tears slipped down her cheeks, mingling on their lips. She'd never believed she could look that way. She was just Danielle Wind Dancer, a woman of the people, a ranger, Silver Fox's granddaughter, nothing special—until now. He'd shown her so much about herself. Until he had walked into her life, she had never admitted that she had a poor self-image, or flinched when she glanced towards the mirror.

Focused on Love

But now she realized she had nothing to be ashamed of. She believed him more than she had been willing to believe her gramps—her excuse had always been that the old man was biased. "Yes, I believe you now."

"I'll never lie to you, Dani," he murmured against her lips, holding her firmly against his chest. "Ask me anything you want and I'll answer you, even if the answer might hurt me. That's why I couldn't walk away from you after you told me about you and Aaron—it would have been hypocritical of me to do that. You don't deserve things like that, from me or anyone else."

"Bear lied to me for years," she admitted, looking up into his soft blue eyes. "I never knew until the morning I met you. He wrote to me, admitting it. We've been apart a year, and it took him that long to finally get the guts to let me know."

Her hands clenched at the memory of the letter. He could have sent that a year ago, when he first left. But to wait so long to send it, to leave her lingering, waiting to find out what was going on....

"I could have written to him beforehand, but I never did."

"I think you knew he wasn't coming back, though he should have told you years ago." His fingers played through her hair, unweaving the tight braid, leaving it loose down her back. "He should have been honest, been a man and let you know instead of a child. That's what he did—he acted like a frightened child."

Silver Fox would agree: men took responsibility for their actions. No, not just men, adults did. That was part of what made them adults, instead of children playing the role. Bear had never taken part in the sun dance ritual, nor had he stepped foot into the sweat lodge; only now did she finally accept some of the reasoning behind the disapproval she had felt emanating from her gramps every time he had met Bear.

Steven smiled, his lips covering hers, a soft kiss as light as the butterfly she prayed would keep her dreams safe in the coming nights. With a soft moan she pressed tightly to him, reaching up to curl her arms about his neck, her nipples pressing against the inside of her shirt in throbbing pebbles. She felt safe in his arms, desired in a way she had never hoped for.

Her lips parted beneath his as she suckled hungrily on his tongue, thighs pressing together as a soft rock moved through her hips against the growing swell of his cock. They didn't have time now, but she wanted him, needed him.

Soon, though, once the work had been done for the day, they would be able to enjoy the night together. Her bed, her home; it would be cleansed with him in it if she had to do it that way. She wouldn't waste one more night apart from him when they needed to be together.

"I won't ever lie to you, Dani. On that you have my word."

Chapter Fifteen

They'd talked about a dozen things on the drive to the logging mill, about their shared interest in the world around them, the sense of peace they both experienced in the park and their differences—most of all, they had spoken about those. If they were to have any chance of working things out between them, then it would be the things they didn't have in common that needed to be discussed.

Could it work between them? She wanted to believe that but the doubts were obvious. The biggest of all had to be their choices in lifestyle. His love of travel and her preferences to remain close to home and her gramps would clash. He'd let her known about the trips he had coming up over the next six months, some he knew about for certain, and others he still waited for confirmation on. As he spoke about the places he would be going to, the areas he would see, Dani found herself facing a growing urge to travel that she had never experienced before. Seeing how he viewed her and the park in those few photographs had opened her eyes to a world of possibilities. She couldn't imagine leaving for good, but the thought of taking the occasional trip with him, if he didn't mind, now felt enticing.

"What if I wanted to come with you on a trip—just on occasion, I mean, not every time?" She glanced towards him as they pulled off the main road and headed down the wide road towards the logging mill. Locally, private roads were seldom more than dirt tracks, but with the heavy vehicles that had driven back and forth from the mill, a more permanent road had been built. The location had been ideal for the construction of the mill: at the bottom of a hill, close to the river, but in a wide enough part that it was unlikely to flood except under extreme weather conditions.

"I think we could arrange that, if it was what you really wanted to do. I've got a trip coming up to the Painted Desert in Arizona later this year. I'd love for you to come with me." That energy she had seen reflected in his work still danced within his eyes.

"I'd love to, if I can get the time off. When are you planning on heading out there?" Debris crunched under the tires as she pulled up in front of the mill.

"It won't be for a few months yet, but I'll have the details of the trip in about three weeks' time. We can sort it out then," Steven said, falling quiet as her radio crackled into life.

"Dani, you there?" Henry's voice broke through the static.

"Here." She picked up the handset.

"We've had a small fire. Nothing more than a dozen trash cans, but it spilt over this time. Looks like some sort of accelerant was used, judging by the burn pattern. I'm calling out a team from the city, see if they can find out what was used."

Her throat clenched. "How bad was it?"

"Broke out of the cans, hit a patch of scrub. We were lucky the bad weather here stopped it from turning into something far worse, but it means that whoever is behind this is getting worse." She could hear the worry in Henry's voice. "Keep an eye out during the shoot today."

"Will do; anything else I should know? Steven's here, by the way." She glanced towards the photographer, seeing the frown that now creased his brow.

"Nothing else I can tell you. We caught a lucky break this time; next time, though, I don't think we'll be as fortunate. The person behind this is stepping up each time they do something, so just be very careful out there today." He paused for a moment. "I'll try and get out to the mill this afternoon, during the shoot if I get the time. If not, then try and stop by my place on your way home."

"Will do." That was rare—normally she'd meet him at the Ranger Station. She could count on one hand the number of times she had been at Henry's house. It wasn't that she wasn't welcome; it just made more sense to meet at the Station the majority of the time.

Still frowning, she set the radio back down on the hook on her dash board, glancing towards Steven as she did so. "There's been some minor vandalism of late."

"I remember you saying, but by the sounds of things it's changed from minor to major." He nodded towards the parking area in front of the mill. "Looks like we have company."

The rest of the team were waiting at the logging mill when they arrived, and the look on Karol's face made it very clear she had not enjoyed the wait one bit. They'd barely stepped foot out of the truck when the blonde launched into her tirade. "I can't believe you dragged me all the way out here, Steven. Have you any idea just how badly this place smells? And there are machines everywhere; you can't be serious about using this as a location."

"I can and I am." Steven didn't give her more than a sideways glance. "The old machines will be a fantastic backdrop, and what you can smell is sawdust, perhaps some oil from the machines, the smell of years of honest, hard physical labor. Not that I expect you to recognize the smell for what it is."

"Are trying to say that models don't work hard?" she snapped, glaring at him. "How dare you insult us all like that? If you think Diana, Anna and I will stand here and let you degrade us in this or any other manner, you are sorely mistaken."

"I never said that." He gave Diana and Anna, who hung back, a quick wink. Their choice to stand back gave the appearance of physical as well as emotional distance between themselves and Karol, a choice Dani knew to be a wise one. Aaron remained conspicuously absent at the moment, but small sounds of equipment being set up and new sources of light shining from within the mill gave her a good idea where the other brother would be.

"But you said we didn't recognize the smell of hard labor." Karol looked back at the other two women. "You heard him say that, didn't you?"

"Not at all, Karol," Steven spoke before either woman could. "I'm saying you don't. There isn't a man or woman here who isn't aware of how you have used the work of others to get where you are today. So don't try and pull that line on me." He pulled his pack out from the truck.

"We have two days work, maybe three left to get this shoot finished, and we will get it done a lot faster without you complaining every other breath. You used to be fun to work with—you knew how to offer suggestions, you listened to others' advice—but all that changed after you did that shoot in Europe." He closed the door, looking directly at her now.

"You went away to that assignment as a lovely woman and came back a bitch queen who thought she was better than everyone else. If you took a good long look at yourself in the mirror once in a while, I mean a *real* look instead of just to get your hair or makeup in place, then you might realize what you've become."

She stuttered, her lips moving without sound, her ability to protest lost under the intensity of his gaze, the uncompromising words he had forced her to listen to. "Now you can either work with me and get the rest of this shoot done, or I will do the rest of it without your help."

"You wouldn't. You need me for this assignment," she protested, finally regaining her voice. "You can't just toss me out of the rest of the shoot like that. I know what you've been doing, Steven. Spending all your time with that woman. The whole town knows about it by now, you've not been very careful in covering your tracks, and now you're taking it out on me. Well I won't stand for it; there is no way you'll cut me out of the shoot."

"I can and I will. I should have done that months ago, but I'm going to give you one last chance. If you bitch, moan, complain or make anyone's life here uncomfortable again, then I will keep you out of the rest of the shoot. That means you keep that perfect little mouth of yours from spilling the venom that has become such a great part of your life." He didn't waver, neither in gaze nor stance, as she spluttered.

"You cannot deny that you've been spending a lot of time with that Ranger woman," she growled, seeking a target to lash out at.

"Why would I deny the obvious truth?" Steven smiled, his amusement clear. "And her name is Danielle Wind Dancer—she's standing right there and can hear every word you're saying, but of course you're quite aware of that. You just don't believe she's worthy of being addressed directly by you."

Standing back and not becoming directly involved in the argument was one of the hardest things Dani had ever done. If she had dived in, spoken, given Karol the sharp end of her tongue, all she would have succeeded in doing was stooping to the other woman's level. Besides, Steven was dealing with the matter far better than she could have done. Personal attacks, in the snide way that Karol used them, were enough to trigger Dani's temper; and as long as she represented the park, she couldn't permit herself to get involved in what would quickly turn into a shouting match.

"You're screwing her," Karol stated.

"What she and I are doing is private. We are involved, we are going to keep in contact after the shoot, and if you want to define that as us 'screwing,' you're just continuing to show everyone here how low you've sunk."

He looked over the assembled group and then nodded towards the logging mill. "We have work to do. You've had your say, Karol, and that is the end of the matter. Unless you really would prefer to return to the hotel now?"

Karol opened her mouth to speak again, perhaps to begin a new round of protests, but the cold look in Steven's eyes finally silenced her. In an obvious rage she turned, stalking towards the mill with Anna following in her wake. Leaving only Diana, Steven and Dani remaining by the truck.

"You really would have sent her back to the hotel?" Diana

spoke quietly, her face pale as she tried to avoid Dani's gaze.

"Yes. I've had enough of her games over the years to last me a lifetime." He started to walk towards the Mill as he spoke. "And I will be very glad to see the back of her. She's one of the reasons I'm getting out of this side of the business. I found out a while back that Karol had struck a deal with the agency—the only assignments they will now send me are ones involving her, so she has crossed the line from being a model into a stalker of sorts."

That had been something Dani hadn't expected to hear. "Can she do that, pull that kind of weight?" she asked, trying to learn a little more about the world Steven was involved in.

"Yes, unfortunately, as she is their top model. The higher up the ladder you get, the more demands you can make," Diana explained as the three of them walked towards the building. "I'm nowhere near that level yet, and though I don't like what she did I can understand why she would want to work with Steve. He is one of the best there is, if not the best." There was no denying the hero worship that touched every word Diana uttered. "I can't imagine working with someone else, and I don't know what I'll do now that you're retiring from the business, Steve."

Her focus was on the photographer, and Dani could see that the other woman's interest in him had not faded. Had he done anything to lead her on? Not that she had been able to see.

"I don't think he's leaving the business, Diana. He's just changing his area of interest."

"What if Karol was never able to interfere with your work again; would that help?" Diana ignored the comment.

"It might, but I can't see the agency dropping her, and I really did lose a lot of my other contacts in the business when I focused that side of my work with the one company. It's a mistake I will pay for; but life is about learning from your errors."

Steven snaked an arm about Dani's waist as they walked into the Mill. "Now we need to put aside the problems of earlier and get to work. The sooner we get this shoot finished, the sooner

I can be done with Karol's tantrums." The cold look Diana shot Dani's way was missed entirely by Steven, and with the stress he had already been under, she didn't want to bring his attention to it.

"Then I'll have to hope that Karol sees the error of her ways and either retires or changes agencies," said Diana as she headed into the mill and gave one last quick glance towards Steven. "I would hate to have to give up working with you just because one or two silly women got in the way."

A sharp sound caught her attention as they stepped inside the mill: the familiar but grating noise of a crow. She turned enough to see the lone bird fly low across the parking lot, winging in on soft breezes before arching upwards into the sky, carrying with it the memory of Silver Fox's warning....

Hours passed as models danced to Steven's subtle tune directing them across the open work area of the mill. Small rooms led off from the main equipment area; large saws with great circular blades still remained in place, though sawdust had been swept to corners in the mill. There wasn't enough to be a breathing hazard, but the scent was ever-present as the shoot continued.

As the work continued, Dani's tension eased. Of Aaron there had been little sign, except as a shadowy figure moving behind the mobile lights, running for water when one of the women called out for a drink, and that didn't change until halfway through the shoot.

"How are you doing?" Aaron sat down next to her, giving her a passing glance over. "I tried calling you this morning, but some old man answered the phone."

"You mean my gramps—he's doing some work out over at my place today." She fought not to flinch at his presence, but the slow itch that worked its way down her spine made that difficult at best.

"You mean the old man from the diner?" He edged a little closer.

"Yes, that's my grandfather. He drops by at times, more often than not without warning," she said, taking a risk in playing up that part of the relationship. If the thought that Silver Fox would drop by without warning kept Aaron from stopping by the cabin again, then so much the better. "I said he could do some work there over the next few days." It might not take that long for the cleansing to take place, but again, it might keep Aaron away.

"Pity about that; perhaps you'd like to meet me for coffee then? Tonight? I think we have some things to talk about, clear up a few rumors. I heard that you and Steve are becoming a permanent item, and I know you're not stupid enough to fall for his lines." He reached out, squeezing her knee. "Especially not after what we shared last night."

"What we shared was a mistake, Aaron. I'm sorry; I should have told you to stop, or asked you to leave. I'm not into the casual sex thing—thought I could be, but it's just not a part of my nature." She avoided talking about Steve right now, not wanting to step into a full blown argument. If the shoot had been over, it would have been another matter; but to disturb the work that was taking place was not an option, not in Dani's book.

"We've got the chance to have more between us, Dani. A lot more than casual sex, as you put it. I want to get to know you, spend time with you, I want to be able to have you in my life." He didn't move away from her, his voice taking on a possessive tone that made her increasingly uncomfortable. "You're the woman I've been looking for, and I never even realized it until last night. I've never known someone like you. You're beautiful, confident, at ease with your body, with the world around you. You don't need any false pretenses—you don't wear makeup, you're not a slave to fashion or fads, and being with you, I feel as though I have the chance to see the world in a different light.

"Sure, making the adjustment to moving out here will take

a while. Or maybe you'd come to the city with me; either would work. Though you moving with me would be easier, I'm sure you could easily fit in with some other line of work, after all," he rambled on, oblivious to her discomfort.

"I don't want to leave my home, not for you or anyone else." She kept her voice low, wincing when the grip on her knee increased.

"You might change your mind after you've been exploring with me. I know some wonderful places in the city; it's not all that bad." He'd moved closer, until their shoulders touched.

"Aaron..." she tried to interrupt him.

"There are parks. Sure, they aren't as interesting as this one, and nowhere near as large, but you'll love them. I'm sure of it."

"Aaron, I'm not going," she tried again, shaking her head as she carefully lifted his hand away from her knee. "And you're hurting me."

"Sorry; I don't know my own strength at times." He didn't draw back but didn't try and replace his hand. "What do you mean you're not going—you wanted me to move in with you?"

"No, I never said that either." She fought to keep the exasperation from her voice. She had to tell him the truth, no matter how brutal that made her seem. "There's nothing between us, Aaron. I tried telling you what happened last night was a mistake, nothing more. We agreed to a no-strings moment; you want more. I don't. I've a life out here, family, friends, and I can't see you being a part of it."

"There could be—something else, I mean—if you were willing to give it a try." He reached for her hands, trying to take them in his. "You and I could be happy, very happy. Think of everything we could explore together. I'd love to see the park with you; I haven't had the chance to do that. You've been so busy with the shoot and Steve...." He voice trailed off, the grip on her hands tightening until she let out a short gasp of pain. "It's Steven, isn't it?"

"Even without Steven in my life, what you want couldn't

happen. It's just not something I feel towards you, Aaron." She pulled her hands free with a wince. "Please don't feel bad about this—it's really not you, it's just how I feel. I can't force myself into trying to be with someone I don't connect with." *Connect with*; she sounded like a telephone operator from an old movie.

"How can I not feel badly about this? You won't even let me touch you!" His voice rose, carrying across the mill. "What was last night, just some mild amusement to you? A distraction because you'd had some argument with my brother?"

"No, nothing like that at all. It was something we both wanted to do at the time, or so I thought." Twin points of heat rose in her cheeks. "We agreed that it was a one-off, just...."

"Well, I changed my mind, and like an idiot I thought you'd want to do the same thing. What is it with him? What can he give you that I can't?" he growled, grabbing her shoulders, forcing her to her feet in a painful grip. "He's nothing special—he's a lying, cheating, arrogant asshole who'll leave you when the next pretty face comes along, just as he always has done!"

"Let go of me." She tried pulling from his grip, barely aware that the sound of the camera clicking, the soft talk of the models, had all faded into silence. "You're hurting me; let me go."

"No, I damn well won't. All my life I've lived in his shadow. Not this time." His fingers dug into her shoulders, pulling her closer. "I want you, Dani, and I'm going to make you see that you need to be with me."

"No!" His lips pressed down over hers, claiming them, his arms tightening about her body, crushing her against his chest until she fought for breath. She struggled, kicking against him, her teeth sinking into his bottom lip, panic fueling her fight.

"You bloody bitch," he growled, letting go of her, his lip bleeding from the bite. His hand rose, coming down towards her face in a backwards blow; she flinched, tensing, one hand half-raising, hoping to block at least part of the blow,. She closed her eyes as she waited for it to land—what other choice did she have, with nowhere to back away from the slap?

It never landed.

"You keep your hands off her," Steven demanded. "I don't know what idiocy you think you are committing here, but I don't want to ever see or hear of you laying hands on a woman like that again. Nothing ever gives you the right to hit a woman."

Shaking, she opened her eyes fully. Her left hand had clenched and was still partially raised, though she doubted even if she could have blocked the blow that she would have done anything but increase his anger. Now, with Steven gripping his brother's arm in a vice-like hold, she slipped sideways along the log she had been sitting on, moving out of reach.

"That's rich, coming from you. How often have you lost control of your temper, how many messes have I cleaned up for you, how many men have you hit or come close to?" Aaron yanked his arm free, turning his gaze towards Dani. "And her—what lies have you told her?"

"I've hit men, not women. One man at that, and for trying to get one of the models he was working with into bed when she didn't want him." Steven moved in between Aaron and herself. "And I haven't told her any lies; if anything, I have been brutally honest with Dani. Can you say the same thing?"

"So you've told her about the other women?" Aaron glared past his brothers' shoulder towards her. He tried pushing past Steven, but his brother kept between them both. "Has he?"

"What few there have been, yes, I've told her about; but I've not done half of what you've told Dani. You went out of your way to make me look like some damn player." Steven didn't get out of the way, no matter how hard Aaron pushed. "You knew from day one I was interested in Dani. I made no secret of that with you—why would I hide it from my own brother, the one person I thought I could trust."

"Why should you always be the one who gets what you want?" Aaron had turned his full focus on Steven, though with the anger she could hear in his voice, the pure venom that she never thought she would hear thrown at a family member, she found no way to relax. "You've had everything you have ever wanted in life. Your career, beautiful women, traveling the world…. And I have been the one to tag along after you, picking up your messes, carrying your boxes, driving models around, acting as your damn gopher. Just once, I wanted something for me."

"You had something for you; you had a wife, children," Steven protested. "You lost them because you couldn't stay around. You had to take on jobs that forced your wife to become more and more independent after marrying a woman who made it clear she needed her husband around the majority of the time." He didn't hold back this time—what felt like years of unspoken rivalry between the two men finally escaped into the full light of day. "You screwed up that relationship, no one else."

"And Dani, what did I do wrong there? I'm sure you have the answer—you always have an answer, don't you. You're never in the wrong, you've never made a bloody mistake in your oh-so-perfect life." He snarled, stepping back, turning to face the three models. "Get the hell away from me—what do you think you are staring at?"

His hands clenched into fists, the reason lost from his eyes. She'd never seen a man become that angry before. She'd been lucky; violence had become a rare thing in such a small town. People tended to watch out for each other, and to come that close to being hit had left her shaking.

"They're looking at a man who has lost control of himself." Steven spoke quietly, his voice dropping into little more than a whisper. "They're watching a man who tried to hit a woman because she told him no. Aaron, this isn't you—this anger, you nearly hitting Dani, it's not you. Get a hold of yourself. You know I am in love with her, and if you have any doubt about her returning those feelings, then ask her for yourself. But you have to accept what she tells you."

Focused on Love

"Do you?" Aaron turned, his fists slowly un-clenching, tears shining within his eyes, his entire body trembling as he finally forced himself to meet her gaze. "Is it true; do you and he love each other? Tell me the truth, Dani. That's all I ask for—the truth."

She waited, taking a slow breath before answering him, doing her best to keep her nerves under control. He'd frightened her; no man had done that before. She'd faced bears, floods, small fires, nature at her worst, but never before had a man tried to hit her.

"Yes, I love him, and I believe he loves me." She watched as the impact of her words sank in, a reluctant acceptance, regret mingling with tears that he shed without shame.

"And what do you plan on doing about that love?" Aaron looked over towards his brother.

"If she will have me, then I hope we can marry. Not straight away, not even this year. There is a lot to sort out between us, but I hope one day to be able to call Danielle my wife." He smiled, looking back towards Dani as he did so. "I know there have been some rough times between us, and I don't blame you for wanting to lash out at me. She's a beautiful woman with a graceful spirit. I just hope she and I will one day be able to marry, and when we do, I'd like nothing better than to have you standing there with us."

He reached out towards his brother; the temper they both shared had faded in the light of a few calm words. A quicksilver temper—easily lit, but quick to pass with the right care. Despite everything, she knew they loved each other. "Do you think you could see that happening between us one day, Dani?"

"I would like nothing more than to one day be able to become your wife, Steven. And he's right, Aaron—I would love for you to be there."

"No." A low breath carried the word to the small group. Only it didn't come from Aaron. This time the single word of denial came from Diana, her small frame tensing with a growing fury. "No, you can't mean this, you can't. I thought all that time together, the work, the encouragement was because you believed in me! I thought you loved me."

Chapter Sixteen

Dani starred at the shaking woman in shock. After the talk earlier in the parking lot, the way Steven had made it very clear that there was something between him and Dani, the last thing she had expected to hear was an outburst like that. "Diana, I thought you knew?" she stated calmly.

"I assumed—I mean, I remembered what Aaron had said about his flings, the local women he tended to pick up, and I just thought that you were his latest. I never thought...." She trembled, looking from Steven to Dani and back again. "How could you do this to me?"

"Diana, I've done nothing to lead you on. Not so much as a kiss or anything beyond a friendly hug," Steven replied. "I'm not sure where this came from."

"You can't tell me that all the time we've spent together over the last year, those shoots, the advice you've given me, those small moments we've shared over coffee or a light lunch, have meant nothing at all to you?" Diana all but ignored Dani's presence, leaving her bemused as she watched the woman tremble, trying to find her balance. "You can't be with someone like her; you and I, we've shared...."

"We've shared what I have shared with a dozen other new and not-so-new faces, Diana," he tried explaining. "I've helped a lot of models, and I take care not to press the line between helping them and abusing them. I've been a friend to you, nothing more than that."

Had some madness seized the group? First his brother, now Diana; but as she watched the hundred small glances she had seen Diana cast towards Steven, the way the woman had hung on his every word, it all began to make sinse. Blind, they had all been blind not to see the infatuation she felt towards Steven. It had been her voice in Steven's room that night, but she'd trusted him, trusted that Diana had been there on nothing more than business. "I would never use you that way, Diana. I don't want to hurt you either, but I'm not going to hide my feelings for Dani."

Diana didn't move for several long moments, her hands clenching and un-clenching in slow tight grasps, the color draining from her face as the words sank in. With a low cry she turned, running from the mill without another word.

"Diana!" Steven called after her, taking a step forward.

"Give her chance to calm down. I'll go bring her back," Aaron offered. "The last person she will want to see right now is you, unless you're going to tell her that you're mistaken and want to be with her instead."

"No, I need to...."

"I'm partially to blame for this, Steve. Let me do my part to fix it. I never thought that what I said would have her thinking she had a chance with you like that." Aaron shook his head, glancing in the direction that the young woman had run. "I'm sorry, Bro. I should have kept my mouth shut or been honest with you about my feelings for Dani. Instead, I said a few things that I shouldn't have...."

"I know." Steven nodded, his voice calmer than she would have expected. "Go and find her; then we can head back into town and sit down. We all need to talk about this, and I see no point in pretending to work anymore today. Do you?" He looked towards the remaining two women: Anna, whom Dani had barely spoken to other than to say hello; and the silent Karol, who had made no snide comment during the two confrontations.

"No, we'll start packing things up," Anna agreed, taking hold of Karol's arm as they both turned towards the makeshift set. "For what it's worth, Steve, I never believed the rumors about you."

"Thank you," he replied as he sat down on the same log Dani had watched the shoot from. "I never saw any of this coming. When you told me about Aaron's lies, I assumed he had some other motive. A personal grudge, or he was bored—anything but this. And Diana, I had gone out of my way with the models I worked with to make sure I kept things on a professional if friendly level. After making the mistake I had with Karol, there was no way I wanted history to repeat itself." He hiked up one leg, resting it against the log. "How could I have missed so many things?"

"I should have told Aaron no the other night." Dani glanced over, watching the two women working with the remaining crew to clean up the set. Even though Karol kept silent, she could feel the cold glances being thrown her way, those unspoken accusations of being a slut, a local whore who'd be forgotten in a day or so. "I let myself believe his words. Sometimes it's easier to believe the worst of people instead of the best." She wasn't going to let him take all the blame.

"I'm sorry for dragging you into this. I came out here hoping to end my working relationship with the agency by doing the shoot of a lifetime. Using nature's glory as a backdrop for my own vanity. Instead I met you, and all those plans disappeared with that first kiss at the edge of the river." He reached out as she sat down next to him, pulling her close against his side, his lips brushing against her cheek as he spoke. "You changed that, changed me in a way I had never expected."

"I think we've both changed," she said, looking up into his eyes. So much had happened in the past few days that she barely knew where to start. "I'm not sure if it was all for the good or not, but I don't wish to change what has formed between us."

Neither of them spoke further as they sat on the log. The only sounds came from those clearing the set of lights, coolers and props. He pulled her in closer, until she rested her head on his chest, no longer caring about the unwanted, hateful looks from Karol or the whispered comments she would have otherwise strained to hear. There they remained until Aaron finally returned, sweaty and out of breath.

"I can't find her." He gasped, leaning on his knees as he tried to catch his breath. "I looked all around, but she must have headed into the trees. She's nowhere near the cars, and I have no idea how to find her."

"She doesn't know the area—if she just ran blindly, she could end up badly hurt." Now she had to move. Regardless of what Diana might think of her or whether she was someone the model wanted to see, she had no choice but to go looking for her. "I'll grab my radio, let Henry know what is going on out here, then start looking."

"I'll go with you." Steven started to his feet.

"No, your best bet is to stay here. Aaron, I'll need you to make sure that Anna and Karol make it back to the hotel, and then I want you to come back out here. By then I should have the immediate area checked out—if she's within shouting range, I should be able to find her. But Steven, I need at least one person here with my spare radio."

She didn't wait to hear their answers as she sprinted out towards her truck. However upset Diana was, she couldn't be left to wander the forest. Even those who knew the area would be likely to make mistakes when they were as upset as Diana had been. She didn't have time to waste, or to dwell on her part in Diana's rash behavior as she reached the truck and pulled out her small pack, along with the spare radio.

"Henry, are you there? Pick up, Henry."

"I'm here, what's up?" he answered almost immediately.

"We've got a missing woman out here, Diana, one of the models. She ran out into the park upset over something and hasn't come back in yet. I'm heading out to find her," she explained, shouldering the pack.

"Preliminary search already done?"

"Yes, by Aaron Black—I'll be redoing that before heading out on a wider pattern. She doesn't know the area, so I'm expecting to see some sort of trail left behind." She glanced towards the mill. "I'm having the other models head back into town, and Steven

Black will be staying at the mill in case she returns to base."

"I'll gather up some extra people and head out your way. Are you leaving a radio with Steven?"

"Yes, that's one of the reasons I am making him stay behind." She was already heading back to the mill as she spoke. "I'll check in every fifteen minutes."

"Counting on it. Out."

"Are you sure you want me to wait here? I know how to look after myself out there," Steven protested as she handed him the radio. "I'm very sure. I need one person to stay here with a radio in case she makes her way back here, but I don't see a reason to have Anna and Karol hang around. They can't help with the search if it gets to that point, but they can stay at the hotel. There's a slim chance that Diana might hitch a ride back into town. If so, one of them can use the emergency radio at the hotel or call the ranger station to let us know what is going on." The chances of the woman doing that were slim, but she had to cover all the options. "I need you here, Steven. Trust me on this one; I know what I'm doing."

He nodded, fixing the radio to his belt. "Just look after yourself out there. It's not that I don't trust you I'm just going to worry the entire time you're out there."

She stopped in her tracks. "I'm not used to people worrying about me, other than Gramps."

"Get used to it." He pulled in close, leaning down to press a deep kiss against her lips, cupping her ass in both hands, his fingers massaging her taut cheeks. "It's part of falling in love with you."

"I'll be fine, and I've already agreed to check in with Henry every fifteen minutes. It's standard check in; if the weather was bad, or there were other risks, I'd be checking in every few minutes." She stepped back from his grasp despite the fact she wanted to remain held within his arms. "I promise you I'll be fine. Check the radio before I go."

"I'll hold you to that. Come back safely to me, Dani." He spoke into the radio, smiling. With that she turned, heading out of the mill at a rapid pace, already scanning the ground for signs of Diana's hurried passage into the tree line. For a woman who didn't know the area, she hadn't left a clear a trail as Dani had been hoping for. Worse still, it looked as though Aaron's attempts to find the woman had disturbed the path.

Dani cursed under her breath. She should have gone right after Diana and not left the matter in Aaron's hands, but she hadn't thought Diana would be so foolish as to run headlong into an area she didn't know. The self-recriminations were pushed to the back of her mind as she spotted the first mark on the trail that gave a hint to which direction Diana had headed in.

Despite the upset the woman had been suffering from, the tracks were neither clear nor as random as Dani would have expected them to be. It appeared as if Diana had had some form of purpose in running into the forest, though what that might have been, Dani had no idea. Nor would she until she caught up with her and had the chance to ask a few questions.

The small signs became scarce; the paths Diana had taken into the tree line were well-used ones, making it harder to see where Diana had gone. By the time she did her first check-in with Henry, Dani was having problems following the woman.

"Check in," she spoke into the radio.

"How's it going?"

"Not that good. I would have thought she'd leave a trail a mile wide; no such luck." She turned down one of the smaller paths, finally catching sight of a more obvious set of tracks. Here Diana had rushed, seemingly headlong, through an overgrown section of the path. Strands of hair had caught on the brush, and many of the smaller branches had been broken in her flight.

"Okay, found her trail again. I'll check in shortly."

"Every fifteen minutes, remember?"

"I'm not likely to forget; how's it going getting other people together?"

"Not much luck there, but I should have a small team and be able to come out within the next thirty minutes, if you haven't found her by then...." Henry's voice trailed off.

"If it gets to that point, than we know we're looking at a long search. Check in soon." She settled the radio back on her belt, continuing down the trail. She stopped a moment later to check in with Steven—if she didn't, he'd start to worry and eventually come out after her. "Steven?"

"Here." She could hear the smile in his voice.

"Any sign?"

"Not really, but Aaron mentioned something odd before he and the others headed out. One of the makeup kit bags had been rummaged through, and a small pack was missing. Just one of the basic canvas ones we'd been using for the shoot. Is there a chance she could have grabbed them?" he asked, the concern growing with each passing moment.

"Yes, but why would she unless this had been planned?" She looked over the trail, catching sight of another too-obvious marker of Diana's passage. They were few and far between, but when she did discover one, it was almost as though Diana had planted them.

"Maybe it was planned," she said, tugging the piece of cloth from the brush. It looked as though it had been cut from something rather than snagged. "I'm not sure what she's doing, but this is looking more and more like some form of bad joke. Let me know if you find out anything else. Dani out."

The further she followed the signs of Diana's flight into the trees, the more uncomfortable she grew with the situation. For a woman who didn't know the area, Diana seemed to stick to the paths that would keep her away from danger and lead.... Where did they lead?

Thirty minutes into the search and two more check-ins later, Dani stopped, taking a breath as she tried to make head or tails of what Diana was up to. She was traveling in the form of a circle, leading outwards into the forest, but the outer edge of the loop left her open to return to the mill at a moment's notice. If she did head back to the Mill, at least Steven would be there to meet her.

After another fifteen minutes, Dani had confirmed that the trail was nothing more than an elaborate circle of the mill. It didn't make sense.

"Steven?" She spoke into the radio, looking over the trail. Static crackled back at her instead of his voice. By now she knew that Aaron and the models would be back in town and Henry should be heading out to meet her, but that didn't explain why Steven hadn't replied yet. "Steven, are you there?" She could feel a knot growing in the pit of her stomach as she waited for him to reply. "Steven? Come in?"

The soft crackle of static was the only answer, just as it had been earlier on. The knot turned into a rock settling in her guts as she turned towards the mill. "Henry?"

"Here."

"I'm getting no answer from Steven." She took a step down the trail, back towards the mill. "And all the signs I am finding on the trail are giving me a sick feeling. It's like she knows the area, or at least some of it. I don't think this was the headlong run I first thought it was."

"Where's the trail leading to?" Henry inquired.

"That's just it. It's not really leading anywhere—it's taking a large circular path around the mill, at least on the landward side. She's avoiding the river completely. I'm heading back to the mill to see what's going on with Steve's radio...."

There through the gap in the trees, she caught sight of it: a small finger of white smoke drifting upwards into the sky. "Fire."

"What?" Henry exclaimed. "Diana? No, that doesn't make sense. The criminal record was for Karol years ago; why would Diana be behind this?"

"Well, I'm not seeing things. We've got a fire at the mill, and right now I don't care who's behind it." She barely had the words out of her mouth before she broke into a run, following the trail back. "I can see smoke coming up from the mill, one… no two plumes, neither are large, but with the seasoned wood still there and the old dust, that place could go up fairly easily."

"We're on our way, Dani. Be careful." His end of the radio clicked off, leaving her to focus on the run back to the mill. Diana, Karol…if either of them were responsible for the fire, she'd tear their damned hearts out. Fear clenched at her guts, the trail little more than a blur beneath her feet as she ran. All her thoughts now focused on the fire, on Steven, on what she would find when she reached the entrance of the mill.

It wouldn't take much for the fire to spread out of control, not with the sawdust still there. When the place had been in use, there had been buckets of sand, hoses, fire extinguishers in easy reach. From what she had seen during the shoot, they were still there, so Steven might have been too busy putting the fire out to answer her call on the radio.

Fire; of all the things she hated about this job, this one was the worst. Just the glimpse of it had been enough to bring back memories of the last fire at the edge of town, the one that had finally taken her mother from her life. The one she had been unable to save her from. No, she couldn't think about that now. With her heart pounding, her pulse a raging torrent that blocked out all other sounds, she broke out of the tree cover.

Flames flickered in darkness beyond the open entrance of the mill.

"Shit." She darted towards the opening. Even now the heat was growing quickly. Within a few more minutes, it would be too much for her to attempt to enter. "Steven! Answer me, Steven! Where are you?"

Don't enter a burning building without backup; how many times had she been told that? The same applied for a forest fire. Make for safety, water, rock, something that wouldn't burn if you couldn't get out of the way completely. You could fight it on your own if it hadn't spread too far. If all you faced was a small fire, a few trash cans, or it was still small enough that the extinguisher from your truck could handle it—but more than that, you waited for help. Waited and prayed.

With Steven in there, waiting wasn't an option.

She darted for the truck, yanking open the door as she grabbed for the small extinguisher and a blanket. The iron drums outside the entrance offered a supply of water and an option. Enough to give her a few minutes in the building, the chance to find Steven. The blanket she dunked into the barrel, soaking it fully, along with the large handkerchief she carried. The hankie she tied over her face, covering her from the eyes downwards; the blanket she then threw over her head, wrapping the sopping wet material about her shoulders before heading inside, clutching the extinguisher in her hand. Foolish woman; Henry would have her head for this.

"Steven!" Vile fingers of heat reached out to embrace her, steam rising from the blanket as she hurried through in search of him. "Steven, where are you?" He had to be in here—otherwise he would have answered her on the radio, or she'd have seen him out at the truck. "Steven!"

Smoke curled along the walls, chased by eager flames offering a terrifying source of light, illuminating the vast building as she darted through in search of him. She couldn't breathe; even with the soaked cloth across her nose and mouth, she was fighting for every breath.

Panic gripped her. She couldn't search for much longer now, not with the way the heat and smoke grew with every passing heartbeat. Where was he? A slumped figure caught her attention, lying prone on the floor next to the log they had both sat on earlier in the day. Steven.

She darted forward, barely avoiding an explosion of fire as the flames leaped into a pile of sawdust, feasting hungrily on the new source of life, licking towards her legs in the moment she grasped his arm. The back of his head was matted with blood. She wanted to stop, check he was alright, but there wasn't time. She had to get him out of the building before the fire trapped them within. Behind her something crashed to the ground, beams giving way, or a part of the walls, either way she had to move fast.

Heavy, she'd forgotten how much an unconscious body weighed; each step backwards tugged painfully at her lungs, forcing her to breathe more deeply in the smoke-filled air. At least his body was closer to the ground, giving him more chance to avoid breathing in so much of the smoke. Her eyes stung, watering from the cruel onslaught. Her lungs burned, her body ached as she dragged him back towards the safety of the open air.

"Please, don't leave me!" A small figure crouched close to the floor caught her attention. Diana? "I can't move, I'm trapped, you can't leave me here!" Diana pointed to her legs, her ankle caught between two beams that had fallen. Perhaps the very crashing sound she had heard earlier?

"I'll be back for you, I promise!" She couldn't leave Steven to go after her, not until he was out of the building. With a grunt she hauled him backwards, out into the daylight, coughing hard as her body gulped for the clean air. Trembling, she propped him at the side of the truck, checking his pulse. Alive, at least he was alive.

She turned, running back for the entrance, barely aware of the sound of vehicles pulling into the lot behind her. With the blanket re-soaked, she headed in. Common sense said stay out, wait, but she'd promised. However foolish that promise had been, she had made it.

"Dani, wait!" Henry called out as she darted inside.

Where had she seen the woman? It hadn't been that far into the building. Heat clawed at her waterlogged frame, steam curling upwards from the blanket as she searched for the woman.

"Please!" Diana clawed out towards her, desperately trying to tug her leg free. One end of the beams that trapped her to the floor was already on fire. "Please, I don't want to die!"

"Hold on, I'll get you out." She dropped the wet blanket over the prone woman, searching for something to use as a lever. Small drifts of sawdust were catching light all around them, new blossoms of flame reaching out to both of them, seeking a deadly embrace.

Dani didn't stop to think. Tearing off her jacket, she used it to wrap around a metal rod, one of the bars used to help roll logs, propping it under the edge of the beam. "When I get this lifted up, you scoot out."

"I can't... it hurts, I can't move!"

"You have to. I can't pry this up and pull you at the same time!" Dani forced the edge of the bar under the beam, her muscles screaming as she pressed down, using every ounce of strength she had. "Move!"

"I can't!" Diana screamed, her face pale, eyes wide as she clawed at the floor. "I can't move."

"You have to or you'll burn to death. Move! I can't hold this thing forever. If you don't move, you'll die. I can't hold this up and drag you out!" She couldn't stay there much longer; flames danced across the floor towards the both, threatening to lap at her legs. Without the protection of the soaked blanket, she could feel the effect of the heat on her skin. "Move or I'll leave you here!"

With a cry of pure terror, Diana scooted backwards from the beams, breaking free moments before Dani's grip on the rod gave out, sending the beams crashing back to the floor. She didn't hesitate, but moved, grabbing Diana under the arms as she pulled her backwards, not even waiting to see if the woman had the ability to get to her feet. There just wasn't the time to spare. Flames shot across the floor, chasing them out, leaping from one source of fuel to the next, hitting a large pile of sawdust behind them both.

Fire and light exploded, heat, pain, smoke all combined in a violent blaze. Dani turned, half-throwing Diana out towards the opening as the world erupted into a fire-filled hell around her. She darted for safety, her shirt crackling on her arms, the fire seeking a new source of fuel, barely aware of the scream that tore from her lips as a sharp pain struck her from behind....

Chapter Seventeen.

Flames licked at her legs, eating into her hair as she stood frozen in the middle of the logging mill. She couldn't move, no matter what she tried she couldn't move, ropes of fire held her in place, forcing her to watch as he pulled Diana into his arms. Her hair turned into a cascade of flame as he kissed Diana the same way he had kissed her. Her lips melted, hands curling into claws, her skin blackening, molten tears streaming down her cheeks as the cruel bondage forced her to watch him slip a ring onto Diana's fingers.

"After all, how could I ever marry a woman who looks like you do now?" Steven looked directly at her. "A woman as scarred and destroyed as you are. You were beautiful once, but now you're damaged goods, Dani."

"Stupid woman; did you think he'd stay with you anyway? A passing moment, a roll in the hay—call it what you will, but he was always going to be mine. It just needed the right circumstances to show him. And you provided that so willingly, didn't you, coming in to save me? I couldn't have planned it better if I had tried." Diana's cruel smile, Steven's devotion, the kiss they shared...it all became too much.

She tried to scream, but her lips weren't there anymore. She pulled against the flaming rope, but it cut through her body until all she could do was scream....

"Dani." A cooling sensation washed over her face. "Dani, wake up, it's just a dream." His voice—Steven, but that couldn't be, not after what she had seen. "Wake up love, I'm right here, thanks to you."

Slowly her eyes opened, blinking as she focused on the room around her. "Where am I?" The light hurt her eyes, a bed squeaked under her as she shifted, trying to sit up.

Focused on Love

"Don't move just yet, you've still got an IV in you." He pressed her back to the bed. "You saved us, Dani. You got me and Diana out of there. Henry told me how afraid of fire you were, yet you still did it, you still pushed past that and came in to get both of us." She wasn't imagining it—he was holding a cloth and using it to wipe off her tears. "I am so proud of you, love. So very proud of you."

"Diana? Is she alright?" Her throat felt tight, and her eyes still felt sore from the smoke that had clouded her vision. The IV needle pressed into her arm as she tried to move again, and only then did she become aware of the light bandages that wrapped about her upper arms and back. Her body felt numb, as if she had been wrapped in a thick cotton wool. "What happened to me?"

"One of the beams came down and caught you in the back. You were lucky, though—just a few bruises from the blow, and it knocked you out cold, but...." He looked away from her for a moment.

"But what?" What was he hiding from her, and why couldn't she really feel much of her body? The more she thought about it, the greater her concern became. Something was wrong. "Am I hurt, more than the bruises?"

"Henry didn't get to you before some of the flames did. You've got some burns, upper body mainly. Most of them are light, you'll be fine, but the ones on your left shoulder might scar." He turned back to face her, cupping her cheek gently. "It's nothing severe, love, a few marks that show just how brave you were. It doesn't change how I feel about you."

But it did, it had to—people didn't look at women with scars in the same way. Even if they could be hidden under her shirt, unseen except in rare moments, they would know about them. There would be pitying looks, comments cut off as she came into hearing range, just as there had been when she had been a child and her mother had been killed. Those half-heard whispers of sympathy for the poor orphaned girl who'd stood and watched her mother burn to death.

"It changes everything," she murmured, fighting to keep back the tears. At least she couldn't feel the pain yet. The doctors must have plied her with morphine or something of that nature in order to keep her from feeling it just yet. Or had shock taken its toll?

"How much was lost in the fire?" She tried to think about other things and not nagging doubts that now she was scarred, he would leave her.

"Not much. I'd shifted my camera and gear out to your truck after you headed out to find Diana." He set the cloth to one side, reaching for a glass and straw. "You should try sipping some water. The doctor said you'd need to regain the fluids lost in the fire, and they can only pump so much into you at a time."

He pressed the straw to her lips, urging her to drink. Her body craved the fluids, her throat raw from the smoke that had scoured her lungs. Even after a few sips she started coughing, lung-wracking hacks as her system tried to recover from the smoke she had inhaled.

"Take it slow, love. With everything you've been through, it's going to take a while for you to recover."

"What happened with Diana?" She needed to know.

"A few scrapes, and her ankle is broken from where the beam landed on her, but she'll recover well enough to stand charges for arson." His words confirmed the worst.

"Then she started it?" She took another sip of the water. "Diana, and not Karol?"

"Ah, you know about Karol's record. Well, as I understand it, that was a one-off Karol did as a late teenager." He set the glass down, pushing a loose strand of hair away from her eyes. "How much do you know about Karol's interest in fire?"

"Only that she has a record." It hurt to talk—the medication was slowly easing off, and with each beat of her heart, she became more aware of the pain that blossomed to life across her arm. Thick cotton pads lay beneath her shoulder, the wrappings light enough that the air could get to them without leaving her open to infection—or so she believed. Not that she was a nurse or had any idea how she was being treated beyond the wrappings and medication.

"Yes, she has a record; so do I. A lot of people do." He settled down on the edge of her bed, taking her hand in his. "I've made mistakes in the past. Karol's was a little more obvious than most, and I've always known about it. She was eighteen, got into an argument with her mom. This was when she was working with another agency—one with a habit of not caring what a model did to keep her figure to the level they wanted. She was taking a mix of anti-depressants, alcohol and who knows what else. One thing led to another, and she set fire to her mother's office. No one else was in the house at the time, and her Mom had been one of the people pushing her into the business." He almost sounded as though he were defending her. They could have both lost their lives in that fire, and he was defending an arsonist?

"You feel sorry for her?" She couldn't keep the accusation from her voice.

"I've met her mother, and people like her; so yes, in a way, I do feel sorry for her. I guess it's one of the reasons I've put up with so much from her over the years. It might even be the real reason I dated her. I'm a sucker for thinking I can fix people at times." He stroked her hand lightly.

"She lit a fire, destroyed things, and you thought you could fix her?" She wanted to ask if he now thought she was a project to be fixed, but feared what the answer would be.

"That was years ago, Dani. Before you ever met her. She went through counseling for what she did, paid the fine, did her probation, and hasn't stepped out of line like that since." He smiled, watching her face carefully.

"And no, you're not some project for me to work on. I outgrew that stage with Karol—or so I hope. You, Danielle Wind Dancer, are the woman I love. Now, did you want to hear the rest of this, or do you need to get some sleep?"

She tried to ignore the growing pain that now burned across her shoulder. Sending him out now would leave too many unanswered questions. "No, I want to hear the rest."

He nodded, looking towards the clock. "They'll be in soon to change the dressings and give you some more meds. I should have told them you were awake, but I wanted some time with you before they chased me out. Selfish, I know," he admitted, looking back at her. "I'm almost afraid to kiss you in case I hurt you."

Dani chuckled, the soft laughter bringing a fresh wave of hacking coughs. "I'm sure there is at least one safe place you could try and kiss me."

"After your next set of meds—besides, that way you can't fight me off." He grinned, teasing her. "Back to Diana, yes?"

"Please." She settled back on the pillows, wincing.

"You're hurting already; I should call the nurse in now." He started to rise, but she caught his hand.

"No, wait. Fill me in first and then send for one, please." She pulled him back to sit on the edge of the bed. "I'd rather know what is going on than have so many unanswered questions plaguing me."

"Okay, well, Diana had been working with the agency on and off for the last two years. Long enough that she knew Karol's history. She'd also had a crush on me since the first assignment, but like a fool, I never noticed. I guess I didn't want to see what was right under my nose. At first she thought Karol was the one standing in her way—when I didn't respond to her interest, she had find someone to blame, and Karol was the natural target." He fell silent for a moment. "Maybe if Karol hadn't become so possessive when we had been dating, if she hadn't viewed me as her property even after we broke up, then who knows...."

"You can't think that way, Steve. You'll fall into the pattern of blaming yourself for what has happened, and you're not to blame." She wanted to pull him in close, hold him tight and find a way to help him forget the small part he had played in it all, but her body shook with the growing pain. "Tell me what I need to know."

He took a slow breath and then nodded, continuing as he did so. "She had been trying to find a way to get close to me for years, and when this assignment came up, she made a choice to actively step in between Karol and myself. I guess she thought we were still involved, despite everything I had said to the contrary." That made sense, especially after the way Diana had reacted in the Mill. "She began a slow campaign to get Karol into trouble, feeding into my concerns about her, then taking it one step further with the small fires and the slashing of my tires."

"That was Diana?" She'd seen all three of the women there, standing close to the cars at one point. "They all have those nail files, don't they?"

"It's pretty much a standard for quick fixes on broken nails. Though I've never seen you with one," he teased. "You'd make quite the sight standing there, fixing your nails in the middle of a hike across the park."

"Oh yes, I can just see Henry making my life a misery over something like that." She grinned, then nudged him to continue.

"She didn't see or didn't want to see that you and I had become close. Diana just saw you as another way of pulling me further away from Karol. When it became obvious that Karol had major problems with the amount of time you and I were spending together...well, she fed into that, urging Karol on behind the scenes to pick more fights with me. At the same time she was coming to me, saying how sorry she was that Karol was behaving like this, how she couldn't believe such a wonderful woman had turned into a raving bitch."

He rubbed his head. "I owe Karol an apology as well, for letting myself believe half of what was being said and letting it taint how I viewed her actions." It didn't mean that Karol was in the right, not by a long shot, Dani could see that in his gaze. "It turns out she had been the one feeding Aaron snippets of information over the years as well, feeding into his insecurity."

She listened, trying not to hiss at the mix of heat and pain that had surged into life. "It sounds as though she was a world-class manipulator."

"Yes, sad to say, she had us all fooled." He lifted her hand to his lips, pressing a soft kiss across her knuckles. Even with the pain she was, in her body reacted, her thighs tightening as she squirmed under the light sheet. "When she realized it wasn't going to work, that she couldn't turn my attentions to her, she took it one step further. I don't think she planned on hurting me—not at first—but she wanted you out of the way. I believe she thought you would be gone for hours searching for her, and by the time you returned, the blaze would be well set in the Mill. She used nail-polish remover to start the blaze, it didn't take much from her to get the fire going, and by the time I caught her, it was too late."

"How did you end up hurt?" She could clearly remember him lying prone by the log, blood matting his blond hair. "Are you okay? It wasn't anything serious?"

"I had a headache for two days, a stitch or two but I'm fine now." Two days; she'd been asleep for two days? "You've been half-awake, half-asleep during the last day. I think one of the nurses told me that it was fairly normal for the body to want to sleep during the first stages of healing. It shuts everything down. I'm not sure how accurate that is, or if they were just telling me that so I wouldn't worry too much."

"I'd have worried if it had been you in this bed, unable to wake up." She squeezed his hand.

"I know. I've barely left the room since they let me out of E.R. They wanted me to stay overnight in one of the observation rooms, but when I said I'd be in your room until you woke up and told me to go away, they relented." He grinned. "Are you telling me to go away yet?"

"Not yet," she admitted, though it wouldn't be long before she had to. She didn't want him to see her in tears. "How did you end up hurt, though?"

"We got into an argument. I tried telling her I wasn't going to leave you for her no matter what was said or what she tried to do. She didn't like that and tried to grab me, I stepped back out of the way and must have slipped, as that's the last thing I remember before waking up outside and seeing Henry pulling you out of the flames."

He pressed a finger to her lip. "I know what's coming next, and no, Henry is fine. No one else was hurt."

She couldn't hold back the tears any longer. Without warning, they slipped free down her cheeks, all the pain, the strain of the past few days finally released in soft gulping sobs. "I couldn't bear the thought of losing you." Her skin burned afresh in the memory of the flames' hungry embrace.

"You're not going to lose me, Dani. Not now or ever. But now you need to rest. Let me call in the nurse, have them check you over. I'll be back shortly. I just need an hour or so to get some food in my system, take a shower, then I'll be back. I promise I'll be back."

He rose, pressing a soft kiss against her cheek. "You need to get some sleep again. I know you feel like you've slept for too long, but you're already tired again. Trust me on this one." He pressed the button calling the nurse in, lingering by the side of her bed until he had no choice but to head out under the instant instructions of a middle-aged nurse.

"Now we need to get those dressings changed, and the doctor will want to come out and see you first. He's on his way, though. When I saw the light go on at the nurses' station, I paged him." She set the tray down on the small table. "So if you can hang on a little longer, we can get you changed and some fresh pain meds in your system. You've become quite the celebrity around here."

"I don't understand?" Pain clouded her judgment, a deep

shudder claiming her body as she tried to shift on the bed.

"Dani, you saved two lives. You went into the fire and pulled them both out despite the risk to yourself, and you can't understand why the town would view you as a hero?" The nurse gave her a hard look. "I think the pain has chased away your good senses here. You're a hero, Danielle, regardless of whether you believe it or not."

Chapter Eighteen

Six long days she stayed in the small hospital. Perhaps if she had been closer to the cities, she would have been released sooner; but the local hospital had played on the side of caution, keeping her in several days longer.

Steven had been right: there were going to be some small scars, but by day five, the pain had eased to a low ache that cream and oral medication kept under control. She'd need to come back in to have it checked out in another week's time, but she was finally fit enough to be sent home.

"I'm proud of you, Dani." Silver Fox shouldered her small bag, opening the door for her. "You did well, very well, and faced the fear in you. Not everyone could have done as you did." He pressed his hand to her good shoulder, walking out of the room that had been her home over the past week.

Steven had been in every day but was now absent having been called back to the cities the night before. He'd wanted to stay, but had already gone long past his deadline to hand over the photographs from the shoot. Despite the fact the fire hadn't been his fault, he had been worried they would fine him for the failure to complete the work. She'd tried easing his concerns, but it hadn't helped, and by the time he had left the night before, he had been a nervous wreck.

"Henry would have done the same; so would you have done, Gramps." One thing she had been grateful for had been the shelter from prying Rangers that Steven and her Gramps had provided. At first they hadn't tried to get into her hospital room, but as word had spread beyond the town, the first of the outside reporters had made their way in. If the models hadn't been involved, if Steven hadn't been one of the two people she had pulled out of the fire, then she doubted anyone outside of town would have taken interest in what she had done.

"Maybe this is true, but you pushed past more than one fire—you defeated the fire within you as well." The double doors of the hospital opened up, and there in the parking lot, she saw them: the gathering of reporters, cameras and more, a small camera crew from an out-of-town station.

"Danielle, how did it feel when you realized there were two people trapped in the mill?" one voice called out, a camera flashing in her eyes.

"Did you hesitate? Or think that waiting for the other Rangers to arrive would be a better idea? Or did you just dive in?" A woman's voice reached her ears as a microphone was shoved under her nose.

"I'm sorry? I need a moment before I..." She didn't get the chance to finish; three quick flashes from a camera and a hand grabbing for her arm stole the remainder of her words.

"Look this way, please!" another demanded, a forth and fifth voice melding in words she didn't quite understand. From each side came cameras; the pressure of the photographers, questions, all pushed against her until she felt she would be squashed in the wave of people.

"Give my granddaughter a little time to catch her breath, and at least let her sit down before she answers any questions. If you will give her a moment, then she'll be able to do that—if you promise to leave her alone afterwards?" Silver Fox kept a protective arm about her, watching for signs that the reporters would do as he asked. "If you cannot do that, I will take Dani back to my cabin and you will go without your questions answered." If nothing else, that threat had them backing off.

Slowly she settled down on one of the carved benches that decorated the park-like entrance of the hospital, watching as the reporters circled her. It was like watching vultures circle a wounded animal, waiting for that moment of weakness when they could feast.

Focused on Love

"One at a time, please—even after a few days rest, my throat is still sore." She spoke quietly, hoping they would understand her request. It wasn't a lie, either—her throat was raw, and until only a day before, she had been coughing every time she had tried to raise her voice.

With a little more concern than the reporters had shown before, the questions began, focusing on the fire at first. Then came the more personal questions.

"Is it true that you and Steven Black are lovers?" the woman with the television crew asked, thrusting the microphone closer.

"No." She didn't even hesitate. Despite every ounce of her that screamed to tell the woman to go and fuck herself for prying that deeply into her private life, she managed to answer with a smile on her face. "No, we're not lovers; we're planning on marrying when the time is right, so that makes us more than a casual love affair."

There was no ring, not yet, and she struggled daily to keep the fears at bay. He'd not yet seen the scars she had been left with, however small they were. The Doctor had made it clear that she had been lucky—the fire could have taken her life, or left her body scarred far worse than it had been. Her answer had been the right one, stunning the small crew into silence for several long minutes.

"What about his well-known relationship with one of the models, Miss Karol Serenity?"

Strange—it had taken a trip into the fire for her to learn Karol's last name. "I know about that, and I am well aware that it has been over and done with for some time. Close to two years, as I understand it."

She wanted to tell them to take the rest of their questions and shove them where the sun didn't shine, but that wouldn't have done any good for either Steven or her. Whatever questions they wanted to ask of her then faded under the protective glare of her grandfather.

"If you've all finished, I will be taking my granddaughter to rest. It has been a long few days for her, and she needs to take it easy for a week or so yet." He dismissed them with a near-arrogant wave of his hand, helping her to her feet as they parted before him. Even with his age, he had a presence of spirit that few had the ability to stand up to; and she was grateful for his strength now more than ever.

They didn't speak through much of the trip back to her cabin. Just small things here and there, nothing more than passing comments about the weather, how her cabin had stood up over the last winter, what repairs would be needed before the next one. He didn't talk about the cleansing, and she felt too uncomfortable to ask, even though she had known it would have been needed.

Her shoulder ached as she stepped out of the truck. The short ride had jolted it more than once, sending small surges of pain through the healing skin. They'd given her a large tub of some sort of cream that would help the skin heal to some extent, but it had also been made painfully clear that no matter what she did, how she took care of herself, the scars would remain in some form.

A welcoming smell of fresh coffee greeted her as she walked into the cabin, her Gramps setting the bag down on the counter. "I had the pot set on that timer thing you picked up last fall."

"Thanks." She tried to smile but couldn't stop the disappointment from building. Though she hadn't seen any signs of the SUV, she had hoped, with the smell of the coffee, that it meant Steven had returned. It would be hours before he would return, if he managed to return at all tonight. If work kept him busy, then it could be days before she would see him again. "Has there been any word from him?"

"Steven, you mean? No, there hasn't been. But he went into town last night instead of waiting for the morning." He looked around the cabin. "I finished the new dream catcher—the day of the fire it was finished, then I took it to some of the elders to look it over. They each added something of theirs to make it more powerful after the fire. To stop the dreams from coming back."

The dream catcher waited on her coffee table, larger than the one she had had before, decorated with feathers, braided leather, beads that had been hand-bored and polished, and three butterflies. It was easy to see the amount of work that had been put into the catcher. The love her gramps had for her had been worked into every piece of soft leather, ever small knot and feather.

"It's beautiful, Gramps. Thank you." She traced her fingers over the leather, smiling. "For my bedroom?"

"Yes, that would be the best place for it; do you need help hanging it?" He watched how she was moving, she knew that. "You will need to be careful over the next week or so and not stretch things too far." He would end up mothering her if she gave him half the chance. He had every reason to that much, she accepted—but it didn't mean she had to like it.

"It might be for the best," she admitted after picking up the dream catcher. Even something as lightweight as this pulled at the still-raw skin. "I'm not sure I'll be able to lift it up. Was the cabin cleansed, or does that still need to be done."

"I did two passes through, but you will need to do one yourself as well—you know how that works." He smiled, taking the dream catcher from her hands. "I've taken a little time in here every day, making sure that nothing has disturbed your home, getting it ready for when you would be able to return." Silver Fox followed her through into her bedroom. "

There were bad spirits here, Wind Dancer. I don't know if the brother brought them in or if they came in with the fire-starter. They can cling to others, following them in. Maybe that is what happened; we have no way of knowing for certain. The Elders and I have spoken long about this. We think the fire-starter is very sick, very sick indeed. It is one thing to want another when they do not want you; it is another to try and destroy the world around them in order to win them."

He spoke in an easy tone, relaxed despite the topic. "If she were one of my kin, I would take her to the lodge and see if she could be helped. Instead she will go to a hospital in the cities and another form of help." She knew very well what her Gramps thought of treatments like that. For some people they worked; for others they didn't. She wasn't a doctor, and neither did she want to get into an argument with her Gramps.

"It looks good, Gramps." She smiled, watching the old man as he carried the catcher to the wall over her bed. He'd already put three nails in place, which she didn't see until he reached up and hooked it against the wall.

"You prepared for this earlier, I see."

"Well, if it were left to you, then it would sit on the table for six months before you put it up." She began to protest, but he cut her off. "And don't try telling me otherwise, Dancer. I know you better than anyone else—remember that. So if you want to try telling someone else your excuses, go ahead. But don't try them with me."

He grinned, stepping back from the bed now that he was satisfied the dream catcher was in place. "Now we get you settled and you can get some rest."

"I feel like that is all I have been doing over the past few days—sleeping, resting, having the dressings changed, taking more meds and falling back to sleep." Sleep; she didn't want to sleep any more, no matter how heavy her body felt. "Maybe I'll take a long bath."

"Remember not to use any of your bubbles or salts, just water. And you won't be able to do one that's too hot right now—the Doctor warned you about that." He looked towards the bathroom. "Did you want me to run the bath for you, and stay with you, Dancer?"

"You're hovering, Gramps." She almost laughed; the last time he had been like this had been just after her mother had died. "I'm not going to do anything foolish. I know what the Doctor said, and I just need some time in a bath without someone walking in on me."

"Yes, I'm hovering, and I'm overprotective, and I want to keep an eye on you. You can't blame me for that. You are the only family I have left." He caught her arm, gently turning her to look at him directly in the eye. "I have always loved you, Dani, and I will look after you for as long as I can, for as long as you will let me. Even if you and Steven forge a life together—which I believe you intend to—I will be as much a part of your life as you are willing to let me be."

She didn't want to send him away, not even so she could have a bath in peace. He was a stubborn man, one she could understand even if he drove her insane some days with their constant disagreements. They argued back and forth, debating her way, his way, the life ahead of her, the choices they had both made, and the ones she would yet make after he was long gone.

"I know, Gramps, but give me a night to unwind by myself—that's all I ask." She pressed a light kiss against the soft, wrinkled skin of his cheek. "I'm old enough to bathe myself, after all."

"Are you sure? Well, you look like you are well out of diapers, but you never can tell with some people." He grinned but headed for the kitchen. "Let this old man have one coffee, and then I will leave you in peace. I deserve one cup of hot coffee before being thrown out into the snow, don't I?"

"Okay, one cup of coffee, and then I get my bath...and what snow? It's still summer." She laughed, following him into the kitchen in search of two cups.

"Well, I am old—it only takes a small breeze, and these frail bones start shivering."

She came close to scooping up a cushion and throwing it at him. "And you are far from being frail, Gramps."

"Well, I hope you remember that the next time you tell me off for seeing to the repairs at my cabin." He had her there, and the grin made it clear that he knew it.

"You sly old...."

"Fox? Why do you think I was named after him, Wind Dancer? One day you and I will sit down and talk about our names, our family and our people. But for now, I will be happy with that cup of coffee."

Warm water molded about her body, oddly cool still against the burn on her shoulder. It could have been far worse, but still she didn't want to look at it, didn't want to be reminded of how badly she had been marked. In time she might be able to look at the wrinkled burn scar without regret. For now though, she wanted to forget it had ever happened, reach out to find a way to make him ignore the marks when he next saw if.

Would he understand if she turned him away? No, he wouldn't; she wouldn't if she were in his shoes. Not after everything they had been through. Her hands slipped over her body, caressing across her stomach, lifting under her breasts. At least the scars were at the back, where she couldn't see them, or feel them unless she stretched to touch behind her back. She had to get this out of her mind, once and for all. With a sigh she let her eyes drift closed, sinking further into the bath, resting her head against the edge.

"Thinking about the time we shared the bath together?" His voice pulled her from her thoughts. "I hope you didn't mind me walking in like this—your gramps seemed to think it would be alright."

"He was there when you arrived?" She sat up, heat coloring her cheeks. Without bubbles or the cloudiness from bath salts, her body remained fully revealed to his gaze.

"Yes, we stood out there talking for a while." He leaned against the door frame, smiling as he let his gaze linger on her wet body, trailing down from her breasts to the soft-trimmed triangle of hair between her thighs. "I think he wanted you to become settled in your bath before I walked in."

Focused on Love

"That sneaky old…." She couldn't help but laugh at the idea that her gramps had set her up like that. "Did he know you were on your way back?"

"Yep—I called ahead before you got out of hospital. He knew and wanted you home in one piece before I arrived. Yes, he is a sneaky one, but he loves you very much, Dani." He moved over to sit on the edge of the bath, trailing his fingers through the water, tracing up over her stomach, teasing a light touch around one ripe nipple before leaning up to cup her face. "You're beautiful, Dani. Nothing has changed there; you're still as beautiful as you ever were to me."

"I've changed," she protested, leaning into his touch. "The fire changed me."

"Life changes us all." He didn't pull his hand back away from her face. "It changes everything about us eventually. Small steps, large ones, but nothing ever remains the same."

Tears stung in her eyes, slipping down her cheeks to mingle with the bath water. "I want to believe you."

"Then believe me." His hand moved into her hair, just as it had done before, tangling in her loose damp locks, tugging her up out of the bath with a firm but gentle grip. His free hand moved under her arm, supporting her as he lifted her dripping body out of the bath, carrying her back through into the bedroom despite her murmured protests. "If you won't believe my words, then maybe you'll believe actions instead. I've never lied to you, Dani, and I never will."

He lowered her onto the bed, silencing her protests with a kiss that stole her breath, his tongue dancing with hers, stroking within the depths of her mouth, his free hand tugging at his own jeans, his boots hitting the floor as he discarded his clothing, never breaking the kiss.

With a soft moan she arched into his touch, her thighs parting with the light pressure of his fingers. She wanted him; despite the scars he would see, she wanted him. Her pussy tightened at the soft kisses he laid over her breasts, and a low groan released eagerly as his lips closed about one firm nipple.

Her fingers curled into his hair, playing through the soft blond strands, tightening as he suckled her nipple hard into his mouth, drawing pleasure and low moans from her trembling body. He shifted on the bed, moving over her, pressing her back against the soft quilt, trailing heated kisses over her breasts, up along her neck until he bit against her throat. "Mine." He groaned against her neck. "Mine no matter what."

"Yours, for as long as you'll have me." Her grip tightened in his hair, tugging him upwards along her body, seeking out his lips with a kiss that threatened to bruise her lips. The hunger that rose within her knew no control and sought only a release within his arms.

"Forever; that's how long I want you in my life. I want you with me forever and a day." He growled into her kiss, wrapping his arms about her body, breaking away from the kiss as he pressed her back to the bed, slipping between her thighs. Slowly, with teasing kisses, he trailed back down her body, licking over the swell of her breasts, tracing around one nipple then down over her stomach. Lower and lower he went, until she finally realized where he was going. His breath caressed across her inner thighs, brushing over her mound, down between her thighs until she felt it in soft heated gasps on her clit. He growled into her vulva, capturing her clit between his teeth, tugging her clit into his mouth hungrily.

A jolt shot through her hips as she pressed forward against his lips, her hands falling away from his hair to grasp claw-like at the bedding beneath her. With a low moan she parted her thighs fully, his head buried between them, squirming at the feel of his tongue slipping into her cunt.

Each soft breath surged against her sex, teasing into her cunt, vibrating against her sensitive clit. She tried holding back, but heat surged between her thighs as they tensed on either side of his head, her breath coming in soft, low gulps of delight.

Focused on Love

"Gods!" She hissed, her back arching from the bed, nails caught in the bedding, surges of pleasure rocking through her hips.

"More?" he purred directly against her clit.

"Yes!"sShe cried out, her hands loosening from the bedding, reaching for his hair, holding him tight against her cunt as her hips rocked, pressing back against his lips, rocking down on his tongue, her walls clenching tight on his seeking tongue. She wanted so much more than she was able to beg of him. His tongue plundered into her cunt, pressing against her throbbing walls, slipping free to circle her clit in quick flicks.

He reached up, grasping her breasts with both hands, growling into her sex, drinking from her as her body offered up slick, heated juices for his hungry search. Pressure built deep within, a need she understood but wasn't ready to give in to. She wanted to make it last, to enjoy hours if possible under his seeking lips, delighting in the play of his fingers over her body. A soft cry tore from her lips as he pinched both her nipples, suckling hard on her clit at the same time, matching the pattern on all three pulsating points on her eager body.

"Now?" he teased, pulling away from her cunt, his breath warming her inner thighs. "Do you want me now, or shall we wait a little longer?" She groaned, unable to offer him any other answer, her voice stolen by the waves of intense pleasure he forced her to feel.

"Ah, well, as you can't give me an answer, I'll decide for you," he growled, lowering back to her cunt, licking slowly over her lips only to pull away again. Before she knew what he was doing, he'd flipped her onto her belly, urging her knees up beneath her breasts. Her hands dug into the bedding, arching as he licked slowly from her ankles, up along her calf, tickling into the back of her knees before he continued a slow, lingering licking path over her thigh.

She moaned, fighting to keep still under his tender

ministrations to her naked body, a soft low sound gaining strength as his lips pressed small, biting kisses across her taut ass, his hands grasping her hips. Now, as he moved closer, tracing his tongue along the length of her spine, she could feel the press of his cock against the back of his thighs, throbbing with each breath.

He wanted her, yet he held back; she could feel his desire, his hunger to seek out her cunt with his engorged cock pulsating against her body, but he waited. Only when she felt his kisses seek out the still-tender flesh of her burned shoulder did she realize what he was waiting for.

"Don't." She regained control of her voice enough to plead that single word.

"Why not? This is as much a part of you as everything else. It doesn't frighten me, it doesn't disgust me. I love every part of you, Dani." He licked slowly over the raised mark, his tongue lingering in the ridges that had already formed. "This, or anything else, won't change how I feel about you."

Her breath caught in the back of her throat. Every kiss sent fresh tingles down her spine and jolts of pleasure into her clit. Her back arched, nipples pressing to the bedding, scraping softly with each rock of her hips. She couldn't wait any longer, not now, not with the way she felt.

"Please, fuck me, please, Steve." How she found the ability to speak she would never know. His answer came in a swift move. He shifted behind her, his cock slipping between the slick lips of her vulva, one hand reaching forward to grasp her hair as he pressed deeply within her cunt. As one they cried out, her body tightening on his cock, the walls of her sex rippling along his length as he rocked within her.

She didn't even care about the tight grip in her hair; it was a part of how he was, loving and possessive at the same time. There wasn't anything threatening about him doing that—she knew that now—he simply claimed her, protected, desired, and loved all at the same time.

Focused on Love

He stroked into her, his teeth nipping against her back and seeking out the back of her neck; nipping, licking over it, finding that spot that sent shivers down her spine, into her cunt in clenching waves of pleasure. Faster it built, burning within her, a need to cum that outreached anything she had expected.

Her body knew better than she did what she needed giving itself over to his touches, rocking back against him as he pressed deeper and deeper into her tight pussy. She couldn't hold back, didn't want to hold back; her breath came in sharp gasps. Even with the grip on her hair she lowered her head, pushing back against him, feeling his cock burying deeper into her cunt, bottoming out.

"Going to cum," she growled, her nails digging into the bedding. "Have to cum."

"Cum with me, then." His teeth caught the back of her neck, growling into her, a sound of pain, pleasure and need rolling into one as she felt his cock swell against her tight walls. She couldn't hold back. With a scream she lifted her head from the bed, almost pushing back to sit back onto his cock, her cunt squeezing tighter than she had ever known, threatening to push him out of his body as she came.

His arms wrapped tight about her waist, releasing his hold on her hair as he knelt up, pulling her back to sit impaled on his cock, holding her against his chest as they both caught their breath. She didn't move—the idea of leaving the safety of his arms as she rested with him was almost unthinkable.

"I love you, Dani. I always will." As he pressed one soft, lingering kiss against the raised mark on her shoulder, she finally accepted that he meant every word.

She didn't know if she should laugh, cry, or scream at the world. "Stay with me, Steve. I don't care about when or if we get married, but stay with me, make a life here, please."

"I already have."

Epilogue

Summer was almost over. The fall colors had invaded the park, turning the trees into living beacons of red, orange and gold, reflecting the last flames of summer in their own tribute to the change of seasons. There would still be a few warm days left where she could enjoy the park; then fall would be over too quickly, the first snows of winter fast on its heels, ready to coat the world she knew in a blanket of white. A low breeze tugged small clouds across the sky—no sign of rain, nor would it be a late summer where she could swim in the river well into October. She'd be lucky if the chill would hold off into September, with the way Silver Fox had been talking.

The dreams hadn't come back. Her gramps had taken pride in that, stating it had of course been the work of the dream catcher and white sage smoke. Perhaps that had been it, or the knowledge she had been accepted, fully, by the man she loved.

Silver Fox still came out here, to sit on the ridge and watch the world go by; so did she when Steven was away.

"I can see why you wanted to bring me up here." Steven circled her waist with his arms, pulling her back against his chest, his breath warm against the back of her neck. "There's something magical up here, a sense of being on top of the world."

"You can see for miles, even on a cloudy day." She smiled, looking back up at him. It had taken nearly two months for her to gain the chance to show him the ridge. The eagles had returned fully, the lone male having found a mate, though there had been no chance for a nest and young this season. She could only hope the following year would change that. Now she rested against Steve as she watched the two eagles dance on the air currents, courting each other time and again, although they were already an established mated couple. "It was up here that I first saw you."

Focused on Love

"This is where you were when you spotted me by the river?" He nipped along her neck, one hand cupping her breast through the jacket. "I remember that day. Didn't you come barreling down in search of me in case I was some fly-by-night hiker who didn't know how to look after himself?"

"Hey, careful, someone will see you." She laughed, half-pushing his hand away. "Yes, I was up here, looking out over the river. I was so used to having to warn people to be careful down there that I assumed I would have to do the same with you; and I used to come up here a lot to think."

"No one is going to see us without binoculars." He grinned, but moved his hand away. "Not that I care if they see us or not."

"Well, I do—I am supposed to be working." She turned, looking up into his eyes. "I don't want to end up losing my job for being caught in a compromising position up here."

"Oh, you mean as opposed to one in the grove?" He pressed a soft kiss against her chin, a teasing light shining in his eyes. "Or should we head down to the caves this time? You did promise me a better look at them."

"Maybe we'll do that when you get back." In the two months since the fire, he had been away more often than he had been home, and the cabin was home to him now. He'd sold his apartment in the city, renting a small unit in town to change into a studio and darkroom set-up. In every way except marriage, they had become husband and wife—but that didn't stop her regretting each time he had to leave. "You'll be heading out early tomorrow?"

"Yes, to catch the early flight. I'd rather have a partial night with you then no time at all." He cupped her face, nibbling a line of gentle kisses over her jaw. "I'll only be away for a week this time. Maybe less if I can find the right locations."

"I have every faith in you, Steven, and I'm not going anywhere."

"And I will always come back to you, Dani. No matter where I go in the world, I'll always come back to you." He pulled her closer, slipping his hand into the base of her braid. It no longer mattered if someone else saw them or not.

She leaned up into his kiss, her arms slipping about his neck as she felt the world drift away in the safety of his embrace.

Terri Pray

Terri Pray is a stay at home wife and mother currently living in Iowa with her second husband. She was born in England, only moving to the States in 1999. They have two children together and share a love of writing and role-playing that brought them together via the Internet. Together they not only run a chat site, Dark Fantasy Chat, but also work in the RPG industry and Terri can often be seen at such conventions as ValleyCon, Gen Con and Origins at the Final Sword Production booth.

Visit Terri on the Web at www.terripray.com.